ger. fict.   1/ 00

CHEZ MOI

AGNÈS DESARTHE was born in Paris in 1966 and has written many books for children and teenagers, as well as adult fiction. She has had two previous novels translated into English: *Five Photos of My Wife* (2001), short-listed for the Independent Foreign Fiction Prize and the Jewish Quarterly Fiction Prize, and *Good Intentions* (2002).

ADRIANA HUNTER has been working as a literary translator since 1998, and has now translated over thirty books from the French, including two other novels by Agnès Desarthe. She lives in Norfolk with her husband and their three children.

Praise for *Chez Moi*

"*Chez Moi* is a delectable confection of renewal and hope, peppered by surprises and sweetened by friendship, set in a little restaurant in Paris. Agnès Desarthe's mouthwatering novel, like an innovative menu, introduces scenes and sorrows and characters in unexpected flavors; culinary ingredients rush in by flurries of musical aromas. The pages beg to be licked!"

—Cynthia Ozick, author of *Dictation: A Quartet*

"Thank you, Agnès Desarthe, for letting us into the imaginative mind of this wacky, philosophic, good-hearted, and altogether brave woman. I loved her from the piquant start to the satisfying finish, like an inventive meal with a deliciously perfect dessert."

—Susan Vreeland, author of *Luncheon of the Boating Party*

"Sometimes—very rarely—a book comes your way that is so deceptively approachable and sastifying, it is only when you are finished that you realize it has offered profound human wisdom and a refreshing new way of looking at life. This is such a book."

—Linda Olsson, author of *Astrid & Veronika*

"*Chez Moi* is full of surprises and delights. Myriam is the sort of friend we'd all like to have—smart and determined, eccentric and brave—a person who will serve you fine coffee and praline raspberry mousse while she listens to your story. Her own story, with its pleasures of discovery and piercing losses and errors of the past, will catch your attention and make you want to linger in her restaurant over yet another cup of coffee, and then one more."

—Kim Edwards, author of *The Memory Keeper's Daughter*

Chez Moi

Agnès Desarthe

Translated from the French by Adriana Hunter

PENGUIN BOOKS

PENGUIN BOOKS

Published by the Penguin Group

Penguin Group (USA) Inc., 375 Hudson Street, New York, New York 10014, U.S.A. • Penguin
Group (Canada), 90 Eglinton Avenue East, Suite 700, Toronto, Ontario, Canada M4P 2Y3 (a division
of Pearson Penguin Canada Inc.) • Penguin Books Ltd, 80 Strand, London WC2R 0RL,
England • Penguin Ireland, 25 St Stephen's Green, Dublin 2, Ireland (a division of Penguin Books
Ltd) • Penguin Group (Australia), 250 Camberwell Road, Camberwell, Victoria 3124, Australia
(a division of Pearson Australia Group Pty Ltd) • Penguin Books India Pvt Ltd, 11 Community
Centre, Panchsheel Park, New Delhi – 110 017, India • Penguin Group (NZ), 67 Apollo Drive,
Rosedale, North Shore 0632, New Zealand (a division of Pearson New Zealand Ltd) • Penguin Books
(South Africa) (Pty) Ltd, 24 Sturdee Avenue, Rosebank, Johannesburg 2196, South Africa

Penguin Books Ltd, Registered Offices: 80 Strand, London WC2R 0RL, England

First published in Great Britain by Portobello Books Ltd 2008
Published in Penguin Books 2008

1 3 5 7 9 10 8 6 4 2

Originally published in French as *Mangez-moi* by Les Editions de L'Olivier, Paris.

PUBLISHER'S NOTE

This is a work of fiction. Names, characters, places, and incidents either are the product
of the author's imagination or are used fictitiously, and any resemblance to actual persons,
living or dead, business establishments, events, or locales is entirely coincidental.

LIBRARY OF CONGRESS CATALOGING IN PUBLICATION DATA
Desarthe, Agnès, 1966–
[Mangez-moi. English]
Chez moi / Agnès Desarthe ; translated from the French by Adriana Hunter.
p. cm.
ISBN 978-0-14-311323-2
I. Hunter, Adriana. II. Title.
PQ2664.E7375M364 2008
863'.64—dc22 2008006677

Printed in the United States of America
Set in Garamond MT
Designed by Richard Marston

To Dante
To my friends, for whom I love to cook,
and to Claude, at Le Passage.

Am I a liar? Yes, because I told the man at the bank I'd been on a hotel and catering course and done an eighteen-month work placement at the Ritz. I showed him the diplomas and contracts I'd made the day before. I also brandished a management training certificate, a really good fake. I like living dangerously: that's how I lost my way in the past, and why I'm on a winning streak now. The banker was completely taken in, and gave me the loan. I thanked him without turning a hair. The medical check? No problem. My blood, my precious blood is clean, nice and clean, as if I hadn't been through anything.

Am I a liar? No, because I can actually do everything I claim I can. I can wield spatulas like a juggler with his batons. Like a contortionist, I can supplely activate several different parts of my body independently: thickening a sauce with one hand while separating eggs and tying filou pastry parcels with the other. True, teenagers with fuzz on their lips, spots on their foreheads and greasy hair under their kitchen boys' caps can master the amber colour of an impossibly unctuous caramel, they can fillet a mullet without losing one milligram of flesh, and stitch their crepinette sausages with all the dedication of Penelope. But. BUT! Stick them in a kitchen with five starving bawling children who keep getting under their feet and need to be back at school within half an hour (one's allergic to dairy products and another won't eat anything), throw our splendid young apprentice chefs into that lion cub's den with an empty fridge, pans that everything sticks to and a desire to give the little darlings a balanced meal, and watch them cope. Watch those chubby-faced boys toil away and fall apart. Everything they've learned in cooking school I've learned from my different lives: the first one, in those far off days, when I was a housewife and mother, and the second, more recently, when I earned my crust in the kitchens of the Santo Salto circus.

My restaurant will be small and inexpensive. I don't like frills. It will be called *Chez moi* because it really will be my home, I'll be sleeping there; I don't have enough money to pay for the lease and a rent.

It will serve all the recipes I've invented, the ones I've transformed and the ones I've worked out for myself. There won't be any music – I'm too emotional – and the light bulbs hanging from the ceiling will be orange-tinted. I've already bought a giant fridge on the Avenue de la République. They've promised me an oven and a hob at a good price. Does it matter if it's scratched? It doesn't matter at all, I'm pretty scratched myself! The salesman doesn't laugh, he doesn't even smile. Men don't like it when women do themselves down. I also order a fifteen-setting dishwasher, the smallest model they have. It won't be big enough, the man says. It's all I can afford, it'll have to do to start with. He promises he'll send me some customers. He promises he'll come for supper one evening himself, without any warning: as a surprise. Now he *is* lying, that's for sure, but I don't mind, I wouldn't exactly have loved cooking for him.

I cook with and out of love. How am I going to manage to love my customers? The sheer luxury of that question makes me think of prostitutes because that's precisely what they don't have – that luxury.

I didn't let my friends or family know about the day of the opening. I gave them the wrong date. This time, there's no denying it, I lied too. The shopping's done. I've written my menus. I've prepared everything that could be prepared. The rest is last minute work. But there is no last minute. I'm still waiting. And there's no one coming through the door. No one knows my restaurant exists. I shake with anticipation from quarter to twelve till half past three. It's very tiring and my navel, which is the epicentre of frequent nervous spasms, is sorely tested.

When someone stops outside my door or hovers at the window I mentally shoo them away. A restaurant should be either full or empty. A single customer is worse than no customers at all. I've decided I'll be open at lunchtime and in the evenings. Maybe that's too much to start with. But I don't see how I can avoid mistakes. I've never run a restaurant. I don't know how it's done. I've thought at length about stocks and leftovers. How much should I buy? What should I cook? How long should I keep it? I've thought about it and found an answer: do what you would for a large family. With fish: raw on the first day, cooked the next if it hasn't been eaten, made into terrine on the third and soup on the fourth. That's what my grandmother does. That's what most women do and no one's ever died from it.

4

How do I know? It would have been in the paper. With meat it's the same, except I think tartar is a bit vulgar, so I cook my meat the day I buy it, then it becomes meatballs, soft little meatballs with coriander and cumin, celery tops, fronds of chervil, cream, lemon and tomatoes, roasted in garlic. There's no third chance for meat. Well there is and there isn't. I'm not allowed to write about it. With vegetables it's even more straightforward: raw, cooked, puréed, in soup, as stock. It's the same for fruits. Dairy products are such a help: they hold up well. I have a particular weakness for them. I trust them completely. Juices, of every sort, are kept separately in glass jugs. Very important, glass jugs. That's something else I got from my grandmother.

The first sitting hasn't happened. I'm exhausted. I hope this evening I'll see the chock-full tables of my dreams. Mind you, I'm even more frightened of streams of customers arriving than none at all. I'm not ready. Will I ever be? I have a nap from four o'clock to six o'clock. The banquette I got from a charity shop proves a very good bed. I sleep without really sleeping, my eyelids fluttering like butterfly wings. I keep going over things, checking through everything I have to do. The moves and the words: 'Have you reserved a table? What would you like to drink? The bill? Certainly, I'll bring it straight away. Go on, give in to temptation, the desserts are all home-made.' Impossible. I'll never be able to say things like that. Luckily, there are no more punters in the evening than there were at lunchtime. I close at twenty-five to eleven without clearing the tables and with no washing-up to do. I lie down on the banquette again, this new life is so draining – and it's only day one! I think about bills, working out everything I've got to pay when I haven't earned a thing. I feel I've been abandoned by everyone. Punished. At five o'clock in the morning I'm woken by the dustbin lorry. So I must have slept. Good news. I'd better get up, have a shower in my huge sink – I shouldn't write about that either – and get to work. Today's the real first day, the launch.

My friends think the food is delicious. They've brought champagne. My parents think the tables are too cramped and the chairs not comfortable enough. I feel like telling them it's not a restaurant for old people and they don't know what they're talking about. But they're right. I don't like my tables; I don't like my chairs either. It was the man on the Avenue de la République who gave them to me. He took pity on me, he was going to throw them out. 'They're all wonky,' he said, 'uneven. But just ask your husband to put a few bolts in them, tighten the odd screw here and there.' A bolt and a screw, me and my husband. Oy oh-yoy. Just the thought is embarrassing. I change the subject, asking when the dishwasher will arrive. 'Soon enough, soon enough,' he assures me; this time, he's not lying. The day he comes to deliver the furniture he brings the machine too.

'What's that?' he asks scornfully, pointing at my nice green banquette from the charity shop, soft moleskin set off with gold piping.

'It's a banquette. For the ladies!' I add to shut him up.

He shrugs and starts methodically filling *Chez moi* with furniture so that it suddenly looks very cramped to me. That's worrying, I think. Has it got smaller? Have we got bigger?

'It's nice,' he says when he's finished. 'It's cosy.'

'What can I offer you to eat?' I ask, hoping he won't want anything too specific.

'The best you've got,' he replies.

I think: me, eat me, but I don't say that because it all comes down to the same thing anyway. I serve him a portion of chocolate, pear and pepper tart with a glass of chilled rosé. I watch him eat, and think that, in the end, he didn't lie: he is eating in my restaurant. Except it's not supper time, so he did lie. I look at him and think he's feeding off me because I put all of myself into that first tart, that inaugural dessert. I kneaded gently, melted patiently, saved the juice as I sliced, then incorporated it into the pastry, with the Massai-black chocolate, my brown pastry in my hands, rolling it out and shaping it, rolling it out and shaping it, the pepper over the pears because I believe – in the kitchen as in other areas – in the mysterious power of alliteration. The peppercorns are dark on the outside and pale yellow on the inside, not crushed or ground. Sliced. My pepper-mill is a grater, creating tiny slices of spice. The man eats and I can see it has an effect on him. It breaks my heart. Why? I have no idea. Neither of us is worthy of the exchange.

My friends think my chairs and tables are fine as they are. 'Why's the pavement on this chard tart all green?' my mother asks. She's never trusted me and probably thinks I've let it go mouldy. 'Because I've put chopped dill and chives in it. It looks better and it makes it lighter too.' My father spits it out. He doesn't like herbs. He thinks they're for girls and for cattle. My mother's the only person I know who calls a pie crust a pavement. I think it's sweet and can pardon her the offence.

Has she forgiven me mine? The raw tuna marinated in cébette onions is a success I regret. It cost a fortune and it's so easy to do it's soulless. It's the sea they should be thanking, not me. My own vanity is intoxicating. I've made the decision: no more raw fish.

My first two customers are schoolgirls. They come through the door at quarter past twelve. *Chez moi* has been open for several days. I've had a visit from the florist next door who has bad breath and claims to be very *persnickety*. He announces the fact proudly, as if it were some sort of prestigious pedigree. I think he chose the flower trade in the hope of masking the wafting bile that creates such a stench on his palate. If you were really so *persnickety*, I feel like telling him, you would make up your mind to be a bit less so. If it goes too far it just makes you grumpy and generates black bile. A hair on the television screen provokes stomach cramps, a paper plate for a salade niçoise and the vice squeezes tighter and your oesophagus flares up, a customer who confuses ranunculus for anemones is enough to taint your saliva. If you weren't so *persnickety*, you would smell better and the world would be cleansed as a result. But I don't say anything.

The silence makes him uncomfortable and he feels he has to offer me something. 'To decorate the place,' he says, 'I could keep my unsold flowers. With a reputation like mine, I can only sell flowers that will last a week, I can't keep them in the shop more than four days…'. He expects gushing gratitude, but I don't say anything, don't show anything. I don't even manage a smile. It's because of the smell, as if a tiny corpse were rotting inside him. 'They won't be wilted,' he assures me. Perhaps he read the disgust in my eyes.

When I close the door behind him I can finally breathe through my nose, and I think of Leslie, the tight-rope walker who used to wind me up with her constant complaining, languid mutterings melted into the bland sauce of her American accent: 'Meat again!' she would moan. If there were vegetables she would complain they gave her wind. When I cooked pasta she snivelled, saying it all went straight to her thighs. I explained that pasta didn't make you fat. She laughed her funny laugh like a sheep with melancholia and shook her head, casting her eyes to the heavens.

My first two clients aren't like her. They're schoolgirls. Their trousers hang from their well-padded hips. My little poppets, I think secretly. I find their bodies charming, like giant apricots. I can't help wanting to prod the perfect flesh of their stomachs, offered so openly, bulging under their gleaming skin. Of course, I do nothing of the sort.

When they order only a first course I don't try to hide my surprise.

'It's too expensive,' they explain.

'But you'll be hungry, afterwards. Have you got lessons this afternoon?'

'Yes, philosophy.'

'You need to eat before philosophy. I'll cut all my prices in half. Let's say it's my contribution to the future of world philosophy. What if one of you becomes the greatest thinker of the century? '

I've said too much, they're bored. They think I'm mad, but that doesn't mean they won't make the most of my generosity. As I watch them drinking their avocado and grapefruit soup I wonder whether I like them or loathe them. I notice I've left a bra drying on the gas tap. That's the drawback with an open kitchen. I put it in my pocket and open the fridge to get out my old steak aiguillette – a waste that would break many a house-wife's heart – because it's meatball day. But with me it's different. I run a restaurant. I can do what I like with expensive cuts of meat. It's not a waste, it's a sign of quality. I mince the luxury meat and, so as not to disturb my two young philoso-phers' chat, I take the processor into the toilets. That's the other drawback with an open kitchen. For a moment I picture a full restaurant, twenty-five covers, orders piling up, and customers using the toilets stopping me from taking refuge in there to do the noisier jobs. I could always just close, I tell myself, reeling at the thought.

When I come back out, I notice they've taken out a packet of cigarettes. I am gripped with an irresistible urge to announce that *Chez moi* is a non-smoking establishment, but that would be stupid: I smoke myself and it would be unbelievably bad for business. The gluttons have already finished their first course. Didn't their mummies teach them to eat slowly, putting the spoon down between each mouthful? The scrolls of Camel smoke merge with the clouds of steam from the saucepan. We become ghost-like figures, lost in thick mist. They don't seem to mind and I congratulate myself that my first two customers aren't persnickety. Passers-by have started gathering, intrigued by the mysterious fog. This is the beginning of my glory. A man rushes in to save us, looming out of the mists yelling 'do you want me to call the fire brigade?' Startled, we burst out laughing. You know, there's a wonderful atmosphere here.

After reassuring him that everything is all right, I suggest he sits down. I open the door to create a draught, and offer him an ice-cold beer. 'While I'm here, I'll have a bite to eat,' he says, loosening his tie. I catch him eyeing the girls' amber-coloured hips, and make up my mind to give them their desserts on the house.

'This is too good!' one of them exclaims, dipping a piece of bread in her sauce when I go over to clear their plates. I do like them, actually. I make a mental note that they're my lucky mascots. I think I can picture a particular way of running the business: I could attract pretty women by offering them certain advantages and privileges. Crowds would converge on my restaurant to feast their eyes and my profits would be guaranteed. Any kind of sale, as a matter of principle, eventually reminds us of the slave trade or immoral earnings. I try to think of a counter-example but cannot find one. I'm not ashamed: I knew all that when I opened *Chez moi*. It's fine with me. Absolutely fine.

Last night I dreamed the Beatles came and had supper in my restaurant. All four of them. Paul McCartney, John Lennon, Ringo Starr and the other one, the one whose name I can never remember. I was really pleased when I saw them coming in but worried too, because of this recurring memory lapse. What if I have to introduce them to someone? Just as I am about to name the fourth Beatle, bang, I go blank, nothing comes to me, or actually it does, but it's worse than nothing: Jim Morrison, Jimi Hendrix, Lou Reed. Luckily there aren't any other customers so I don't need to worry about being caught out like that. I tell them how much I like them, and they answer with touching modesty and sit down at the table closest to the kitchen. We're instantly immersed in a radiant familiarity, with me at my oven and them at their table but all in it together as if they chose those seats specially, so they could talk to me. I feel honoured, but at the same time I think their consideration for me is quite natural; this is a dream, remember.

I take their order and that brings on more worrying: Paul McCartney wants fish fingers (I forgot to say they all speak very good French, without a trace of an accent). Fish fingers don't feature on my menu and I immediately hate myself for the arrogant way I put my menus together. What makes so-called serious food, dishes that are meant to be refined – cod loin in blackberry jus with wild mushrooms, millefeuilles of lamb and aubergines, torte of mascarpone with grapes and cognac – what makes them any more worthy of being served at *Chez moi*? I find my own elitism repulsive. To crown my embarrassment, Yoko Ono, who I hadn't even noticed until then (she probably wasn't there at the beginning of the dream: that's the problem with dreams, people come in and out at the wrong time), stares at me sternly. She's right. I've slavishly followed bourgeois notions of cooking when, when… stammering won't get you anywhere, come on! Get into your kitchen! I go to the fridge and take out a beautiful slab of monkfish. Armed with my thinnest knife I cut into its rich dense meat, well away from the central bone, which is too bloody for my liking, and the stomach where the flesh becomes softer, floppier, thinner, like wide ears on some washed-out sea monster. I cut out a rectangular piece which reminds me of those little blocks of wood I used to buy in loads of five hundred for my son so that he could build wonderful fortresses. It shouldn't be allowed for real memories to get mixed up in the flimsy structure of dreams because the pain it causes is unbearable. This fish 'block' is perfect: smooth, white and supple. I make a thick coating for it, browning some breadcrumbs in butter. The crumbs aren't quite rounded enough for my liking, not as rounded as on the fish fingers I remember from the days when I used to fry them up for my son, who loved them, secretly congratulating himself for living in a world where shapes were governed with such stupefying coherence: building blocks were followed by fish blocks and, at bath time (he liked having his bath after tea), blocks of soap. What am I talking about? I've no idea what went through my son's head. That's the other drawback with dreams, the propensity to hallucinate, the illusion of intellectual omnipotence. My golden breadcrumbs are ready. I dip the fish in a touch of egg-white and roll it in them, and it works: when I've run over the plate of tiny nuggets four times it is perfectly disguised, perfectly unrecognizable as a monkfish fillet and perfectly recognizable as fish fingers. When I lay it on Paul McCartney's plate, he shrieks with joy and, probably by way of thanking me, starts singing 'Norwegian Wood'. They all sing along with him. Even Yoko Ono. Guitars and other instruments join in, somewhere in the wings. It's wonderful. It makes me cry. It makes me cry because that's the record that was playing the first time I made love.

I remember it very well. I was on the floor on my back. The urge had been getting stronger for months and months. I kept laughing, not because it was so strange, not because I felt ashamed (I didn't at all) and not because I was embarrassed. I wanted to laugh because it made me so happy, that discovery, the intoxicating belief that I was inventing something. I thought of Archimedes and Copernicus. I thought of Newton and Einstein. I thought of Galileo. In the depths of me, just like in the universe, this untapped seam, like gravitational force, in me, just like the earth, this inexhaustible source of energy. Why hadn't anyone told me about it before? How could I not have guessed? And was it for free? And could everyone have it? And was it really that easy? So easy? I didn't think about not being on the pill, or that the boy hadn't used a condom, that I might get pregnant or catch God knows what. I just thought this is crazy. And while all this was going on the Beatles sang 'Norwegian Wood'.

How come we live several different lives? Maybe I'm generalizing a bit. Maybe I'm the only one who feels like this. I will only die once and yet, during the time I'm allotted, I will have lived a series of related but clearly distinct existences.

At thirty, I wasn't the same person I am now. At eight, I was a very individual little thing. I see my adolescence as quite autonomous in relation to what followed. The woman I am now is rootless, unattached, incomprehensibly alone. I used to have lots of people round me. I had become very sociable. Initially I was shy, then reserved, then sensible... finally mad.

It's a quarter to midnight and I run a tiny bath in the giant sink. Only newborns are given baths in basins. Newborns and me. I put in the plug and let the warm water fill up till it's twenty-five centimetres deep. There are another thirty centimetres to the edge. I climb onto the work surface. The metal shutters are closed. I am standing here naked on my draining board and I'd like someone to see me because it's an unusual situation and it deserves an audience. I sit down with my back against the smooth steel, and it doesn't overflow. I like the arithmetical precision of the thing. Being quite incapable of calculating anything, I used guesswork and it didn't let me down. In order to take up less space I put my arms under my bent knees, ending up – more or less – in what's called the crow position. In the days of the Santo Salto circus I used to warm up with the performers. We did a sort of yoga, stretching and pushing exercises. My limbs, which had never been subjected to any form of discipline, made cracking noises and my muscles trembled but I didn't let it put me off and no one made fun of me. Pretty much all of us had some previous conviction, had gone astray, and not one of us would have dreamed of commenting on someone else's behaviour. We had no choice but to tolerate each other. It was a world within a world, oblivious to the rules governing the rest of society and indifferent to its conventions. You could become a mother at fourteen or forty-eight. Stay single or have three husbands. You might be an aunt of the children you were bringing up, and you could work in the kitchens one day and on the till the next; and that never stopped anyone pampering the horses or feeding the dogs. Our animals were particularly intelligent. We liked to take in a great variety of species and didn't believe tigers necessarily made for a better performance than dogs or cats. The frontier between the domesticated and the wild was unclear. We constantly blurred it, allowing some to be wild while firmly believing in our own ability to subdue the untameable. No one spoke, we all shouted, rarely using verbs or adjectives but relying heavily on names, nicknames and onomatopoeia. Hup. Bang. Woah. Half an hour before going into the ring we were a bit like stick insects, motionless, alert, subsumed into our ropes, batons, poles, nets and barres, indistinguishable from our own accessories, camouflaged. Our animals fell silent and we all exchanged looks exhaustively: men and dogs, goats and young girls, snakes and women. It was a cold world but not chillingly so. We didn't have time for feelings, but physical contact compensated for the shortcoming. There was always a hand on your back, your shoulder, your elbow, an instep on the inside of your thigh, a head against your stomach, a knee wedged in your groin. We formed a collective Karma Sutra peculiarly devoid of eroticism. Skin is a platform, a flat surface but, like the earth, it is also rounded and self-contained and made up of interdependent elements. We take a long time to understand our own skin, the paradoxical way it's both a surface and an envelope, its singularity and multiplicity: the skin on our feet, the skin on our necks, our chins, genitals, ribs, the sole same organ keeping itself constantly informed. I thought I knew my skin but one day a hand on the back of my neck – an unexpected, or should I say un-hoped for, hand – showed me I was wrong: there was a whole world left to discover. That was before Santo Salto and it's a long story which I will have to go into, but at the moment I'm talking about skin which, like the wild animals we lived with, can be domesticated and tamed.

My first week at the circus I was electrified by the constant hugging, the warmth exchanged, taken from someone else, sold on, lost, then found again. When the circus manager, who everyone called boss, explained what he wanted me to do he put his hands on my shoulders and looked me right in the eye. I couldn't see why he needed to be quite so emphatic. It was only a question of the right amount of meat and carbohydrate, of vegetable supplies and limiting the use of spices. It was only later, after a few days, when I had a pot of cayenne pepper in my hand, that I understood the point of his touching me: it was a way of physically imprinting his words in my skin, because things were only ever said once. If I hadn't remembered the weight of the boss's hands on my shoulders as I sprinkled the pepper I would probably have used too much, the dish would have been sent back to the kitchen and I would have been fired. I couldn't afford to be. I had no money, no home and absolutely no structure left in my life. If I had left the circus, it would have been only too easy for me to dissolve into the streets, to disappear because I had been disowned, no one wanted to see me, no one, not my family nor my friends. I had become such dubious company that no one would have noticed if I had run away, dispersed into thin air or died. What sort of thread did I manage to cling to? We always think there's a thread until the day we meet a truly good magician or a truly good acrobat. Sometimes there's no trick, sometimes it all comes down to training. I suppose I had been well-trained for survival. Yes, that was it. That's my skill, or perhaps it's a gift.

It's not just that I adapt easily, it's that I revel in adapting. Does it go back to my early childhood? Is there a doctor or a fortune-teller who could establish that? This sink here, for example: when I step into it, I don't think about the fact that I haven't got a bath; instead I'm delighted by the telescopic tap and the shower head that the facetious manufacturer thought of adding. When I'm in a bath, I don't think enamel, oh, a lovely enamelled bath (actually, I don't know if it's enamel or china, that smooth heavy substance which makes me think of unpasteurized milk and is such a heartbreaking white). No, I don't miss that noble surface; instead I wonder at the versatility of stainless steel: sturdy but light, hollow but undentable, neither hot nor cold by nature but successively hot and cold depending on the temperature of what is in contact with it, like an echo of my own system for thermal regulation – cold with cold people, warm with the warm, no little nuances, no balancing out, just joining in. It's what some people would call flexibility, the same flexibility that means I'm quite happy to take a bath in a sink fifty centimetres across. I sometimes construct complex day-dreams on the subject: I'm on a desert island, I've been abandoned on top of a glacier, I'm stuck in a cave several hundred metres underground. The most worrying thing is that these nightmarish imaginings don't arouse any fear in me. Quite the opposite: these disastrous scenarios with me as their heroine help me defeat the endless banalities I have to get through every day. Just living, now that's difficult, away from whirlwinds, away from danger, calmly looking at the cork board with bills pinned to it and telling yourself you'll honour them on the ninetieth day and that, if there's not enough money, you'll use money you don't even have and risk going bankrupt, like a surfer in the tube of a giant wave, except he's risking death whereas I'm not risking anything: at worst repossession, failure and extreme poverty, and, even though these spectres are terrifying, even though I know how bitter they feel from having come too close to them already, they're nothing compared to death. So yes, that's what I have to do, every day, follow the straight stretch of road onto the next day, get up – early, very early – do the shopping, clean, chop, think, warm through, fry, defrost, strain, count, serve, count again, clean some more, throw away, take back, scour, peel some more, press, blanch, break up and knead. At night, sitting in my bathwater, I go back over it and the list of my daily activities, the sum of all those things is nothing, and yet it's everything. I try to define my reason for living. It can't be formulated or pinned down, it's a kernel of pure joy that I never quite reach and is linked – although I don't know how – to sensations in my skin. I get out of my sink, dry myself carefully and rub myself with oil that I don't use for cooking, because I do still have some boundaries, in spite of everything.

The florist arrives armed with his first salvaged bouquet.

'I don't open till eleven,' he tells me.

He's got time for a cup of coffee, then. That is how I interpret this information he has given me and which would otherwise be pointless.

'Would you like some coffee?'

'If you like,' he says, as if the pleasure would be mine.

He sits down on the moleskin banquette for women while I nip behind the counter to get away from his breath. I adore my percolator. And that's not too strong a word, I really adore it, like an idol. There it stands, gleaming, with its handles and buttons, its tubes and grids like the dashboard of a private jet. I can't get over the luxury of it. My percolator is a Hirschmüller, that's a German subsidiary of the original manufacturers Kruger, based in Neufchatel in Switzerland. I've got quite hot on kitchen equipment thanks to my new friend the salesman on the Avenue de la République. It's an old model but nearly new, and he gave me fantastic credit on it, the sort of credit to make me think he was in love with me if I weren't so lucid: what he likes is the use I'm putting my machines to, and that's a step in the right direction, I tell myself, as I slot the little receptacle into the breech.

'I like it strong,' the florist says. 'If you don't mind.'

I'm tempted to give him some coffee beans too, for him to chew on to purify his exhalations.

'No problem,' I tell him. 'I'm the same.'

'I'm Vincent.'

'I'm Myriam.'

I tear open the brown paper packaging.

'I haven't got a vase,' I say apologetically, looking at the flowers: grim-looking auriculas, carnations with brown-tipped petals and gypsophila so ready to drop its flowers that my draining board is instantly covered in a pretty carpet of snow. There are also two tall stems of some plant I don't recognize, probably something exotic, which culminate in a sort of wrinkled scarlet quiff which, in spite of myself, I think looks like you know what.

'What a pain!' he says instead of running back to his store-room to offer me his chipped pots, out-dated single-stem vases, rusty buckets, I don't know, all those containers probably cluttering up the back of his shop which he keeps for some inexplicable reason.

I sacrifice two wine carafes and three glasses.

The coffee's ready. The floral ambiance is a bit exuberant for my liking, and the bouquets give off a smell of tired gardens which has a powerful effect on my sensitive nerves.

'How's business?' Vincent asks, dipping his pale lips in his strong coffee.

I think for a moment: it's the eleventh day since I opened and I've got €300 in takings and €4000 in debts, not to mention my various loans.

'Good,' I say with a smile. 'Very good, even. It's weird. It's going better than I hoped. I used to have a *salon de thé* in the Seventh Arrondissement. It was too tiring but, my God, we made a lot of money!'

I fan myself with my hand as if feeling the heat from this past – fictitious – fortune.

'In the Seventh Arrondissement?' Vincent says, impressed.

Don't let him ask me the name of the street.

'Yup, near Invalides.'

I'm such a daredevil.

'I don't really like it round there,' he says sulkily and I remember he has his reputation for pernicketiness to live up to.

'You're right. The customers were horrendous. Here they're much more… much more…'

I'm struggling to find the words because my customers are so few and far between it would be difficult to define them.

'They're more like family,' he announces.

'That's it!'

And a brilliant idea suddenly seeds itself in my mind. But I let it get away. I don't have time to deal with it straight away, it'll just have to come back later. It's the eleventh day since I opened and things aren't going well at all. There are leftovers piling up in the fridge, I'm chucking out shoulders of beef, binning leeks, throwing away tomatoes. Every time I lean over the bin my conscience is streaked by the whip marks of guilt. I feel as if someone's watching me, and they're not happy. This threatening presence might just be my own shadow; like when you frighten yourself walking through an empty house at dusk, glimpsing the white of an eye in a mirror. It's your own face that has appeared in the mirror, but by the time you realize this your blood has already run cold. It could be that this critical eye watching me is my own, it could be that the courtroom in which my trial is being held is my own conscience, my poor whipped conscience. But then, standing facing Vincent who recycles his rotting flowers by giving them to me, a second brilliant idea suddenly comes to me. This man's doing a lot for me, I tell myself. He's giving me inspiration. He's my muse. I get the feeling Vincent wants to ask me about my private life. He would love to know, for example, whether I'm married. Single women don't make him very comfortable and there's nothing odd about that – they're bad for his business.

'And you've reinvested it all in… in your…'

Why's he having such a struggle calling *Chez moi* a restaurant? If people have trouble identifying this as somewhere to eat, where you pay for food, it'll never take off. It's true I don't have a sign. It's true it doesn't say 'restaurant' on the front, or 'cafe-bar' or 'brasserie'. It doesn't even say *Chez moi*, I haven't had the time, or the ladder or the paint. But I do have a big window with the menu written on a slate and, just behind it, tables, chairs and a moleskin banquette and, right at the back, the dazzling nickel of my percolator. Shit, I think. That's it. It's as stupid as that: people don't realize I've opened a restaurant. Oh, Vincent, Vincent, you're such a help to me!

'In my restaurant, you mean?'

'Yes, well, in your – erm – business.'

'No I put all the money from the sale of the *salon de thé* into the Stock Market. I felt happier taking out a loan to buy this business,' I say, to impress him.

'Clever', he says softly, sketching a wink.

I'm beginning to like my new personality, that's one of the difficulties with being so adaptable: any set-up will do. I don't feel cramped in a businesswoman's smart shoes. I have a sudden urge to talk to him about my family, the family that would suit my new personality: I would have a lawyer husband, five children – yes, it turns out we're Catholic (quite modern, granted, but we do insist on certain values). It would be a bit of a scrape, what with the holes in my apron and the scuffing at the bottom of my cords. And because of my face too, which – I'm well aware – looks more like a squaw who's been around the block a bit or a gipsy on an assignment to infiltrate the ranks than some pious stalwart of the PTA. Adaptability and compulsive lying don't make good bedfellows, contrary to what you might think. For a compulsive liar the pleasure isn't just in catching out the person they're talking to, it also draws on the fibber's own astonishment at believing their fabrications themselves. With me there are no surprises. Whether I'm one thing or the other, it couldn't matter less.

There's no coffee left in our cups. We can't pretend to drink one last mouthful.

'Do you like reading?' Vincent asks me.

He could have driven a knife into my heart and the pain wouldn't have been more acute. I clench my jaw, don't say anything. Can't say anything.

He gets up and casts an eye over the room.

'It's unusual,' he says, 'to have books in a… in a… Have you read all of them?' he asks, taking one of the thirty-three volumes I've lined up on a shelf opposite the banquette.

'*The Sorrows of Young Werther*,' he intones. 'That can't be much fun. And what's this, *The Wild Palms*? Is that English or German? How many languages do you speak? Ah, now, this is more me, *Kingdoms of Elfin*, have you read *The Hobbit*? I see you've got some children's books, *Alice in Wonderland*, I think I must have read that when I was little. It was a talking book. Do you remember talking books? They're useful for children who don't like reading; and adults too, but you wouldn't have that problem. Still, it's quite surprising in a…'

He's going to mess everything up. If he opens one and starts reading, breathing into it, tainting the lovely smell of old paper with that foul stench in his mouth… but no. He isn't that curious and, in fact, he's very careful. Don't let's forget he deals in flowers. He sells living things, ones that die very easily too. He asked me whether I like reading, but he couldn't care less about the answer and that's just as well because it would take me too long to give one and he wouldn't be back in time to open his shop. I know I'm safe not saying anything, he's still got plenty to say. He's perfectly capable of producing enough little remarks to punctuate the ten minutes till he has to leave quite comfortably. I let him get on with it. I let him talk. And, while he does, I think of one of my precious books, one that isn't on the shelf, it didn't come with me, I've lost it and I could almost cry if I didn't secretly believe it will come back to me one day. Someone will bring it back to me, a messenger, an envoy from the past, in the last act, almost at the end, like in a Shakespeare play. I couldn't buy this book again because I don't know what it's called or who it's by. You think that's odd. Yes, especially as I've read it several times. It's a problem I have. Neurological. Neurological that is, not psychological (that's a terrible word, it really is). I'm absolutely hopeless with book titles. I get all the authors confused. Just then, for example, I mentioned a Shakespeare play but it could be that the one I was thinking of was by Molière or Ibsen. I can only cope with the thirty-three volumes of my nomadic library. The rest is just a great heap, a muddle and, in my eyes, the site of all beauty. The book I'm thinking about, while Vincent explains the relative merits of slot-in record players and the sort with an arm, the book I've lost is a philosophical treatise. My favourite chapter is about dogs. In it the author explains that dogs are not animals. According to him, or her (I don't know what sex authors are in the same way I don't know their names), dogs are a concept. A Doberman is not much like a Cocker Spaniel which shares few characteristics with a Chihuahua; a Saint-Bernard can meet a Pekingese and, theoretically, they can mate, but does that ever happen and would it be a good thing? Because, although zoologically they belong to the same species, in practical terms it's blindingly obvious they're not made for each other. The author went on to say how amazed he (or she) was that his three-year-old daughter (the tendency to mix personal life with reasoning makes me incline towards an Anglo-Saxon writer) could always recognize a dog when she saw one in the street, even though the animals she pointed at so enthusiastically –

delighted by an opportunity to display her combined mastery of language and categorization – didn't look anything like each other. If a cat appeared, even a big beefy one, she would not be fooled. If a pony turned up, even the smallest of its lineage, smaller at the wither than a Great Dane, she would not cry 'Dog! Dog!' She knew. Even if they don't bark, have their ears trimmed so they prick up, or are bundled into miniature anoraks to protect them from inclement weather, dogs maintain their conceptual integrity. A thought which, although confused, really bothers me in the context of the indiscernibility of my establishment. Vincent can't say I've opened a restaurant. He doesn't have a word to describe the place we're in, and it makes me feel like a dog which doesn't fall into the concept, the only dog that three year-olds sometimes mistake for a bear or a cat. I don't understand how I could have created such an awkward situation.

I wonder exactly when I realized I would have to work much harder than before to carry on living. Just living. I had always imagined, I have no idea why, that our existence was shaped like a mountain. Childhood, adolescence and early adulthood corresponded to the upward climb. Then, at forty or fifty, the descent began, a vertiginous one, of course, towards death. This idea, which I think is fairly common, is quite false. As I am discovering a little more clearly every day. It all starts with the descent, feel-wheeling, no effort required. We have all the time in the world to look at the scenery and enjoy the smells – that's why childhood smells stay with us.

The real slope only appears later, and we take a good while to recognize it for what it is: a hard climb with the same outcome as the steep drop we all imagined we would be projected into at top speed. And you wonder, one autumn evening, with your hands in a bucket wringing out the floor cloth before dragging it – is this the fourth or fifth time today? – over the filthy kitchen floor: how come sorrow is as heavy, lumpen and impenetrably black as an anvil? You wring out that grey rag which has picked up baby sick, their pee, spilt tomato sauce, wine, birthday champagne, thousands of droplets from a water fight enjoyed by some children who couldn't bear the heat, and that horrible pavement grey which everyone takes home. You wring out that poor rag which has seen so much, and it's your heart and your liver and your stomach that contort, spreading acrid thickened blood through your veins, blood which – if you could see it – you'd expect to be the same colour as the filthy water in the pail. Sadness wells up and you'd drown in it if there weren't things to do, letters to post, bills to pay, holiday time to allow for. We all know that if we don't put our lives together as we go along no one else will do it for us.

I remember a cartoon from my childhood, called *La Linea*, I think. It was my favourite programme. It featured a little man in profile who was depicted by a line which came up from the ground, traced round the contours of his body and head, then went back down to the ground again, so that everything was jumbled up in the same line: the character, his setting, the horizon. The little man walked along, humming and mumbling quite happily and suddenly the line, the line drawing him, would stop two paces in front of him. And he would cry out in near gobbledegook tinged with an Italian accent, 'Hang on, why isn't there a line here?'. Quite often he would fall down the precipice, unravelling like unfinished knitting, screaming, 'Aaaaaaah!'. Sometimes he would climb back up. He even occasionally managed to form the path in front of him by using some that he'd already walked over. He was the human equivalent of a train that has to lay down its own tracks every day. The adult human, it goes without saying, the human in the throes of that exhausting climb towards oblivion. One day that's what happens: you end up, like *La*

Linea, with nothing in front of you and there's no one to blame. You're horrified not to have seen it coming, incensed that no one's doing anything about it. 'Hang on, why isn't there a line here?' you ask as you wring out the floor cloth. There isn't a line because that was false too, that was all a dirty trick too. If we want to get on, just following the road isn't good enough, we have to spend our every moment covering it with the unctuous Tarmac of our hopes and dreams, tracing it out in our minds, striving to anticipate the inevitable corners and bumpy patches. Sometimes, when things are going well, when by some miracle we've managed to get a little way ahead with this terrifying work of art, we enjoy a little respite and it all goes smoothly. We might even start thinking the worst of it is over, that from now on everything will be all right. We're so naive and our memories are so short that we forget the ground ahead of us was put together by our own hands and our own minds – always so quick to imagine all sorts of things. We glide along gently until the next hole, and then peer down it in dismay. I haven't got the strength any more, we think, and I deserve better than this, it's about time someone helped me, it's about time there was a hand to guide mine. And all around there are nothing but arms swinging aimlessly. Everyone's tired. Husbands, wives, friends, everyone's had enough at the same time and that's when – but only if we're very lucky, only if we're not afraid or if we're mad enough to pounce on the furtive bait – that's when love comes along. And then it's no longer Tarmac we throw into the void, it's a suspension bridge opening the road up to infinity.

This evening my brother has invited me to a restaurant. Charles, my brother, is a good man, everyone says so and it's true. He has nothing but good qualities: he's calm, sensitive, trustworthy, funny, inventive and – whatever the situation and wherever he is – he always feels comfortable. I sometimes think he's like a version of myself that went right. When I was a child he irritated me because he never got annoyed. I would foam at the mouth, rage and scream, drum my fists and sob. Not him: he smiled, that mysterious smile perched at the top of his long neck like an unfurled sail. He's four years younger than me, but I think he seems so much younger. He rang me this morning just after Vincent left.

'It wouldn't by any chance be your day off today, would it?' he asked.

'I don't have a day off.'

'Exactly. Seeing as you don't have one, we can make it whenever we like. If a whole day seems a bit much, let's just say it's your evening off.'

'Why?'

'Because I want to take you out to a restaurant.'

'Is this a joke?'

'No.'

'You didn't even come to the launch of mine.'

'I was in Toronto.'

My brother travels, a lot, and very well. He doesn't get sea-sick and isn't affected by jet lag. He never talks about it, doesn't boast about it. I only know these admirable details because I've travelled with him in the past.

'And now you're home,' I say, 'so you ring me because I'm at your beck and call. You just have to ring and I come running, I even shut up my restaurant. I'm about to go bankrupt, you know.'

'Exactly. One evening off isn't going to change anything. I'll come and pick you up.'

'On your motorbike?'

'On my motorbike.'

I'm the elder but he's in charge because he's more intelligent than me. That's just how the cards were dealt, very early on. Even as a baby he impressed me. He was placid and did every-thing babies are supposed to do with bewildering skill. He ate well, slept well and made delightful comforting little utterances. I would look deep into his eyes, my heart constricted with loathing. His lead-dark irises reflected my image and, as I moved closer to get a better look at myself, he would reach out his hands, take hold of my cheeks and suckle absent-mindedly on my nose. Even though I was only young, I felt there was something inappropriate about this – which I loved and interpreted as a very individual brand of humour.

The restaurant my brother has chosen is extremely sophisticated, not the sort of place I go to. Unlike him, I frequently feel uncomfortable. Everything here has been wonderfully thought out and designed. I notice that the table-cloths are short, revealing elegant legs in carved wood. I find this detail touching: if you have lovely legs, why hide them? The cutlery is unusual too: it has the snowy gleam of old silver but is very light, almost weightless, so that it feels a bit like eating with your fingers, with nothing weighing you down; the food glides to your mouth. I wonder what the manager of this restaurant would think of *Chez moi*. I'm ashamed. The pitiful shame of a non-concept dog.

I've ordered ice-cold ficoide in truffle vinaigrette. Ficoide is a rare kind of salad with thick fleshy leaves prettily arranged round a delicious pulpy stem. I don't know where you buy the stuff. At *Chez moi* I have ordinary lettuce and romaine lettuce, and also rocket which I toss into gravy because I've got an idea rocket is a meat-like plant: I'm keen to reconcile it with its animal tendencies. It's a waste because most people leave it on the side of the plate, shrivelled and pathetic as if it were a failed garnish. Still, I press on with my attempted trans-categoriza-tion: I feel it's what the various foodstuffs expect of me, what I'm supposed to give to the world. Rocket with meat. Avocados with fruit. White wine with cheese. I realign friendships, cheat at Happy Families.

I don't know how they do the lighting here. I can't see any lamps and there isn't a single candle, and yet there's light melting over us or, rather, we're melting into it. We're clothed in a golden glow, my brother, the other customers and myself. The waiters are haloed too, as if by a permanent sunset. We all look so gorgeous I wonder whether we've been transferred to paradise. Each of us a little figurine dipped by some deft and kindly hand into a pool of forgetfulness and languor, with iridescent crescent shapes highlighting our cheek-bones and foreheads. I eat my magic salad – for, now that I think about it, I realize ficoide can't be bought, it's picked in the forests of Brocéliande by the light of a torch which burns with a cold flame – and I think it tastes better than any of the dishes I make, the dishes I'm so proud of. I didn't think it would happen so soon, being sanctioned like this, being informed that I'd lost the plot and that, at the end of the day, I'm not cut out for what I thought I was. This chic restaurant, whose identity and purpose no one would ever question, this perfectly conceptual restaurant presents me with an unbearable comparison. I'm not a Poodle faced with a Doberman or a Pekingese faced with a Labrador: at a real pinch I'm a cuddly toy dog, but an ugly one, the one no one wants, that sits gathering dust on the shelf in a village shop where they once thought they should get into toys to attract more customers. I wouldn't have guessed that this bitter revelation would come from my brother, either. What was he thinking? Why has he brought me here? Perhaps he thinks the fall won't be so painful if it's very quick and very sudden. But no. Because he's never been to *Chez moi*. He doesn't know what you can eat there, or where you sit. He is talking to me, he hasn't stopped talking since we got here and – and this is terrible – I haven't heard a thing. I was aware of the sound of his voice in the way you can be aware of waves in the background, intoxicating or irritating, lulling or invigorating, but who would ever think of working out what they mean?

'I haven't listened to anything you've said.'

I'd rather things were clear between us. I just hope he hasn't told me his fiancée's died, he's about to be fired or, even more scary, he's got some incurable illness. I shake at the thought of my prognoses. He's smiling.

'Couldn't matter less,' he says. 'If you want a summary, I talked about the new gym I go to in the morning, and I also told you how I found this place. Do you like it?'

'What?'

'This place.'

As he says this, he gives a discreet sweep of his arm to point out the walls, furniture and even the people working and eating here, as if it were all his.

'It humiliates me,' I tell him, too quickly.

My answer is both hurtful and unfathomable.

But Charles is still smiling. He's not upset. He thinks it's interesting, wants to understand why I feel like that. He wants to know whether it's connected to our mongrel origins, whether I've become more left wing than him, whether there was something wrong with my salad.

I explain that I feel stupid because... oh, how come he's even asking me that? Has he forgotten I've just opened a restaurant or what? I work myself to death from morning till night, my back hurts all over and so do my wrists from standing whipping up sauces, I think my cooking's boring and haphazard, I'm not an experienced waitress, I spill the soup, I'm a complete shambles, I'm too slow, even when I'm being quick, I don't know how to deal with customers, I'm no good at the art of conversation, and the lighting at *Chez moi* is two neon strips on the back wall and two huge orange lamps which I loved on the first day and have sincerely loathed ever since. I feel humiliated because I now see I don't know anything about restaurants, that it's a profession, a profession I haven't learned, and – actually – I never learned anything, ever, in this bitch of a life, I'm incompetent, I'm going to throw in the towel and…

I've managed not to raise my voice, but can't hold back the tears. I start crying just as the waiter, a beautiful young man with dark hair and eyelashes that go on for ever, comes over to clear the first course.

'Thank you,' says Charles, 'it was very good.'

He comes across as so convinced, he manages to slip such a credible note of emotion into his voice that you would think that was why I was crying, because it was so good. In a few words he's given my tearfulness a new meaning, transposed it, made it far more sophisticated by attributing an aesthetic explanation to it. He's delivered it of its triviality, dissolving away my lack of discretion. The young man smiles at me, sharing with me – or at least so he believes – the silky soft but devastating pleasure afforded by the perfect combination of the special lettuce and its vinaigrette. Back in the kitchen he'll be able to tell the boss that he's made yet another customer cry. And the latter will sharpen his big knife, his full lips reflected in its flashing blade, and drive it into the tender flesh of the veal he's intending for me.

I can't bear to think what I must look like to my brother. I want to be strong and sound of mind. I wish I could reason in the same good-natured way as my lost philosophy book. I want to inspire respect, not pity, not even compassion. My tears dry up. I straighten my shoulders, look at Charles, and we both burst out laughing.

'I love the way you always do the most ridiculous things,' he says.

'Sorry?'

'When you said you were going to open a restaurant I thought it was a joke.'

'Didn't you believe me?'

'Not for a minute.'

'That's upsetting.'

'Well, it shouldn't be. Because you've done it. I was wrong and you were right. You've won.'

'Why did you bring me here?'

'To prove how little imagination I've got. If I opened a restaurant it would be like this. I bet yours is different. I bet your restaurant isn't like anywhere else. I don't understand how I can be such a conformist and you're not.'

'You're jealous.'

'No. I couldn't live your life.'

'Neither can I.'

Charles shrugs his shoulders, and I think I wouldn't like to live his life. A first wife met at university, not very pretty but a good sort, with whom he has two brilliant children brought up on the tried and tested recipe of after-school sports lessons, long meaningful conversations and weekends in the country.

Leaving her because she feels unfulfilled and her psycho-therapist leads her to understand that her marriage is an inhibiting factor. Meeting another girl – a prettier, younger one – and torturing her by refusing her a child. And all the while earning enough money to live and take your sister (and other people, I imagine) out for sumptuous meals in perfect settings. I couldn't do it. I've tried. There's something stopping me. A force. A tide. My brother's a yacht and I'm a steamship, but my keel's too shallow and my rudder too long. The slightest movement of the tiller drags me thousands of miles from my intended destination. I have the sluggish inertia of a great big ship. When the port's in sight there's no point aiming for the harbour, I'll pile straight into the sea wall. Even though it's slow and unremarkable, my existence has caused terrible damage. And yet I did see the lighthouse flashing its anxious message in the distance. I got its warnings and said, yes, yes, I know, I'm going to break everything; but it was too late.

'What's it like in your dive, then?' Charles asks me.

'Why do you call it a dive? You haven't seen it.'

'That's what Dad calls it: your sister's dive.'

I feel as if I've opened a brothel.

'And what else does he say?'

'Nothing. As usual. Rubbish. He talks and all you get's that droning fa-deva-fa-deva-ba-deva.'

That is absolutely exactly the sound my father makes because he decided a long time ago that muttering was all the world deserved from him. I smile.

'And Mum, did she say anything?'

My life suddenly hangs on my parents' opinions.

'She said… hang on, I'm going to get it right, are you ready for this, I'm letting her come to me for a minute, just wait…' He concentrates, closes his eyes, screws them up slightly and when he opens them again he is my mother. His cheeks are sucked inwards, his nostrils pinched, making his mouth protrude all the more, fleshy, clearly defined, and his eyebrows curve up towards the middle of his forehead, half-imploring, half-exasperated.

'Your sister's got so much talent!' he pronounces in a voice ravaged by tobacco, when he doesn't even smoke; ravaged, then, by my mother's tobacco, she of the long cigarillos.

He manages to reproduce every last nuance of her intonation: admiration, anger, a feeling of waste, despair. He's so good at it that it comes as a slap in the face, but I take it without flinching: my mother's slaps no longer get to me. They get lost somewhere between us, in a place where there's no sound and no pain, a place I sometimes imagine – it's white and we drift through it, facing each other and constantly threatening to bump into each other, but we never touch, just smile and avoid each other's eyes.

'Unbelievable talent!' he adds, and the imitation is so accurate I can almost see smoke coming from his nostrils.

I burst out laughing. My brother blinks and turns back into himself, freed from the maternal dybbuk. We're ageless. When we meet up like this and our thoughts slot together like the two halves of a magic ring, time melts away and we relive every period of our existence condensed into the nectar of our shared presence. We talk about baby milk in the same breath as cigarettes, and Mickey Mouse plasters in the same sentence as nicotine patches. We can say Mummy and Daddy, words which are forbidden the rest of the time. We meet on the sibling's playing-field, a stretch of wasteland that lies unnoticed behind a fence buckling slightly beneath the varnish of social expectations. We've got everything we need: stones to throw at each other, clumps of grass to collapse onto in exhaustion, and insects to frighten each other and observe. Sometimes it feels really good to be there, when there are camp fires and we take refuge in their glow, outlining us with a golden igloo and protecting us from the outside world. The twigs we throw onto the fire to feed the flames are shared memories, and jokes that don't make anyone laugh but us. We're neither boss nor employee, divorced nor married, we have no children and no friends, the whole world has been swallowed up into our little pyre, reduced to whatever we want it to be. But there are times when it doesn't feel good: the ground is too dry and the dust whips up off it and stings our eyes, the place is covered in thistles so there's nowhere to sit down, the fire smells of cold cigarettes and the precious sibling is unrecognizable. We realize we have suddenly grown old, and the secret door in the fence slams shut behind us.

Charles didn't come to the field for several years. Or he only went there half-heartedly, as if performing an onerous duty, but his heart wasn't in it because it was consumed with dreams for the future. He had become too ambitious for the two of us and I wasn't what he needed. I would go and sit down alone beside the cold embers, and wait for him to come and save me from the curse of time which only ever goes one way. Eventually he came back, sat down without a word, struck a match, chucked in a couple of little disappointments which went up in flames immediately, and gave me back my childhood.

This evening, in this chic restaurant, we have built a great bonfire of happiness.

'So,' he asks again, 'how are you getting on?'

'Really badly, I think.'

Charles looks amazed.

'There are some things I can do,' I tell him, so as not to give the impression I'm complaining (we can't stand whingers). 'But there are too many things I just don't know how to do.'

'Like what?'

'The paperwork. Filling in forms. I would never have thought there were so many forms, things to pay, expenses you can't begin to understand and huge charges that you can never hope to pay half of a quarter of. And even the shopping. I'm sure I'm not doing the shopping properly. I've always heard people talking about Rungis, that's where you're supposed to go, but I haven't got a car, so I go to the mini-market and the local market.'

'How did you do it before, for the circus?'

'It was different. We didn't buy anything.'

'Well, what did you eat then?'

'Oh, everything, but I didn't go to the shops. This bloke used to come. A farmer. But he was nothing like the sort of farmers you see in the countryside, or you picture in your mind, old peasants in blue overalls and berets. Our farmer was called Ali Slimane, he was very elegant, always in a white shirt and putty-coloured trousers. He came to us. I didn't ring him, I didn't have his number. I didn't place an order. He'd turn up in his blue van, a very pretty blue, somewhere between dark and light, a blue from our childhood. And he had everything in that van – meat, vegetables, dairy products, but no labels, no abattoir stamps: he reared and slaughtered the animals himself. The vegetables were covered in a thin layer of mud. "It protects them. Take the mud off at the last minute. Don't wash the vegetables, just peel or rub." I did exactly what Ali told me. I always felt a slight constriction in my chest when he spoke to me and I don't know whether it was because I felt sorry for him or because I rather liked him.'

'Why should you feel sorry for him?'

'I thought he was lonely.'

'He could have had a wife, at the farm. And children. Three mistresses in the village and fifty-three brothers and sisters.'

'No. And even if he'd had all that there was something solitary in his eyes, the remains of a bright flame darkened by the expression – or rather the lack of expression – in the rest of his face. He also brought me preserved foods, jars of artichokes, marinaded lemons, all sorts of peas and beans, bottles of spices, eggs with rough shells… he kept flour in brown paper bags. At the far end of our plot he'd cleared a little square patch of land and planted herbs: thyme, rosemary, parsley, coriander, chives, sage and mint. I asked him if he was worried they'd be polluted by the city air. "You're all polluted yourselves," he said, but without animosity, not judgemental. "You breathe the air, what difference does it make if you eat it? It's already inside you." At night I used to visit our vegetable patch with a torch. I would crouch down with my feet on the bare earth and watch the velvety sage leaves catching the moisture, covering themselves in it, soaking it up. The rosemary held up its tiny daggers in the darkness as if trying to burst bubbles of water hovering just above the ground. And the tall tubes of chives, the spiky, green, seriously weird hair-style of a sub-terranean onion reaching upwards. Thyme crawled over the soil, like a detachment of the Resistance, grouped together, efficient, close-knit. I used to stay there thinking, resting. I liked being with plants, they're neutral, they don't talk, don't hear anything, have no longings or needs. I'd have liked to model myself on them, to imitate them…'

My voice drifts off, I feel as if I'm leaving the playing-field.

'Why don't you try and get in touch with him?' my brother asks.

'With who?'

'Your farmer.'

'I never had his address or his phone number. I don't know where he was from. I don't even know the name of his farm.'

'I'm sure we could find him. We've got *a* name, his name. He can't be very far from Paris. Why don't you ask the people at the circus?'

'I don't know where they are. When we got the eviction notice things happened very quickly. The next day everything was packed up and they left. When the manager said goodbye to

me I asked him what I should do. "We can't take you with us."
That was all he said. I said I understood but I was worried: how
were they going to cope with the children and animals? The city
seemed such a hostile place but the country was even worse —
people stare at you and don't want you there. I was frightened
the ground would just gobble them up. The manager looked
confident. "Why are you crying?" he asked, "we're lucky, we
never paid for anything here. It's a good site, we made the most
of it. We'll find something else. Why are you crying, my little
Jew?" (It was strange but that's what he called me.) "You
shouldn't be crying for us, you know." I nodded and went and
picked the herbs. I harvested the whole lot, cutting them right
down to the ground. I wrapped them up in paper and took my
little parcels to the manager's wife. She looked at them, hugged
me and chucked them out of the window of her truck as she
left. She laughed and watched those herbs fall onto what was
just a piece of wasteland again. I picked them up and put them
in my suitcase. When I got to the hotel I asked for a vase to stow
my little forest in. It was a cheap hotel and the woman said, "we
haven't got anything like that". I put them all in the basin and
had to brush my teeth without using it. The next morning I
threw them in the bin and cried. I cried about everything that
gets cut down and uprooted. I thought I'd never stop.'

'And you stopped.'

'I stopped.'

'It always stops. Have you noticed that?'

We think for a moment about how sadness inevitably comes
to an end.

'You should have called me,' Charles says after a while.

'When?'

'When you were chucked out of the circus. When you were on your own and you didn't have anywhere to live. You could have come to us.'

'I didn't want to. I think I reverted to a sort of wild state.'

All of a sudden the veal is in front of me and the smell of it is intoxicating. I could pick it up in my hands and bite right to the bone, like the wild animal I have become. But no. I look at it, study it. I analyse how it's been cooked, prod it with the tip of my knife, then make an incision: pink blood – some water, a bit of juice, nothing really – oozes out and blends with the brown sauce where Chinese artichokes drift past green beans so fine they look like chive stems, only firmer. I decide to put off till later my painful deliberations about belonging to a concept, and simply enjoy my meal.

I like winding up the metal shutter to get into *Chez moi*. There's something archaic about it and it affords me a genuine feeling of power. Once inside, I let the shutter back down and feel protected. This steel eyelid cutting me off from the world – in the same way that the blink of an eye is sometimes enough to repress a thought, or a tear – blots me out more surely than a door. Who would think there was someone in there sleeping; that every evening the banquette is covered with a sleeping bag, itself taken from a box cleverly slipped beneath this unsuspected bed? Who would think someone brushes their teeth here, washes their hair, gets up in the night to pee, checks what they look like in the mirror in case the nightmare they have just had has completely transformed them? Who would think that a pot full of pencils graces one of the tables and that someone sits in that orange glow writing and drawing and starting something new while everyone else is asleep? That someone is me. Because tonight I'm not asleep: I'm making a list of my brilliant ideas. I'm also making a list of the things I need to do to help my brilliant ideas see the light of day. So I'm drawing up two lists, and they each have a name: list number one is called 'Brilliant Ideas', and list number two is called 'What Needs Doing'. List number two is much longer than list number one. I don't know whether that's good or bad.

I like writing at night. If I were a writer I would always write at night. That's what Balzac did. Was it Balzac? I can sort of picture a satin dressing-gown with soup stains on it. Was that his? It's what Proust did even during the day because he lived with the shutters closed. I can sort of picture a bed, but — blank! My memory's gone blank! — it's getting confused with the one in Van Gogh's bedroom. That's the kind of jumble my thoughts are usually in; I mustn't let the jumble take over. I must concentrate on writing my lists. With the list of brilliant ideas I think the way they are formulated is very important. I mustn't say too much or be too vague. If it's too detailed it won't really be a list and it could hold me up when it comes to doing the things. If it's too vague — is it really worth my going into that?

Don't let's waste any more time. Brilliant Ideas: 1) A restaurant for children. 2) Restaurant and catering/prepared meals. There, it's already finished, I've only got two ideas. I was prompted to them, both of them, by my muse Vincent-the-florist. The first when he talked about customers being like family: family means children, children means won't eat anything and don't behave well in restaurants. Family means hell, and yet here I am with my revolutionary idea just round the corner from you, with a place where children are welcome, like in a school canteen but better, no more expensive (I know, it doesn't seem possible, but I'll find a way of solving the impossible in list number two), a restaurant where some things have to be eaten with fingers, a place where everything will make them want to eat.

The second idea is, at first glance, less original. A restaurant that prepares dishes for people to eat at home, a sort of posh take-away, yes, but not like other ones. My muse gave me the idea by giving me his rotten flowers. This isn't about serving rotten food at buffets and garden parties. No. This is to do with not wasting anything any more. I won't have dishes for people to take home every day, only when I've got too much food. I won't cater for parties of 500, I'll do micro-cooking for people who don't have time, can't do it themselves, or can't be bothered. It will be very cheap because it will be leftovers and the worst bit is I'll tell people and no one will mind. It will work by word of mouth and people will soon realize that it's a sort of lottery. Sometimes bingo! You get the steak en croute for four with wild mushroom sauce, and other evenings no, sorry, we're fully booked and we haven't got anything, but if you've got five minutes I can give you a recipe that's so easy you'll be able to do it with your eyes shut. When people are really nice and have proved how much they like the place by eating here often and recommending *Chez moi* to their friends, I'll give them a surprise, a gala dinner for a birthday, something extravagant, over the top and unexpected. They like me, the people round here. It's incredible how much they like me. Great streams of love gushing at me. They say, 'But how would we cope without you?'. Housewives say it, and impoverished young couples. It makes me glow, I finally feel I'm me. I give complete satisfaction, I exude goodness, I'm changing the world – changing it into somewhere liveable, at last!

I open a bottle of Bordeaux. I've only had… let's see, how

many glasses did I drink with Charles? How many bottles did we… I can't remember, but I'm thirsty. I need a little something to get me started on list number two, which is much longer and more difficult to draw up because that's where all the problems raised in the first list are supposed to be sorted out.

At the top of the blank page I write 'What Needs Doing'. I decide not to put my thoughts in any order, just to let them come. In a heap. I do some brainstorming and write down: Go to the council to find out about the price of school meals. Get in touch with local nannies (I cross that out straight away, sensing that nannies are my natural enemies because they might think of me as underhand competition). Establish a list of things children like. Calculate the cost of a meal. Decide on a lowest-possible selling price. Invest in unbreakable plates. Don't decorate. Don't put toys all over the place – toys can make a place look awful because they're either too bright or too drab: toys are direct opponents of good taste, even wooden ones which, apart from anything else, bore children to tears and depress them. Find a way to make adults understand that they're welcome here too. Have two different menus? No, appeal to regressive impulses: serious cuisine will be for the evenings and the catering department. Take on staff: a waiter and a girl to help in the kitchen, or the other way round, a waitress and a boy to help in the kitchen. But I'm sure I want a girl and a boy. Why? Because I feel I'd be able to settle disagreements more easily then. Buy cushions so children can reach the tables. Waffle-iron. Pancake griddle. Deep fryer? Deep fryer. And what about an open fire? So I can grill meat on a wood fire: lamb chops, spare ribs, chicken breasts. I look closely at the walls and ceiling, trying to find a flue. With my eyes glued to the mouldings, I don't see the chair in my way, catch my foot in it and fall right over it onto the tiled floor, the fingers of my right hand doing little to deaden the impact between my nose and upper lip and the cast iron pedestal of a table.

I stay there sprawled on the floor for a moment, the way footballers do, with my hands on my face, the way footballers do, and grimacing, like them, with my knees up to my chest, which they do so well. I don't know whose attention I'm trying to attract, there's no ref here. As for whose fault it is, it could only possibly be mine. I'm surprised to find myself regretting married life, a time when any suffering could be traced back to the other half, the evil husband, the wicked man who was so unfair to me. It was so good being able to think *Fuck him!* and feel the pus run out of the abscess. I suppose I could be annoyed with Charles for making me drink so much because I now realize – now that I'm having so much trouble getting to my feet while the walls seem to be dancing round me at hectic angles like a house of cards on the point of collapse, the tables are scuttling about on their feet like giant cockroaches and the chairs, which have turned into dung-beetles, are peering down at me and scowling with their menacing horned foreheads – I now realize that I'm drunk, so drunk I didn't even know I was.

I heave myself onto the banquette and gaze at the crumpled pieces of paper covered in my forger's handwriting: the l's closed to form perfect loops, the dots directly above the i's, the fluid downstrokes, the letters all exceptionally even in size, leaning slightly toward the top right-hand corner, expressing a reasonable degree of optimism, and giving each line a classiness, an elegance as it sweeps smoothly in the direction of the text. I have had many successes thanks to my deceptive writing. Experts have pronounced that I have the natural authority, reliability and enterprise required of a leader, and predicted a dazzling future for me in psychology and psychiatry, guaranteed success in teaching, and tremendous facility for research and engineering. Even when I myself read what I've written, I'm lulled into the illusion of my own abilities. I believe in what's written there and, as blood drips very slowly from my nose and lip (the drips from my nose forming splashy flowers the size of a daisy and the smaller ones from my lip only managing little chickweed buds), I decide to follow my own advice and comply with the instructions given by the excess alcohol.

Before lying down to sleep, I add to the end of list number two: 'Find Mr Slimane'.

I am woken by a rustling, slithering sound and sit bolt upright. The mail is being pushed under the metal shutters. One by one the envelopes peep in, first with just a corner, then the rest follows and, as if suddenly sucked in by the floor tiles, they skid towards me. They're all white, with a window. Envelopes are the exact opposite of bathrooms, I think to myself: having a window is a drawback. I'm amazed how many letters I receive since opening the restaurant. Not that 'letter' is the right word. These aren't people writing to me. It's not sentences that they're sending. I know I should no longer be surprised, I should stop thinking letters are always an opportunity for someone – however close we are – to open themselves up to me. How are you? letters say. I'm feeling much better, the children are very well, my husband's found a new job, I've started reading again, I've enrolled in a wonderful sewing course… Or: I can't really cope any more, I'm in such a mess, every day I think I'm going to walk out, I'm suffocating… News, given and received. I think about Madame de Staël's letters, or was it Madame de Sévigné? I think of Rosa Luxemburg's letters (and here there's no hesitation because her correspondence with Leon Jogiches is part of my nomadic library, the refuge of thirty-three authors salvaged from the chaos of my memory). I get up and pick up the dismal harvest of the day's mail. On offer today: two reminders for unpaid bills with charges for late payment, a request for my compulsory contribution to a dodgy-sounding pension fund, an offer of one month's free subscription to a trade magazine, and a bank statement for my business account. I put them down next to each other, the requests for payments and the pages from the bank screaming 'overdraft!'. Talk to each other, I feel like saying to the two piles of paper. Sort it out among yourselves. One gaping hole to another. I hope this geographical proximity can resolve the conflict. My creditors will give up. The bank will advance some funds. There's nothing I can do, anyway, apart from regret there aren't any other letters, that I only get things with figures on them. In a spirit of revolt, I go over to my book shelf and pick up Rosa Luxemburg. I'll send myself a letter from her. It'll make up for it. I open it at random on page 277, and read:

What really made me happy was the bit where you said we're still young and we'll find a way to sort out our personal lives. Oh, my golden love, I so long for you to keep that promise!... A little place of our own, our furniture, our books; calm steady work, going for walks together, occasionally to the opera, a little circle of friends who sometimes come over for supper, a month in the country without work every summer!... (And maybe also a baby, a little tiny baby?? Could we ever? Ever?...)

I close the book, thinking about that little tiny baby isolated inside brackets, already protected by its future mother – who would never be its future mother because she was childless when she was assassinated in 1919 – in the volatile embrace of two tiny arms of ink. I think a while about a mother's tenderness, about the madness and ferocity of a mother's tenderness. It's nine o'clock. I really must go and do the shopping, at least to get the bread and fruit I need, but I stay there motionless, paralysed by the scene in my mind's eye. My heart beats slowly, my chest constricts. I relive it – yes, I relive my own offhand behaviour when I was in no hurry to erect those vital brackets, and the initial exuberance which cost me so dearly.

My son was the most beautiful baby I'd ever seen. People made fun of me when I said so. Even my husband laughed at me. 'But look,' I told him, 'Look!' I told my family and friends. 'He's exceptional. His head's perfect, his nose, his skin, his body. And his eyes are so kind. Look at him compared to other babies if you can't see it straight away. They're wrinkled with big pointy noses, scratchy little hands and a cowardly look in their eye. Other babies have skinny arms and pigeon toes and bendy, ingrowing nails. They shriek the whole time. My son's the exact opposite, a real pleasure to behold.'

The nurse is worried. According to her, I'm too euphoric. But the fact that she thinks I'm over the top only rallies my fighting spirit. 'Maybe you haven't looked at him properly,' I tell her. 'I'm not surprised, you've got too much to do. If you spent an hour looking at each baby, you'd waste precious time. But this one's different. Look at him, I promise you. I can't take any of the credit, but he's a work of art.' My husband slaps me. With the flat of his hand right across my cheek and nose. The woman in the next bed buries her face in her hands. I wonder whether she's laughing. My nose starts bleeding and the nurse takes my husband by the hand and leads him out of the room. I think none of them have any sense of humour and feel very much alone.

From his see-through crib Hugo gratifies me with his wonderful smile, which I've forgotten to mention. I lie there admiring him but suddenly, unbearably, as if something's broken: I don't love him any more. I look away. Concentrate on the blank wall. I must be wrong. It was just a mental block. I'll get some rest and when I look back in his eyes it will start again, that huge jubilant wave of love. It will swallow me up and pin me down, I'll be ga-ga and triumphant. I wait a while, watching the woman in the next bed suckling her poor little girl, such an ugly scrawny thing with three black hairs on a ridiculous sugar-loaf shaped head but with hair all over her body, on her back and arms. The mother's eyelids are lowered, she sighs with pleasure or disappointment and tries to forget the incomprehensible scene she has just witnessed. But perhaps she's also savouring a sense of victory: I've been punished, me, the mother of the most beautiful baby in the world, right next to her who produced a skinny, hairy frog. I was slapped. I had such a come-down. Was put back in my place. Yes, she'd probably had enough of it too, of me gazing at my son the whole time. But it's not over, they won't get me that easily.

Stealthily as a desert lizard imperceptibly skewing its scaly sand-covered face towards its prey, which mistakes it for a stone until the very moment of capture, I turn my face towards my child, expecting to feel the constantly rising tide of passion. Nothing. Nothing happens. I launch into a detailed examination: dimpled wrist, a tiny soft fold attaching it to the apricot-coloured hand; exquisite padded mouth, flower-like and pulpy, pulpy and feathery, a generous half-open mouth beneath a little round nose, a friendly humorous nose; blue eyelids already edged with lashes; a forehead of unruffled solemnity without even a dip at the temples, solemn then and tranquil, anchored by indistinct eyebrows raised in an expression of indulgent astonishment. An even covering of downy hair whirling round a perfect vortex. His ears as flat, iridescent, restful and calm as clam shells on the shore. A vigorous elastic body in a baby-grow that is neither wrinkled nor gaping in every direction, but instead emphasizes the perfect contours of his limbs attached to his long, powerful and mysteriously convex torso. It's all there, his soothing regular breathing, his eyes which suddenly open, soft grey, looking at me without actually seeing me, the nurses say – because I'm too far away and there's a layer of Perspex between us. He does actually see me, I think. My son's looking at me and he can see me, and he can see in my eyes that it's already over. I can't do it any more. I don't know where it's gone. But indisputably, brutally and terrifyingly it's gone: all my love has vanished; all that's left is a powerful urge to care for him and an appalling pity, but I'm struggling to understand who that's for.

The next few weeks are blank. I can do everything properly. The paediatric nurses congratulate me, I'm discharged, I go home and I wait. I wait for the love to come back. I nip into his bedroom by surprise, catching myself out, and stare into the cradle. Hugo's there, sleeping, gorgeous. And as he grows, a spherical lump swells inside my chest. I never thought heartache would be that shape, or that violent or originate in that way. I start spying on other mothers, the ones with prams like me, the ones who've already got to the buggy stage, the ones walking next to tricycles, the ones carrying sports bags and trotting along behind great bean poles. I'm fascinated by them. They all have the treasure that's been stolen from me. All of them. The strict ones, lax ones, sour ones, annoying ones. I can see it on their faces, in their every gesture, hear it in the intonation of their voices: countless signs of maternal love. And it tears me apart. I don't talk about it to anyone. And no one talks about it to me. Because my infirmity goes unsuspected.

Hugo grows. He plays with his hands, sits up on his own, crawls, stands…. He's never ill, he laughs, laughs from morning till night and starts talking very young, putting together huge senatorial sentences. He grows more beautiful too, his eyelashes getting even longer, his eyes bigger. His hair is a beacon, his body agile. The other mothers at the park envy me. He never cries, even when he falls over. He makes friends easily, and treats them with exquisite courtesy, sharing his biscuits and lending his bucket. He smiles and plays the fool to entertain babies when he's only four years old himself. The other mothers resent me. They think I'm too perfect. We go for boat trips, he goes riding, knows how to steer a hot-air balloon, I pay for a diving course, we read books, we cook, we do silk paintings, he becomes the Capoeira champion. He doesn't do anything with his father. He sits at his feet when he's reading the paper, then curls up against him with his head on his chest and his eyes closed. I've got out of the habit of waiting for my heart to leap again. I've given up on it. Sometimes – like a story-teller who knows ancestral epics by heart – I tell myself the story of my three days of glory. The three days that came between the birth and the slap. I retrace my steps and remember. The wonderment is still intact. I can no longer feel it, but my imagination can synthesize it. It's like looking at photographs of the past, seeing yourself biting into a piece of fruit on a summer's afternoon. It's winter and you haven't got anything in your mouth but if you concentrate you can still find a trace of the sensation, you can identify it without feeling it. It's like working with a stencil. And it's torture, because you keep wanting to thrust your hand into the picture and grab the piece of fruit, take the sunlight, turn back time.

My aunt, who was diabetic, had half a leg amputated towards the end of her life.

'I can move my foot,' she told me after she'd had the operation.

I naturally thought she meant her remaining foot.

'That's great,' I said. 'It hasn't been affected and gone numb.'

She shook her head.

'I mean the other one,' she explained. 'The one that's not there any more. I can still move it.'

She thought for a moment, then asked, 'Where do you think they put it, my bit of leg? In the bin?'

Her eyes clouded. I wonder what sort of bin my lost love for my son could be in now.

It's late and I haven't done anything. I can't afford to shut for lunch on top of my unscheduled closure yesterday evening. I come back to my senses by the dim light of the fridge which I have opened wide to gauge my stocks. My eyes wander from shelf to shelf, from tubs to drawers. On the dairy products side, it's okay, I'll manage. On the fish side, I'm screwed, but it's not Friday as far as I know and if a vegetarian turns up I've got enough in my vegetable racks to keep them happy. The shin of veal is going to turn into Osso buco; I had planned to roast it all in one piece on a bed of shallots confits but I don't have enough cooking time left for that. I take my saw from its sheath and set to work, cutting the joint into sections, first using a knife through the meat, which is pale as a ballerina's tutu, then attacking the central bone with the handsaw.

The telephone rings. Nudging it with my elbow, I knock the handset off to answer the call without interrupting my butchery, then I use the saw handle to push the loudspeaker button. It's Vincent, worried because I haven't opened my metal shutter and it's already ten-thirty. He wants to know if everything is all right and offers to give me a hand.

Now what he wants is a cup of coffee, I think to myself. He's getting into the habit a bit too quickly, he's the Speedy Gonzalez of routine.

'Come over, you know you want to,' I say, glibly introducing a teasing note of familiarity into my voice. If you stay stand-offish for too long, things become stilted and you end up having to sleep with people just to break the ice.

'I can't do the shutter to let you in because I'm a bit busy, but the door to the back stairs is open. Come in that way. Do you know the code?'

He knows the code and comes straight over. All at once I feel both the weight of a new friendship and the relief of no longer being alone.

Vincent is wearing a polo shirt which smells strongly of washing powder. I know this because, probably galvanized by my inviting him over when he knew that I knew it was what he wanted, he gives me a peck on each cheek. It's not very easy kissing me when I'm standing at my butcher's block with a saw in one hand and a shin of veal in the other. Vincent kisses me – how shall I put this? – from behind, which has the advantage of wafting the smell of washing powder towards my nostrils rather than… the other, the fatal, well, you know what I mean. He is, as he puts it, in an epic mood or even, he adds in a 'mega-epic mood'. I realize that I'm duty-bound to ask him the reason for this mega-epic mood.

'Do you want a coffee?' I ask to rile him slightly.

'A coffee? If you like. But champagne would be more like it.'

I finish my slicing and start up my beloved percolator.

'I'm running late,' I tell Vincent, 'so I haven't got time to sit down, but I'm listening.'

'Mmm?' he asks with affected nonchalance, pretending not to know what I mean.

I won't get away without asking him. It's like with the coffee: this isn't to do with what he wants, but with what would make me happy. There's absolutely no question of him pouring his heart out, he's very keen for it to look as if he's merely satisfying my curiosity.

'To what do we owe this mega-epic mood, then?' I ask, defeated.

'A contract,' he replies enigmatically.

I'm going to have to drag this out of him one bit at a time. Still, that's easier than diverting the conversation onto something else. While I slice the shallots I raise my voice above the meat spitting as it browns and the thrum of the extractor fan. 'What sort of contract?'

'Floral decorations.'

I'm not even entitled to full sentences now. No more determiners. Forget verbs. This will have to be a forceps delivery. I allow myself a pause while I take out the meat and put it aside on an earthenware plate, before tossing the chopped shallots and some garlic into the pan along with a bit of rosemary and a bunch of flat leaf parsley. I turn down the heat and put the extractor on a lower setting, then swivel slowly towards my muse who is looking out of the window with an inspired expression and assuming poses like a young pre-Raphaelite model.

'Floral decorations?' I say in my most engaging voice. 'That's exciting. Is this a new departure for you? Have you ever done it before?'

I have opted for what is called a quick-fire tactic, bombarding my target with questions, pretending to be impatient and consumed with curiosity by jumping up and down on the spot a couple of times.

Vincent lazily drags his affectedly dreamy eyes away from the empty street. He's laying this on a bit thick, I think, but I don't hold it against him. Gratitude is a feeling I rate very highly on my personal scale, and I consider I owe him a good deal of it.

'No, I've done it before,' he replies in a blasé voice. 'I do it all the time, but this is different.'

Still facing him, I stir the herbs with a spatula behind my back.

'Go on!'

I gratify him with two further little skips.

'It's for a big company,' he says, closing his eyes so that I can gauge the full extent of his new undertaking. 'Event organizers run by a Jew.'

I freeze. Why is that detail necessary? My face tenses slightly.

'Do you see what I mean?' he asks.

I shake my head.

'Lots of money.'

Really? I think to myself. Of course. Jews and money. I prepare myself for the fun and give up on trying to adapt my expression. It's beyond my abilities. Now I need to deglaze my sauce with some white wine. I turn my back on Vincent and pour in half a bottle of Muscadet, stirring all the time and revelling in the delicious smell. Once I've put the pieces of veal back into the rust-coloured sauce, I flambé it with cognac.

'They arrange weddings, all sorts of parties and... what do they call them again?'

I could supply him with the word he needs, but my gratitude has its limits.

'Bar mitzvahs!' he exclaims. 'No expense spared, I tell you. My first two budgets are around the €3000 mark, and apparently there'll be plenty more where that came from.'

I don't know how to start up my questioning again, suddenly very tired of this particular epic. So I concentrate on the tomato sauce and on making some cremolata, a mixture of lemon zest, basil, olive oil and parmesan that I'll add to the dish when it's served.

'I'm going to do table displays for them with passion flowers,' he coos. 'Circlets of convolvulus for the little girls. I'll use lots of jasmine, of course. I'll have to get used to making crystallized rose petals instead of the usual sugared almonds, they're so much more refined. For big venues I'll use vines and ivy dotted with big blousy roses. Lilies are very tough, very strong. I'll mix wild flowers like cow parsley and camomile with more sophisticated things. Lots of greenery, eucalyptus, ribes...'

There's no stopping Vincent now. I'm touched by his enthusiasm, his genuine love of flowers, how well he wants to do it all. I've poured the tomato coulis over the meat and now I cover it and sit down to drink a toast to him. We clink our cups together. His is empty but mine is still full. Vincent gets a bit carried away and knocks rather too hard, spilling coffee over my fingers and the table, and sending a few droplets onto the white blouse I put on in honour of Charles because I know it's his favourite colour.

'Oh, I'm sorry!' Vincent cries, leaping up to dab me with a cloth which he grabs on his way over. 'What an idiot!' he says heatedly. 'What a prat! I'm so bloody clumsy!'

He can't find insults sufficiently violent for the anguish he feels.

'It's nothing,' I say. 'Really, I promise. Everything's fine. I needed to change anyway.'

His hands are everywhere, on mine, on my chest, under my feet, on the table, between my legs. I like it. But he suddenly stops.

'Are you going to have time to go home?' he asks.

'Home?' I ask.

'To change. It's five to eleven.'

I want to tell him everything. It would be so tempting, right now, to let the truth well up and simply flow, undeterred: this is where I live, I camp in the restaurant. But I restrain myself. It's too soon.

'I've got a change of clothes with me,' I tell him. 'Cooking gets you so dirty.'

I couldn't say for sure whether he believes me. Something in his expression – like a tiny wren feather flitting across a square of blue sky marked out by the bars of a window, and which could so easily be mistaken for a reflection – makes me think he's beginning to guess.

'I'd better go,' he says.

'Mazel tov,' I say as I wind up the metal shutter so he can go out of the front door.

'Sorry?'

'Mazel tov, that's what the Jews say to wish someone good luck. It's what we say when we're happy for someone.'

'You too,' he replies, backing out of the door.

His smile hovers behind him for a moment and I stand there looking out at the street to watch the ghost of his expression. Vincent runs over to his shop, he's late. And, as he does, his smile keeps me company. The street is deserted, this is the lull before the school gates open and offices have their lunch hour. The sun warms my forehead, the tip of my nose and the tops of my breasts, my angled surfaces, the places where my body projects itself forwards. I watch the lab technicians opposite working with acute precision on dental prostheses. I like people working, each in their own little bubble, standing motionless, busy with what they should be doing, tinkering. Workers are well-ordered, calm, and the deserted street is open to offenders: parents of pre-school children, the unemployed, the ill-employed, the idle, the mad and people like me who, despite their best efforts, despite the fact that their days are full and busy, never really settle into the hugely reassuring structure of so-called office hours. The street changes character at different times of day and, now that my observation post is well established, I love watching its every alteration.

I finish winding up the metal shutter and go back to the kitchen. Seeing my reflection in the mirror above the banquette,

I notice there is still a bit of blood under my left nostril and that my upper lip, which split when I fell, is swollen. Vincent didn't say anything. He must have been concentrating on his mega-epic mood. I give myself a quick wash, and tidy away my lists and pencils. I need to make things for people to eat. The sun is warming up, they will be wanting salads. I launch into haphazard peeling and chopping, using an unorthodox technique which probably wastes a fair bit of time, but it suits me. It consists in doing everything at once. I take out salad ingredients, vegetables, herbs and several knives: peeler, smooth-bladed and serrated. I cut half a cucumber into cubes, then move onto the mushrooms which I slice into little slithers, I go back to the cucumber, cutting wafer-thin slices, skip to topping and tailing green beans, pop whole beetroots into the oven, I scoop the flesh out of avocados and grapefruits, and put the chard into boiling water. The whole idea is not to get bored. The theory, because I have a theory about peeling things, is to leave room for random opportunities. With cooking, as with everything else, we tend to curb our instincts. Speed and chaos allow for a slight loss of control. Cutting vegetables into different shapes and sizes encourages combinations which might not have been thought of otherwise. In a salad of mushrooms, cucumber and lamb's lettuce, the chervil needs to stay whole, in sprigs, to make a contrast because the other ingredients are so fine, almost transparent, and slippery. If its thin stems and tiny branches didn't contradict the general sense of languor – accentuated by the single cream instead of olive oil in the dressing – the whole thing would descend into melancholy. Keeping a balance is the key, and I don't think that this balance can derive from premeditation. It's a dangerous thought but one so frequently put to the test that I'm prepared to take on the challenge. Humans lean. They don't know it. But they lean. It's called a tendency, an inclination, a mania. In order for a dish to succeed there has to be a connection between soft and crisp, bitter and mild, sweet and spicy, wet and dry, and that connection has to play on all the tensions in these warring couples. No one is sufficiently tolerant or inventive to respect opposites, so someone has to open up the way for contraband and clandestine activities.

The beetroots come out of the oven and I shower them with walnut vinegar. The chard gushes into the colander and I sprinkle it with lemon juice and pepper. My worktop is a battlefield: pips, tops, droplets, stains, leaves and peelings – everything piles up and oozes. I melt at the sight of pink beetroot blood on a cucumber heart. But there isn't really time. I turn into Shiva, my extra arms popping out from my back, working faster than my brain to clear up, sponge down, sort through, share out and put away.

When my mascot customers – the two schoolgirls with gleaming hips – come through the door of *Chez moi* everything is tidy and ready. The only thing I haven't dealt with is the blackboard, so I'll just have to tell them what's on the menu.

The girls are in a bad mood: they've had terrible marks in philosophy, and they want to eat fish to make them more intelligent. I try to persuade them that Osso buco is very good for the brain, that the unctuous sauce lubricates meningeal surfaces and protects nerve synapses. They tell me it's fattening. I tell them they're beautiful and explain how and why. I talk about how lovely they are for a long time and they say I express myself so well they're sure I could help them with their philosophy. They promise to bring me their next essay topic. I'm terrified to think they actually might. I can remember the torture of quotations. At school. You always had to cite different writers, to say 'like when so-and-so wrote such-and-such' and I never knew who had done what – I got *The Human Condition* confused with Balzac's *Human Comedy* (and, anyway, I thought Balzac was a pseudonym of Stendhal's), I had an idea *The Divine Comedy* was written in Latin by Ovid. And as for philosophy, don't let's go there, the only name I could remember was Plato. So he had written everything from *Theaetetus* to *The Critique of Pure Reason*. But sometimes I also got him confused with Socrates. Who was the puppet and who the puppeteer? Had Socrates written dialogues featuring Plato? I was completely lost.

The girls are hungry. I set the price of their meal at €4 to put a smile back on their faces.

'For the whole year?' they ask.

'For life,' I tell them. 'But that's our little secret. Don't let the others know; don't tell your friends.'

'We haven't got any friends,' they say straight away (which can't be true but they'll do whatever it takes to preserve the unprecedented privilege I'm granting them). 'What if we have desserts? What if we have caviar? And what about coffee?'

They make me laugh. I tell them my name's Myriam. They

shake my hand ceremoniously and introduce themselves: Simone and Hannah.

Two men who have grabbed the moleskin banquette are complaining that the service is too slow. They don't say it openly, but grumble, shoot angry glances, sigh a lot and keep looking at their watches. I've got too many tables at the same time. I waste precious minutes reciting the menu, forget to put the water back on to boil for the tagliatelle and haven't made enough cremolata. One woman sends back her steak because it's overdone. The place is noisy, full of steam and pans clashing together; I drop a cast-iron casserole and it shatters a floor tile, making everyone jump. Simone and Hannah come up to the till to pay for fear of revealing the cut-down price I have offered them.

'You should get a waiter,' they tell me. 'We know a good one, we could ask him to come and see you if you like.'

I'm not listening to them. I thank them and kiss them good-bye. They're my nieces, I tell my other customers mentally in case they get it into their heads to ask for kisses too.

I understand the full meaning of the expression 'it's all go' because it really is all going for me at the moment, only it's all going in every direction as far as I can make out. I write out the orders and pin them to the board, then I carry out the orders I've given myself in the kitchen. Sometimes I'm so quick and efficient I feel I'm on top of things, but I haven't spotted four new customers who have come in and sat down, and I've forgotten the desserts for table five. I feel I'm really turning a corner and euphoria surges up inside me. I'm giving my tables numbers like a professional. It suddenly feels as if there's a giant sign writing itself outside: *Chez moi* is actually becoming a restaurant. I could bark out loud for joy, now that I'm a dog among dogs, but a plate slips out of my oily hand and splatters its contents on the floor. I push the wasted food aside with my foot and make the lost salad again. I've only got three portions of plum and almond tart left. I'm one short. I suggest a praline and raspberry mousse instead, offering it for free, and the jacketed man to whom I'm explaining the terms of this substitution says, 'Well, that's very kind'. I'm thinking commercially-motivated gesture. I'm thinking developing customer loyalty… I'm also thinking improvised prodigality ends in ruin, a proverb I invent for the occasion but whose warning I immediately decide to ignore. I'll have to take my system for what it's worth, it does at least have the advantage of being coherent. I'm banking on the dividends this offer will bring me. This line of reasoning is backed up by countless examples gleaned at random from fables I read as a child. The young girl who agrees to give the old lady a drink at the fountain ends up with pearls flowing from her mouth, the one who refuses spews out vermin.

'Is it too late to eat?' a woman half-opens the door to ask.

I look at my watch, because that's what restaurant managers do. It's quarter to three, *Chez moi* is still half-full, and there's no Osso buco or mushroom salad left.

'It's fine,' I say slightly gruffly, as if doing her a favour. 'But I'm all out of the dish of the day. I've got quiches and a selection of vegetables.'

That's exactly what she and her friend felt like. I find them a table.

The men who were muttering about the slow service are onto their third cup of coffee. They've loosened their ties, they're smoking and chatting. When they ask for the bill, I say 'I'll be right with you!'.

It's half past four when I close the door. I drop down onto the banquette and cry, without tears. A nervous, anxious sort of crying. I feel as if I've been trampled by a herd of elephants. I think it will take me two hours just to clear up and I'm pitifully short of ingredients for the next sitting. I decide to inaugurate themed evenings. This evening it will be various different soups followed by chocolate fondant cakes because I've got some vegetables left and a few eggs. My hand shakes as I write on the blackboard, adding an attractive price at the top (€7 for a set meal of soup and dessert), then I activate my secret arms to fill the bin bags, carry them out to the dustbins, wash the floor and peel another succession of vegetables.

At eight o'clock two women who could be friends of my mother's turn up.

'Do you have any candles?' the taller of them asks. 'It's my sister's birthday.'

I'm embarrassed to have nothing better to offer them than soup for a celebration dinner. But the two sisters think it's perfect because they're both trying to lose weight. Not that that stops them finishing off what little bread I have left, mind you. They order a bottle of Côtes de Beaune, we sing 'Happy Birthday' and I'm just about to offer them champagne on the

house when a searing pain in my back reminds me I do deserve
to earn a living.

They are my only customers all evening. As they leave the
older of the two shakes my hand and says, 'You're very brave'.
I'm not sure what she means by it, what she knows about me,
what she's discovered about my fate and on what authority
she makes this diagnosis, but I feel galled and a sort of
honeyed comfort in equal measures. 'You're very brave' is
what people say to a soldier who has lost both arms, to a teen-
ager who has just been told she has some incurable disease
and is trying to console her own parents, it's what you say to
someone who has lost everything, someone who is about to
lose everything. How did she know? What did she see? As
soon as she's gone I wind down the shutter and run to the
mirror. I want to know where it got out: my eyes? Or perhaps
my grey hairs? I switch on a light to get a better look and am
immediately reassured by my swollen lip. She must have
thought I was a battered wife. I can breathe again. That's
brilliant. Yes, a woman who was slapped across the nose,
punched in the mouth, kicked in the back and the stomach,
cuffed over the head and kneed in the ribs. Phew! The
honeyed feeling is washing over me now. The honey of
admiration. 'You're very brave', that means I'm coping well,
that I've got that little extra something, I'm up to the job and
should feel proud I've done so well. I overcome, endure,
achieve. Her little sentence drives into me like a screw. With
every turn there's another source of pain, with every turn
another reason to be pleased and proud, going deeper and

deeper. Bent double by the pain in my stomach, I finish clearing up and decide to go to sleep without reading, without even thinking, so that I can set the alarm for six o'clock and get things under control again.

We expect sleep to restore us but sometimes it has other plans. I wanted a soft, heavy, velvety night to wrap itself around me; all I got was a few precarious moments on a fakir's bed of nails. My body didn't unwind, staying on the alert, with the ache in my stomach and the blade in my back both active, searing, working together. Only my consciousness broke away, the bolts of reason snapping off. No up or down, no true or false. I'm at home and a woman turns up. When I see her I think, ah, Mrs Cohen, even though I've never met her. Mrs Cohen has magnificent red hair and curved lips that are pushed out slightly by her perfect but imposing front teeth. She has high cheek-bones and her hazel eyes, set deep beneath a huge arching brow, are timid and cunning as a squirrel's. Her tiny little hands, which flit about delicately and greedily, are the sort of hands you want to kiss and hold in yours. Her feet are beautiful too, with ankles the size of a wrist, angular and fragile. Her body bulges softly in clothes that are a little too tight, but its contours are firm and her skin quite lovely. She sweeps aside her curls to talk, and every time her hair falls back down onto her shoulders an amber perfume spreads through the room. She is shy and very worried about disturbing me. It's for a bar mitzvah, for her son Ezekiel, but everyone calls him Zeeky. He's her eldest. It's very important, do you understand? I understand. She's looking for somewhere really original. Her son's very original, do you understand? I understand. Everyone's had enough of fuddy-duddy salons and hotels, all those frills and extras. What she wants is something simple – that doesn't mean she isn't prepared to pay, I should make no mistake about that! I make no mistake. Somewhere simple and fun. She wants to have a look around. I tell her she has, she's seen it all. That there's nothing else, the seating area and the kitchen, that's all. How many square metres? About sixty. I'm lying. *Chez moi* is fifty-three square metres. And there's really nothing else?, she asks. No cellar or annexe? No, I say, I'm so sorry. It's a bit tight for 200 people, don't you think? she asks. Very tight, I say. She wrings her hands for a moment and shakes her head, shifting her red curls and giving off their languid perfume. What about this door here? she says, pointing her tiny and admirably mani-cured finger towards the back of my kitchen. I turn round to discover a door, as if she had just drawn it with the tip of her nail: an imposing door from an elaborate front entrance, carved and painted in sky-blue lacquer. Oh, yes, I say, slightly embarrassed, I'd forgotten the store-room. Mrs Cohen would like me to show her the store-room. No, really. She has a lot of faith in our meeting like this, and thinks there's a good feeling between us. We walk to the back of the restaurant and I turn the heavy brass handle. The door opens without creaking, weighty and well-oiled. We both screw up our eyes, blinded by the sun streaming in through a dome decorated with a mosaic of multicoloured glass. The store-room is about two hundred square metres, but it's hard to gauge accurately because there are private alcoves hidden behind blue velvet curtains in the corners. There is an impressive staircase in dark-brown carved oak to either side of the door, leading to mezzanine galleries hung with ceiling lights in mauve-coloured crystal diffracting the flickering flames of a dozen candles.

How come we can see the candlelight so clearly when the sun's shining? Mrs Cohen asks. I realize that this isn't a question but an enigma. If I can formulate the right answer she won't make any awkward remarks to the effect that it's not very kind hiding such a beautiful back room from customers in need. I think for a moment. Stare at the candles, then study the dome with its coloured panes. I think about death. About the wake it carves through our lives, the terrifying way that wake closes over itself, snatched away by the march of time. And then we realize that the earth which opened up beneath our feet, gaping with sorrow, so deep we thought it would swallow us up, has filled in again. Leaving no trace. The living carry on being with the living. The dead have left us, they're with the dead. But it's not that simple. The dead are with us too in their own way. They speak to us, tease us, visit us in our dreams, they appear in the peculiarly similar features of a stranger on the bus, they make contact.

The candles glow in spite of the sunlight, I tell Mrs Cohen, we can see them, can make them out even in a much stronger light because we've decided, you and I have both decided, not to exclude the dead from our lives. We don't exclude the missing either, she adds. I'm infinitely grateful to her for saying that. I feel soothed and tell her I'll do whatever it takes for her

party to be a success. I give her the use of my back room. I do
need, she adds, still shyly, a guarantee that the food will be
strictly kosher, do you understand? I understand. I'll have
alterations made, double the size of my kitchen, have two
gleaming clean work-tops, one for dairy products and one for
meat, I won't cook the lamb in its mother's milk, I'll ensure
everything obeys the rules of divergence and separation. Two
battalions of sponges, glass plates, different sets of cutlery. I
ring my friend on the Avenue de la République and order an
extra fridge, another oven, hob and dishwasher. I divide the
space I have in two. For a moment, but only very briefly, I
myself become two people: a dairy Myriam and a meat Myriam.

The day Mrs Cohen and I are meant to sign the contract, I
flatten the palm of my right hand on the window and the 'Beth
Din' stamp certifying that everything at *Chez moi* is kosher is
printed onto the glass in black letters. Mrs Cohen is punctual,
she arrives at two o'clock. Everything's ready I tell her, spreading my arms to show off my new equipment. I've spent
€20,000 but I don't regret it. I won't put that in your budget.
That's just as well, says Mrs Cohen, terribly embarrassed,
because, here's the thing, I don't know how to tell you this, but
the whole thing's off. I've had a row with my husband, do you
understand? I understand. When my husband looks at me, she
explains, I feel dead. I can't take it any more. And Zeeky? I ask
her. What's your son going to do? Where's he going to find
somewhere original to become a man now? Mrs Cohen doesn't
answer. She disappears. I turn round and look at my kitchen: a
kitchen designed by someone with a squint, drawn by someone

who was blind drunk – it has two of everything. €20,000. I run over to the blue door, the door to the back room. Convincing myself that this won't be bad for business. If it weren't for Mrs Cohen I would never have discovered I've got a store-room which looks like a Venetian palace. I'll be able to let it out, to expand, hold receptions. The door has got oddly smaller. I turn the handle, the hinges creak and, as it opens, the door gets even smaller. I lean in, almost having to bend double to get through the doorway. I manage to crawl inside. The walls have drawn in, the dome disappeared in the darkness, the chandeliers with drops of crystal dissolved. There is just the flickering flame of a single candle in the dark, so weak one little puff would blow it out. I hold my breath and watch the tiny flame burning in my store-room which is so much smaller and darker it's almost non-existent, imploding and melting into the silent cosmos, the inter-stellar vastness that no light can ever assuage. Little flame. We don't exclude the missing either, do you understand? I understand.

I wake at five o'clock with these words inside my head: 'We don't exclude the missing either'. I think of my son, Hugo.

I haven't seen him for six years. I haven't spoken to him for six years. I don't know where he is or what he's doing. I don't know how much taller than me he is. Has he got a beard? What size are his feet? Did he get his baccalaureate? Has he enrolled at university? Does he have a girlfriend? No one tells me about him and I don't talk to anyone about him. That's the pact. I think he still sees his grandparents. At first I thought I wouldn't be able to stand the torture; I felt it was unfair and disproportionate to punish me like this. I thought the family conspiracy was iniquitous. But I had neither the strength to stand up to it, nor the grounds to respond. I accepted being banished as someone who has sold their soul to the devil accepts being burned in hell. In fact, it's not that they accept, it's that they don't have a choice. My personal hell – and this stroke of luck deserves recognition – was not unlike purgatory.

At first there was a period of drifting: small suitcase, neon-lit hotels, hanging about outside friends' houses, waiting to hear their footsteps in the hall when they didn't even know I was there; friends I could never have looked in the eye, and I would have fled if they had come out. I was petrified with shame for my very existence and for doing what I had done. I was unrecognizable, even to myself. There was nowhere I could put myself, nowhere to sleep: I felt like a hunted animal. I had to find work. My husband, who had also been my boss, didn't want to see me ever again. I went into shops, hoping to find the courage to ask whether they needed sales staff, but my suitcase – which I took everywhere with me – created misunderstandings: people thought I was a tourist and spoke to me in loud, slow sentences. I didn't dare contradict them. I stood gazing at the windows of temping agencies: bilingual secretary, I could do; plumber, I couldn't do; financial manager, I couldn't do; paediatric nurse, hmm… I didn't go in. I was too frightened I might have to put together a CV. I couldn't answer a single question. I didn't want anyone to talk to me. I couldn't look people in the eye. I now know there were people I could have turned to, who would have taken me in, without judging. But my disgrace reared up between me and anyone who might have wanted to help me. So I drifted. From morning till night, wearing out my shoes, light-headed with hunger and lack of sleep. The days rolled into one, indistinct. I don't know how long it was before I gave up looking for work, settling for long, slow, aimless wandering. I avoided the area where I used to live. I would sit and watch teenagers, and their exuberance weighed heavy on my heart.

One afternoon when the storm-laden sky was particularly threatening – thick purple-grey clouds, yellow light and a smell of twilight – I walked down a narrow, sinuous dead-end street with cobblestones snaking between tall buildings so close together they seemed to be in conversation. At the far end, as if leading to a clearing in the woods, it opened out onto an area of wasteland where the big top of a small circus stood proudly, decorated with a string of multicoloured bulbs. I was cold and hungry and curious. I don't remember paying for a ticket. There were only very young children on the rickety tiers, and a few grandmothers. The show had started. All eyes were on the ring, where a poodle was walking on its hind legs while a cat scrambled all over a clown without ever putting a foot to the ground; it trotted over his head and along his arms, clung to his trouser legs, defying gravity, wandering – like me – over a painfully restricted space while giving the impression of never taking the same route twice. The dog made the children laugh because he was wearing clothes and he scuttled about quickly then came to an abrupt stop in front of one of them with a furious look in his eye, only to set off again in the opposite direction. The next act was performed by two elastic young women who walked on their hands, turned themselves inside out like gloves and abolished all sense of body shape so that, after a while, it was hard to tell whether their arms were actually their legs and whether their heads hadn't come unscrewed and taken root somewhere around their abdomens. They smiled all the way through their contortions, sliding over each other, lifting themselves with just one hand, flattening themselves so that they almost disappeared into the ground, and then suddenly springing back up. I started clapping and it was the first time for a long while that I seemed to feel anything. It's hard to say what. Amazement, perhaps. Next came the man I would call boss, standing upright on a horse, smoking a pipe and reading a paper while the animal cantered round. He wasn't holding reins or a whip but he lay down, sat up and got back to his feet without ever losing his balance, and at the end of his act he gave such a convincing portrayal of sleep that I found myself really believing he'd fallen asleep on his horse. As he woke up he looked me in the eye. I don't know how he had time to see me, nor exactly what he saw of me because his head was upside-down and he was going round so quickly he must have been dizzy. Every time he came past he looked for me. When he was taking his bows he stared at me and I felt he was trying to say something.

When the show was over I didn't have the strength to get up. I wanted to stay there, they would have to drive me out. I had seen the elastic girls, the horse man, the clown with the cats, the tightrope walkers with the snakes, the feathered trapeze artists, the football-playing jugglers, the spider man. I, the adulterous woman, the perverse woman, the manipulative woman, the child-eater, had admired them all and was part of their troupe.

The big top emptied. Soon the performers were up between the seats where the audience had been, clearing up. It was more an inspection: picking up the odd orphaned glove or abandoned scarf. I waited my turn. People smiled at me. I couldn't manage to smile back at them. I saw one of the contortionists having a quick word in the boss's ear. He came over and sat down beside me. He sat very upright with the palms of his hands over his knees and his chest puffed out. He smelled of horse manure and oranges. I didn't dare turn to look at him.

'What's your thing?' he asked me.

I had no idea what he meant and didn't know how to reply. He rubbed his stubble and rephrased his question.

'What can you do?'

I can disgrace myself very quickly, was the first thought that came to me.

'Nothing,' I said, so quietly he didn't hear it.

'What?' he said.

'Nothing, I can't do anything.'

I gathered later that this was how a good many of the troupe were recruited. They washed up with no warning like me, sitting on those seats without paying for a ticket, stayed on after the applause had died away and explained their own act. The magician, the juggler, the cat-trainer, the sword-swallower, the girl with the hula hoops. They had all been swept here by a wave and, like seaweed borne on the tide, apparently devoid of free will, they had landed – silent and opaque, keeping their talents hidden – on the tiered seats of Santo Salto. Without realizing it, I had performed the code, said the password and was now expected to demonstrate some sort of miracle. Who knows what I might be hiding under my raincoat? Flame-throwing dwarf rabbits, crystal hoops that I swung round my body without breaking a single one, ropes and rings I used to lift myself up into the air as easily as climbing a staircase? My lined face and tired expression did nothing to belie this hypothesis, quite the opposite. I had plenty of time, subsequently, to watch the performers. There was not one of them whose astonishing prowess could be guessed at first glance (an un-initiated first glance). The boys were mostly short and stocky, sometimes even pot-bellied; the girls, who were almost all very slim, had black teeth. Some of the acrobats seemed damaged, with deeply furrowed brows; the tightrope walker had fat but-tocks and constantly worried about them getting bigger. These people weren't particularly ugly, some of them were even devastatingly attractive, but their bodies were rendered ordinary by the combination of little flaws naturally accumulated over a lifetime. I was like them. I had made no special effort to stop the march of time, with my rounded little tummy, calluses on my feet and bags under my eyes. So there was absolutely no reason why a remarkable talent, a gift like those each of them possessed, shouldn't be camouflaged beneath my semblance of normality.

The boss waited for a moment, then launched into a list.

'Straps in the air? Cannon? Mats? Trapeze? Tightrope? Wild animals? Juggling?…'

They were like the beads on a big, heavy necklace. I didn't interrupt him, sitting in silence, not trying to understand.

'We need someone to cook,' he said eventually, disorient-ated by my lack of reaction. 'Can you cook?'

'Yes,' I cried.

If I could have fallen to my knees I would have done, but I didn't have the strength or the nerve. I could also have kissed his hands or prostrated myself. I had the distinct impression he was saving my life, but I had to disguise this feeling, to keep it a secret for fear of ruining everything.

I squeezed the handle of my suitcase and, as I did, I really felt as if – like Nina or Volsie, the two contortionists – I could have balanced on one arm with my head down and my feet pointing skywards, creating a perfectly straight line like them, a line which they would have rippled slowly and imperceptibly so that, thanks to their orange costumes, they looked like two flames flickering in the wind.

The boss beckoned me to follow him and I discovered my new domain: a very small, very spherical caravan with five gas burners and a wooden table.

'The tap's outside,' he told me.

'What about washing-up?'

'The children take care of that.'

At Santo Salto you were a child until you were twelve, not a day more or less. In winter I would look out of the porthole of my seashell and watch Georges and Rodrigo – four and five years old – running the plates under the icy water, splashing it over themselves. I worried about their health. They were never ill. 'How do you think people managed before?' I was asked if I commented on their methods. And this question, rather than dazing me, raised my spirits. People before, people now, people after, it was all the same. What had been could happen again, what had existed would never stop.

I sit down on the banquette, run my hand through my hair and wait for the pain to go away. It always goes away in the end. I look over towards the wall at the back of the kitchen, wanting to establish whether or not there actually is a magical blue door there. I know perfectly well I don't have a store-room, and certainly don't have a sumptuous back area that looks like a ballroom. I don't know what I'm hoping for. Perhaps a mirage of Mrs Cohen, the frontier guard to that other space, to the world where wishes have performative power. Let there be a door and there was a door. The world of dreams exists just as powerfully as the real world. What's the difference? I suddenly don't know any more. In the world of dreams we don't have anything to worry about, I tell myself. But that's not right, in nightmares we have nothing but. In the real world actions have consequences; but that's also true of dreams. No, I'm getting side-tracked. It's more general than that, a question of continuity. In life everything leads on from everything else, tomorrow's reconciliation from yesterday's mistake, next month's punishment from last month's sin. Whereas in dreams, each slice of life is self-contained. They all start from scratch. Time doesn't exist. We can escape the incurable, even death is dismissed. I'm staggered to think I spend part of my life in a world governed by laws different to those that organize real life. And all of a sudden I can't tell them apart. Why should one necessarily take precedence over the other? Why is it always the same one that wins? Come back, frontier guard, my sideways glance seems to be begging. Come back and deliver me from this tedious here and now. But it's impossible, I'm a prisoner of time.

Yesterday was a good day but I didn't enjoy it. I now see that being a dog among dogs doesn't suit me. I don't want just anyone walking in here. I want them to know why they're coming, for them to realize that everything is different here. I want to fulfil my dream, to see my vision through to its con- clusion, and if success threatens that, then I'll do away with success. Mind you, success is a big word. Yesterday – despite the crowds – I made only half the daily takings I need to pay back my loan. Just half, and I'm already exhausted, ill, good for nothing.

I have a cold shower in my sink, standing there screaming under the blast of water as it freezes and hardens me. I grit my teeth under that stream of arrows in the dark, and my skin puckers and swells, my muscles defending themselves, flexing and bracing, my curves curving out and my hollows hollowing in. I think of christenings, of course, and find it irritating how I always come back to childhood, never succeeding in shaking it off, constantly clinging to it like a pirate to his treasure map. What can I be looking for? Why would anyone turn a restaurant into a school canteen? Why serve sausages and chips when you know how to slow-cook a lamb shank for seven hours? I want to go back, try again, make amends. It's maddening but I can't help it. Now that I've had my brilliant ideas I have to execute them and if that means turning people away – turning away bank clerks to make way for little darlings from reception class – I'll do it. I'm so sorry, I've got a booking for eighteen grated carrots and croque monsieur, I can't take you. I think of this stupid victory: swapping €22 meals for picnics at a fraction of the price. Stand back, here comes the business queen, she's going to teach you a completely new kind of capitalism and re-align your graphs of projected turnover. If anyone ever thought that the shortest route between two points was not, as has always been believed, a straight line, there's no reason why I shouldn't devise a system in which accumulation isn't the only guarantee of profit. I'd like to think that here too, in my little domain, there's something to invent.

I get my lists back out of the drawer where I'd tidied them away, and study my suggestions. The fruits of nocturnal drinking, gleaming in the cold grey light of dawn. Every word I read is like a coloured lantern shedding kindly light. I need to do a certain amount of research on the internet to find prices and addresses but I no longer have a computer: I sold it to Cash Converters for a mouthful of bread. I get dressed and go out into the crisp early morning to go to the market. The boulevard is deserted and market gardeners are just coming to unload. In the clandestine silence hovering before the first customers arrive, I buy kilos of vegetables, meat and fish. I don't count or think about anything, letting my instincts guide me without referring to provisional menus. I move from one stall to another like a ghost. My shopping-trolley and backpack are now both full. Collapsing under all this produce, I strain my muscles like a weight-lifter to make it home. As I reach the metal shutter the sun peeps up between two buildings and draws a golden triangle on the metal. I drop my bag, let go of the trolley and breathe. It's eight o'clock and all the shopping's done. I'm ahead of myself. I'll have time to nip to the local internet café to resolve a few of my enigmas.

'Can I help you?' a voice asks behind me, startling me. 'Can I help you?' it says again.

This is how angels appear to us, dropping from the sky without a sound to say those absurd words we so long to hear. I burst out laughing, just as Sarah did the day the angel announced that, even though she was ninety-nine years old, she would soon bear a son. I feel old and spent too. Who could possibly help me and how?

The young man comes over and holds out a hand towards my bag. He is tall and very slim, wearing flared blue-and-white striped trousers. He is knock-kneed and stands leaning to one side as if trying to get through a doorway too low for him. His torso doesn't fit onto his hips properly and his head is off at a strange angle. My eyesight isn't right.

'Are you not feeling well?' he asks me.

'Yes, yes, I'll be fine. It was all a bit too heavy, I think.'

'If you open up for me,' he says, 'I could take your purchases in.'

This boy seems to talk like an old man. The only person I've ever heard use the word purchases for shopping was my grandfather; he always wore a suit and hat, and never went out without his shopping bag. I wonder whether I too have words in my vocabulary that betray something not quite mastered, something unknown, a truth I can't grasp. I would never notice them myself, in the same way as I will never know my own profile or my back – parts of myself that are familiar to others but not to me.

The young man who talks like a pensioner is called Ben. Simone and Hannah told him to come and see me.

'Simone and Hannah?' I ask.

I can't think who he means.

'Simone and Hannah,' he says again. 'They told me you needed someone.'

'Are you looking for work?'

We're sitting inside *Chez moi* and the sun is spilling great bucketfuls of light onto the tables.

He doesn't answer.

'I can't afford to take anyone on,' I tell him, 'I'm so sorry.'

He doesn't respond to this but gets up and starts putting the shopping away in the fridge. He moves so gently. He kneels down, gets back up, bends and twists, picks up and puts down... all gracefully, even though he looks like a badly-put-together puppet.

'Stop it,' I tell him. 'I've just said I haven't got any money. Your friends didn't understand. They don't know. They've no idea of my circumstances.'

'They told me you needed someone,' he says again.

I can't say anything in response to this: it's the truth.

I watch Ben moving about my kitchen as if he knows it by heart. He puts the food away in exactly the right place, locates the coldest parts of the fridge and keeps the more temperate areas for fragile produce. When he has finished, he slides the shopping-trolley under the counter, folds up my backpack and bundles it inside the trolley, then picks up a sponge and wipes down the draining-board.

'Are you a waiter?' I ask.

Without a word he takes four plates from the cupboard, lays them along his right forearm, his wrist, the pad of his thumb and the rest of his hand, then with the tips of his fingers on his left hand he picks up two long dishes – and I know how heavy they are, problematically heavy – and slips them into a balanced position between his bent elbow and flattened wrist. His hand, which is now free again, picks up two wine glasses. Revolving on his own axis, he whirls from one table to the next, spinning plates, bringing them up over his head and back down to chest height or hiding them behind his back. I tense myself in anticipation of the smash. He looks so clumsy, weedy and misshapen. At the end of this ballet, he puts one plate down on each table and one dish at each end of the counter and then throws the glasses in the air, watches them describe a sort of Catherine wheel through the red morning sunlight and catches them at the last moment. He slips one into my hand and clinks it with the other.

I bury my head in my crossed arms. I try, in my mind, to send him away. I begged the frontier guard a bit too much. Mrs Cohen has sent me the waiter of my dreams, the two worlds have collided. I'm hallucinating. A little snatch of a dream, in the shape of a giant Pinocchio, has worked its way into my everyday existence. It's just that I'm so tired, I tell myself. If I concentrate he'll go away. I close my eyes tight and open them again.

Ben is still there.

He's annoying.

His smile is annoying.

His silence is annoying.

But I can't afford the luxury of coping without him. If he

really does exist he will work for me, starting right now.

'I've got to go to the internet café,' I tell him. 'Could you peel and grate the carrots? The food-processor is in the bottom right-hand corner of the cupboard. If you finish before I get back, wash the lettuce and put the Gruyère in some milk to soak. Take the butter out to soften.'

I don't even need to say he's hired: he's got things to do already.

'I'll be back as soon as I can.'

'Take your time,' he advises amiably.

'How long can you stay?'

He shrugs.

Incredible, I think as I breeze through the gilded chill of morning, I've got a slave! A huge smile breaks my face in two.

No, no! I'm so naïve. He'll rob the till. I've left him on his own, he's got the keys. He'll take the business account cheque-book. He'll take the shopping. The paradise of childhood, the paradise of youth... paradise corrupted. They're all delinquents, the young these days. Rotten through and through, no respect for anything. They'll take everything from us, the bastards. They hate us, they resent us for confiscating wealth and not giving way to them. They've got the vigour we've lost and the audacity we're so afraid of. They're having their revenge. This is a network. Simone and Hannah were just scouts, watching me and passing the information on to Ben. He's making the most of the fact that I'm not there to ransack my poor little restaurant.

There we are, don't worry, I'm back in the real world. The

real world is where things go really badly but follow on from each other perfectly. Dreams, on the other hand, are when everything goes very well, but there's no connection. All the same, I'm still smiling. I couldn't give a damn. He can take what he wants. There's nothing in the till and my cheques will all bounce. I don't believe in angels, but I'm no more afraid of the devil. Let him rob me. I'm happy to be the victim of this scheme.

The internet café smells of cigarettes. Their coffee is filthy, served in ugly chunky cups. The sugar's damp and the spoon suspect. Luckily I'm not as persnickety as some of my new acquaintances. The invidious draft from under the door freezes my feet and it's not long before I'm shivering. But nothing can stop me, not the bland bitterness of the coffee, nor the meagre comforts on offer here. I came to surf and I have every intention of being carried along on this wave. I spend some time on the local authority's sprawling site, explore sporting activities and adult evening classes, and I reinvent a life for myself in which I spend my evenings learning Russian, chi kong and the art of engraving. I make a note of school meal prices and, while I'm at it, find information about nutritional values. The dieticians' recommendations make me quite dizzy – our diet seems to have become our only ideology. It's terrible.

To cheer myself up, I drift over to the virtual islands of various caterers. I'm fascinated by their prices and the names they use. Everything is so detailed, so luxurious. This isn't just

cooking, it's alchemy. It's not just money, it's a budget. I see a
lavish procession of frothy strawberry mousses, strips of
smoked eel, bundles of mixed seaweed and mushrooms,
exquisite spiced biscuits and specialist honeys. The photographs show pyramids, three-arched bridges, palaces with
several floors and balconies and terraces – works of art for
the delectation of the mouth. I admire a Golden Gate Bridge
made of nougatine, an Eiffel tower of profiteroles and a Taj
Mahal in meringue. I'm offered a complete meal for €100 a
head; it consists of bevies of dainty mouthfuls laid out in
rows on a white table-cloth. They are reminiscent of the
improbable hats populating the grandstand of an English
racecourse at the end of the nineteenth century. In my head I
draw in the silhouette of a little woman beneath each
ridiculous headdress. Your wide-brimmed sturgeon-and-
black-radish creation is most becoming, Lady Winchester. I
simply love your salmon-and-samphire number, my dear. The
petits fours have started up a conversation. I listen to them,
holding off till the last possible moment the next stage when
I turn to the yellow pages where I either will or will not find
Ali Slimane.

I feel as if my salvation depends on this search. If I find
him, I will be saved; if he doesn't appear, I'm damned.

After arranging the marriage of a lord in a top hat of
truffles in champagne to a lady in a beret of cucumber and
mullet in aspic, I leave Ascot for the Paris region. I abandon
the grandstand perfumed with wild lemon and draped in
chiffon to roll in the stubble fields of the Beauce and Brie

plains. Slimane. Did you mean Ben Slimane? Widen your search to neighbouring areas. I drift from the Oise to Aisne, go all the way to Aube, get lost in Loiret and go back to Seine-et-Marne. I search by profession, drop the first name. He finally appears in the Eure region: Ali Slimane, Chemin du Vavasseur, 27600 Monsigny-en-Vexin. Alone at the top of a hill, I can see him. His dark eyelids gleaming above his pained eyes, the profusion of lashes like a chestnut husk. With a cigarette in the corner of his mouth, he surveys his autumnal work: the maize that swelled the ribcage of the field right up to the sky has been harvested, the land offers itself up naked once more, dotted with lengths of dry beige hosepipe. The sky can drop right back onto it and lie down, the eiderdown of ears has gone. Mr Slimane gets home to the farm late. He doesn't know I'm going to call him. He doesn't remember me. Never thinks of me. What shall I say? How will he recognize me? I'm the cook from the circus. Then he'll know.

When I get home everything is organized, my orders have been carried out and the chores done. Ben is sitting on the moleskin banquette, straight-backed and with his head at an odd angle like a flamingo. He's waiting for me. He hasn't destroyed anything, he hasn't ransacked or pillaged, he's obeyed me.

'Did it go well?' he asks me.

'Yes. I found what I was looking for. How about you?'

Ben does not reply. He leans his head a little further. I'm worried he'll break his neck.

I explain that we're going to have a double menu. He doesn't understand.

'We're going to do food for adults and food for children.'

'Like at the Hippopotamus?' he asks.

This time I'm the one who doesn't understand. He explains what he means.

'You want to do a children's menu? That's what it's called, a children's menu. Ham and chips or fresh burgers. I didn't like that sort of thing when I was little. I wanted to have what my parents were eating.'

'No, no. That's not my idea at all. I want to make food that appeals to children but which adults can eat too. I want everyone to feel at home here, do you see what I mean?'

'So we won't call it a children's menu?'

'No.'

'What will we call it?'

'It won't have a name,' I say.

And, suddenly, there's a moment of illumination: nothing has a name here.

'Have you noticed? I don't have a sign,' I say. 'It doesn't say "restaurant" over the door.'

'Have you got something against names?' he asks rather dubiously.

'Yes.'

'So how will people know?'

This boy asks good questions. Questions there are no answers to. I bite my lip. He fidgets; I can see that he's looking for a solution, that he wants to help me.

'I'll tell them,' he suggests. 'I'll go out into the street and hand out leaflets. I'll find a way to make them realize. I'll explain without actually naming anything.'

Ben is getting enthused, but I tell him we don't have to go to extremes. I'm against names if names restrict things to categories, but I'm not against words.

He nods vigorously.

'I can stay till four today,' he tells me out of the blue in response to a question I asked an hour and a half earlier. 'I've got lectures after that,' he explains.

'Are you a student?'

'Yes. A waiter and a student.'

'Of what?'

'Political science.'

'That's really hard isn't it?'

'Very,' he agrees with appropriate gravity.

We share the work between us. He takes care of the easier food and I do the more complicated dishes. He butters slices of bread and puts seasoning on the carrots while I prepare the tajine of fish, the minestrone and the goat's cheese terrine with herbs and olives. Ben is so biddable he's exemplary, almost worrying. He's accurate and careful. He doesn't talk spontaneously but answers when I ask him something.

I want to know how he met Hannah and Simone. He can't remember.

'We just met,' he says.

He sees that as an answer.

'Have you known them long?'

'A while.'

'How long?'

'I don't know. Since nursery school.'

He has always lived round here and knows everyone. He thinks it was a good idea to open a restaurant. It's just what was needed. Specially somewhere 'like this'. As we chat I realize he has subtly changed register, shifting from his grandfather-style lexicon to younger, vaguer, less precise language. He uses the words 'thingy', 'whatsit' and 'gizmo' a lot as well as 'like'. I think it is out of consideration for me because he realizes just how hurtful actual names can be, terms that are too precise, too definitive, designating and judging at the same time, identifying and classifying. I ask him whether he still lives at home.

'Yes, but not with my parents,' he says.

'Where are they then?'

'In the cemetery.'

'I'm so sorry.'

'I'm not.'

'Did you inherit anything?'

'Yes.'

'Are you very rich?'

'No.'

'We must talk about your wages,' I tell him.

'You've already explained that you can't pay me.'

'But you mustn't accept that, Ben. This is very serious. I can't pay you, but I can't pay for the two fillets of hake I've just bought at the market either, or next month's rent or the electricity. I can't pay for anything but I pay it all anyway. So I might as well pay you too.'

'It's not worth bothering,' he says.

'Yes it is. It would just be impossible any other way. If you refuse to be paid you can leave straight away. I don't want to see you again.'

Ben looks aggrieved.

'What about the others?' I ask, 'People you've worked for before, did they pay you?'

'Yes.'

'Well, why shouldn't I then? Why shouldn't I have the right to pay you? Because I'm too poor? Because I'm a woman?'

He shakes his head. His eyes dart about wildly and he brings his hands up to his face as if afraid of being beaten. I wonder what he's been put through. How this body of separate elements assembled itself. What treatment he's been subjected to, to be so docile, what upbringing to be so fearful.

'I want…' He hesitates for a moment. '… I want to change the world,' he admits, flushing. 'Hannah and Simone told me about you… how you work. I'm interested in that. I get the feeling you're trying something new. I want to be part of that experience.'

My poor love, I think to myself. What on earth will you get from the experience of bankruptcy?

'What do you mean?'

'They told me about the price for life. They also told me it was a secret. I won't tell anyone. I swear.'

I explain that it's not really to do with a method, it's more a tactic to ensure customer loyalty, that there's nothing new or noble in that, nothing that's remotely like an ideal. 'Don't go hoping you can do a work placement here. I don't do science or politics. I'd be absolutely no use to you for your studies. You'd be wasting your time. All work deserves payment. Have you heard that said before? Even if the work in question is interesting, even if it's a pleasure or an education. You want to change the world and that's all very well, but all I want to do is make my little business work. I don't want any misunderstandings between us, Ben. If you work here, it'll be to earn a living.'

I don't believe a word I'm saying. I listen in amazement to myself as the sentences come out of my mouth: trite sentences, banalities intended to protect us – him and me – from our megalomania, our ridiculous enthusiasm, our pathetic and unjustified faith in mankind's own capacity for progress and improvement.

'What about the food for children?' he asks, making a heart-rending effort to meet my eye.

'Yes, what about food for children?' I ask tartly.

'Well, that's political,' he mumbles. 'You're not doing that to earn money, otherwise you'd call it a children's menu. You're doing it to be fairer, for equality.'

What Ben says is true, but the gravity with which he says it – instead of reinforcing my desire to fight and fuelling my sublime ambitions – dashes my hopes and makes them look pathetic. How did we come to this? How did we create a world in which conspirators get together to talk about recipes?

A few weeks later when I see Simone and Hannah again I ask them whether Ben is normal. They immediately understand the gist of my question and both say together, 'Oh, no, no, no. He's not normal at all. But he's a brilliant waiter, isn't he? Are you pleased? Things are going better since he's been here, aren't they?'

'What about his studies?' I ask them.

'He's skipped loads of grades. Though, he's a bit retarded, but...'

They don't know, don't understand, tie themselves in knots. They clearly don't want me to think they don't like him. They adore him. They think he's the best waiter in the world. They should never have told me that. Oh, why did they say it? They're full of regrets, afraid I'll sack him because of them.

'Why do you think he's the best waiter in the world?' I ask them.

'Because he loves it,' they say.

'How long have you known him?'

'We met him last year, he was working at the Shamrock, the café next to the high school.'

'Didn't you know him at nursery school?'

They don't understand my question. I give up. Ben tells white lies, but he can also tell the truth. He really has been living in this neighbourhood all his life, and it's true that he knows everyone. I can see that from the first day he works for me. As we're finishing tidying up the kitchen Vincent bursts in with a rose in his hand. He doesn't seem surprised to see Ben here. He pats him on the shoulder, offers me the flower and sits down.

'Coffee?'

'If you like.'

'I've taken Ben on as a waiter,' I tell him.

'Good idea,' he comments abstractedly.

He drums his fingers on the table. Slumps. Sits back up. On edge. He hums a tune, then whistles it. He gets up, heads over towards the bookshelf, then sits back down.

I give him his coffee and sit down opposite him. He smiles at me without opening his mouth, which makes him look rather like a toad.

'Still in your mega-epic mood?'

He nods his head without unclenching his teeth.

'You know,' he eventually confides quietly, 'about what I said the other day. I didn't mean it.'

A gap about the size of Lake Michigan appears in my memory. What can he be referring to?

'Well, I did,' he says. 'I did think it but that doesn't mean that... do you see what I mean? It didn't mean anything, it was just a comment, in passing, an observation. I don't go in for generalizations.'

It comes back to me, Jews and money. Poor Vincent. He feels all guilty now.

'I couldn't care less,' I tell him.

'Sorry?'

He's offended now, terribly.

'I couldn't care less about all that. It's much more straight-forward than people think, or much more complicated.'

As we talk, as I try to explain to Vincent that I don't think he's anti-Semitic, while he tries to get me to say that I'm a Jew, while we fight it out over quite separate territories, territories that don't even share a border – him toiling away with his right-thinking ideas and me labouring on with my straight-thinking – while all this is going on something happens in the restaurant. I don't realize straight away because I'm too absorbed in our argument, but while we hammer away, the room fills up. There are customers sitting down, some are even standing by the counter. There are two men in overalls, a woman with glasses wearing a smart coat, a funny little bald man in a raincoat with a scarf neatly crossed at his throat. Ben is serving them, bringing them coffees, a little glass of dry white wine and, I have no idea how, even locating a pineapple juice. I have to face the fact that *Chez moi* has become a bar. Cigarettes are lit, ashtrays spring from nowhere.

A man of about fifty, an efficient-looking sort, comes in and says, 'Hello, Ben, a coffee please.'

'You're on, doctor,' my waiter replies.

The workmen in overalls pay for their drinks. 'See you later, Ben,' they say as they leave.

'What the bloody hell is going on?' I ask Vincent.

I look round slowly, first one way then the other. I look at all the strangers who have come into my home without my inviting them. It's not as if it says non-stop service on the window, I haven't opened a brasserie or a bar. But it's too late. My failure to identify it has produced an unexpected twist. I dare not stand up. As far as the others are concerned, I probably look like a customer because I'm sitting at a table with a friend and a cup of coffee. I don't know whether I like the feeling of dispossession that sweeps through me. I do burst out laughing, though.

'He's a local lad', Vincent tells me, as if that were enough to explain my restaurant's sudden popularity. 'Everyone knows him. He's had a – how shall I put this? – an unusual life. He's hung about in the streets a lot. His parents…'

He stops himself, not because he's baulking at the thought of revealing my new waiter's family secrets, but because I've leapt to my feet to ask Ben how much he's been charging for a coffee. We didn't have time to discuss it. The till has rung several times. How can I treat this all so lightly?

Very quietly, Ben explains that he charges €1 for a cup of coffee at a table, and 60 cents up at the bar. It's cheap and he knows it but he thought this fitted in well with my style. For the dry white wine he went the other way, he reckoned that at €3 a glass. That's very expensive but if we don't use off-putting prices on alcohol we'll end up with all the local drunks. He can see I wouldn't know how to cope with that sort of clientele, so there's no point going down that road.

'And the pineapple juice?'

'€2.20.'

I wonder where those 20 cents came from. They came from his imagination and his business sense. €2.20 sounds right. It gives people the impression they're saving the 30 cents that would round it up nicely so they end up leaving that as a tip but still feel they've come away with a bargain.

When he comes to leave, Vincent puts €1 on the table. I

look at the coin. It shines like a rising moon on the wine-coloured Formica. Announcing a new era. I hesitate to pick it up. I look up at Vincent who's smiling.

'Mazel tov,' he says.

Ben and I have agreed he should work part-time. Vincent has helped me with all the social security contributions and paperwork. I've become a boss. I collect bills, demands for payments and bailiffs' warnings. It's like a sort of un-medicinal herbarium, constantly growing and threatening me. I don't file anything, just let it pile up, charging headlong towards disaster, but the feeling is so familiar I have trouble taking action against it. My life, which I would like to have been so simple, just gets more and more complicated and I have to acknowledge that the distinction – in itself disturbing – between the real world and the world of dreams has company: I now also have to differentiate between the actual universe and a virtual one. The actual one is what goes on in my restaurant every day: customers, orders, food coming and going, drink deliveries, dishes simmering, vegetables peeled, bills given, rolls of coins, banknotes, cheques, reservations, regular customers, the hubbub, that soft hubbub of happy adults and children. The virtual one is what I receive in the post and is instantly lost in my labyrinth of drawers: forms and summonses couched in terms that I find barbaric, and to which I don't deign to reply, figures which always seem to accumulate in the same column, the debit column. I feel like those parched landscapes where the depleted groundwater can no longer hold together the cracked soil, those sterile expanses cleaned out by summer storms but never actually slaked by them. I don't know how but the money that comes into my till never reaches into that dark parched pipe-work, not the tiniest droplet to quench the thirst of the paper monster.

One morning Ben tells me we can't carry on like this. 'You just keep going regardless,' he tells me.

'But it's working, isn't it? The restaurant's still just as busy. Since you've been here people have been tripping over each other to get in. We have three sittings at lunchtime and three in the evening. The mini-canteen's working. And the catering side will be up and running soon.'

Without saying a thing, Ben opens the drawers of the minute cabinet shoehorned between the sink and the cupboard, a piece of furniture salvaged from beside a dustbin on the Rue de la Folie-Méricourt and which acts in turns as my desk, butcher's block and bedside table. As the drawers crawl out along their runners the wads of multicoloured paper spew down onto the floor tiles. My chest feels constricted with shame. I look away, wondering whether I will ever be free of that emotion. I would like to apologize to Ben, to ask him to forgive me for making him take on this role. The world has turned upside-down. I am the older of us, I should be protecting him, teaching him, giving him advice. Ben has no experience, he should be relying on me, trusting in my judgement, listening to me recount my edifying adventures, and reaping the benefits of my wisdom. But no, it's the other way round. He spots the pitfalls better than I do, he's sensible and mature. He asks me for €10 to go to Office Depot.

'What's that?' I ask, terrified – because the words conjure some sort of dumping ground for failed businesses – that Ben is going to denounce me to the Inland Revenue or some such organization, that he'll hand my files over to the police.

'It's a stationer's,' he says.

'Don't you think we've got enough paper as it is?'

He smiles. Reassures me. Claims he can sort everything out.

He goes out and I'm distraught at the sight of his silhouette wavering through the early winter fog. Where are you going, little chick? How are you going to save this feckless old hen?

While I'm waiting for him to come back I make some shortbread biscuits which I will serve with figs in whisky and a vanilla zabaglione. I rub some shoulders of lamb with garlic and harissa, and put them in the oven, then blanch some celery and chard before glazing them with brown sugar. I cut some grapes in half. The word grape is so close to gape, the gaping holes in my reasoning. I look at the inside of the fruit, the smooth watery green flesh. A tear drops onto the stainless steel surface, followed by another, the grape is overflowing. The tide is rising again, I think to myself. Build a seawall, quick! my heart sings. A seawall between me and myself. How can I help the memories welling back up? How do I break my conscience away from the past? What can I do so that nothing evokes, nothing symbolizes, nothing reminds? Why does life consist of this endless rehashing? Do we never recover from our amputations, our mutilations? And why always the same mistakes? As if we were besotted with our own blunders, our own inability to do what we ought to do as we ought to do it. I feel as if anyone else in my position, with the luck I've had (getting a loan on the strength of fake sureties, benefiting from supportive neighbours, taking on the best waiter in Paris) would have run *Chez moi* clearly and efficiently. Anybody, except for me, could have made this the perfect example of a small business. But, there you are, my complete lack of organization always has to play its part. I always end up – and it's like an illness, oh, how I suffer, how I would love to be cured – making a complete mess. I'm unreliable. I'm like someone on drugs, unstable, furtive, dangerous. I watch the episodes as they happen, each a reaction to another, like a point with its counter-point. The characters are similar: they are young and they are here to judge. Ben is so gentle and indulgent but his jurisdiction is a reincarnation of Hugo's, of the trial of the son versus his mother. They were both right and I was wrong both times.

I do make an effort, though; I'm a perfectionist in my own way. In the early stages my energy and inventiveness perform miracles. Was I not an exemplary mother?

I try to stick the two halves of the grape back together. They fit perfectly. The salt from my tears stings my cheeks.

Wasn't I a perfect mother?

Not a trace of the knife left on the skin of the fruit, no scar, the grape is intact, protected by its translucent sheath.

Wasn't I an irreproachable mother?

The tears quicken. My hands are shaking. I drop the grape which falls to the floor, splattering open.

His sweaters always soft. Not one scarf that was scratchy. Not one ridiculous hat. His trousers never too tight at the waist. His T-shirts clean, so clean. His shoes comfortable and welcoming. Every evening a story, a fairytale, a Greek myth. On the table, fresh brightly coloured food, platefuls that looked like flowers, like a patchwork of fields, a landscape. On the ceiling in his bedroom I stick all the phosphorescent stars as per the picture. I almost kill myself climbing up the step-ladder but I don't give up. In the evenings before he goes to sleep we read the map of the stars together. I name the constellations one by one. When we go to the theatre or the cinema we take a picnic to have on the way, a delicious snack of almonds, dried mangoes and Turkish Delight. On the way back we talk. Hugo is wonderfully articulate. He understands everything. He's very quick to establish connections between the different shows he's seen. I'm fascinated by his intelligence, just as I am by the absence of noise in the cosmos. It leaves me with a chill sense of amazement.

For years and years I stay on the look out, waiting to hear the gong sound, the gong of maternal love to set my heart reverberating. Sometimes I forget to think about it, my moment of respite. My every gesture and consideration so perfectly mimes this inaccessible love that I catch myself believing in it. I tell myself I'm a mother like any other, a little more conscientious perhaps. The pain dissipates. I can breathe. But it never lasts; I only have to see a real mother, to hear her talking to her child, watch her gazing at her baby, listen to her singing to her toddler. I recognize all that because the three days I spent loving Hugo left a very particular mark on me, like a burn all along my spine. I watch them and the wound starts to ooze again. I haven't got the flimsy foot-bridge which would get me over that 2000-metre deep gorge. It's barely there. The abyss separating me from my child is so narrow. A rope thrown from one side to the other would do the trick, because it's not a wide breach, it's appallingly deep, but a tree trunk lowered across it, a length of twine… And I'm drawn towards the chasm. Longing to jump, to be done with it, it's exasperating. Perhaps in those moments my expression isn't entirely well-meaning. My eyes might even look like those of a murderer. I resent him so much, this poor child who isn't to blame in any way.

One night I dream I'm delving through his innards trying to find my love, as if he's confiscated it and hidden it inside himself. When I wake up I'm frightened. I take a few drops of Rescue Remedy, tell myself I'm going mad, persuade myself everything's fine and go back to my rituals: perfect care routine, model upbringing. I arrange to talk to his teachers at nursery school, then at primary school. They're surprised to see me, more accustomed to meeting the parents of problem children; they are consulted in cases of hyperactivity, recurring low marks, behavioural problems. Actually, they're usually the ones who ask to see the parents. With Hugo, it's me who wants the meeting and every year it's the same: a stream of compliments. He's bright, he's good at sharing, he has a brilliant mind, he's a kind friend, he has a strong sense of fairness. Some even go so far as to mention his looks, explaining that having such a delightful child in class helps them with their lessons. It leaves me cold, I know all this. I'm waiting for something else. What exactly? I'm naïvely hoping that one of these childhood professionals will uncover the horror of our situation. I picture the scene:

You can't fool me, you know. Everyone knows that the children who look the best looked-after are the ones who suffer the most. All these good results, the fact that your son seems to be flourishing, radiant even, it's suspicious, extremely suspicious. Where my colleagues might talk of good qualities, I would call them symptoms.

I run the gauntlet of paediatricians, anticipating my punishment. Nothing. I'm congratulated on his growth curve, his admirable teeth, his tonsils which needn't be removed. Every appointment is over in five minutes. 'Oh, if only all my patients could be like you!' they tell me.

Have I committed the perfect crime?

Hugo and I never kiss. Until the age of six he holds my hand to cross the road. His palm feels dry and inert against mine. Sometimes I panic: if he falls over, if he hurts himself, if he cries, then I'll have to take him in my arms to comfort him. I can't even imagine it. But Hugo never falls, he's agile and careful. He doesn't cry. He knows what he's dealing with. When he was tiny I gave him his bottles at arm's length, with him on a pillow and me sitting alongside, reaching over. I said it was to avoid backache. Everyone believed me.

He learned to read and write very young. One of the few

advantages of boredom (and it's very boring spending your days with a child you can't manage to love) is that you generate excessive amounts of activity destined to disguise it. At two, he'd exhausted the possibilities of play dough, at three papier mâché had no more secrets for him. Water-based paints, oil paints, pottery. Before he was four I suggested we played with letters. I had bought a wooden alphabet: clowns in red clothes and black hats worked alone or in pairs to mime out the downstrokes and curves. The first word Hugo wrote was 'OR'. I think the position of the acrobats had something to do with this choice: the O was him, a supple little clown closed in on himself, constrained to self-sufficiency; the upright of the R was his father, close-by, straight-backed, stable… and the rest was me, an upside-down clown in a posture of slightly ludicrous flight, with feet stuck to the head of the upright clown, knees bent so that the buttocks were stuck to the father's hips, then the torso and arms launching in the opposite direction as if diving into space. I made no comment. I wrote 'HUGO', he wrote 'MYRIAM'. I wrote 'MUMMY', he wrote 'QTSUBYG'.

One night Hugo had a temperature. It was bronchitis. The doctor had said not to worry. I sent him to school with a silk scarf round his neck as if the luxurious fabric could protect him from a more serious bout. When he came home that evening his eyes were shining. I asked him if he was all right. He said yes and shut himself in his room. He must have gone to sleep because he didn't come to the dining-room at supper time. We didn't worry about it, saying he must have needed the sleep, must have been having a growth spurt. I didn't hear him moaning at three o'clock in the morning. What alerted me was the fact my husband wasn't in bed. I called him. He didn't answer. I got up and looked for him in the kitchen and the bathroom. I didn't think for a moment that he could be with Hugo because the child had never woken us. He'd been sleeping through the night since we came home from hospital. But as I went back to bed I heard a sound from behind the door decorated with the four wooden letters that spelled our son's name. I turned the handle and saw them. Madonna and child, by moonlight. My husband sitting on the ground and Hugo in his arms, streaming with sweat and tears. His father's big wide hands gently stroking his burning head. I closed the door on them and walked back to bed on unsteady knees. With my pillow in my mouth I sobbed, stifling my cries in the feathers. The next day I went to see a doctor and told him I was a bit depressed. He prescribed me some pills. From that day onwards my existence became calmer. I lived underwater, in a submerged cathedral, my sorrow had become inaudible even to me and I smiled, stupidly.

Ben returns, triumphant. He takes four grey files from his bag and brandishes them like bouquets of flowers.

'We're going to sort everything out,' he announces, putting the files down on the desk. He has also bought file-dividers in a range of delicious colours.

'We'll put bills that need paying here. Those that have been paid here. The ones that can't wait can go here, then the ones that can hang on for a while. We'll stick all the admin stuff in the second file. The third is for the bank.'

He punches holes in pages, slips them into place, clears the congestion. Once this work is done, he takes a giant calendar from his bag and hangs it on the wall. 'This,' he tells me, 'is our schedule for payments.' He uses a pink felt-tip to tick off dates.

'Are you pleased?' he asks me.

I can't seem to answer. I'm thinking of the traces of salt on my cheeks, of my eyes which must be red. Ben deserves so much better than this.

Hesitantly, he takes a rectangular package from his jacket pocket.

'This is for you,' he says, his voice unsure of itself.

'What is it?'

'A present.'

I tear the paper. Ben has given me Rainer Maria Rilke's *Letters to a Young Poet*.

'Do you know it?' he asks. 'It's my favourite book.'

'I really like it too,' I tell him.

'But you haven't got it,' he says, pointing to my bookshelves.

'No, you're right. You're so kind.'

I leaf through the book. I know some sentences by heart: 'Force yourself to love *your questions themselves*, as if each of them was inaccessible to you, like a book written in a foreign language.' I would like to tell Ben why this cult anthology doesn't feature in my nomadic book collection. It's too soon. I tell him I've lost it.

We open late this morning but our regular customers don't

grumble. It's impossible to hold anything against Ben. There's a sort of magnetic field around him which makes other people keep a respectful distance. Which is just as well because otherwise, with his uncoordinated limbs and skinny frame, he would constitute easy prey for the dissatisfied of every kind.

It's my favourite time of day, a fully realized glimpse of utopia which happens every morning. Ben serves people coffees, fruit juices, hot chocolates, sometimes they ask for bread and butter. Sometimes what they really want is a boiled egg. Not a problem, the water's already boiling. On the other side of the counter, protected by my zinc work-top, I'm getting lunch and some elements of dinner ready. I work at incredible speed, my hands going more quickly than my mind. This requires tremendous relaxation and enormous concentration. You have to abandon the idea that the brain is in control, staking everything on nerves and memory. It's a pre-conscious state, like reverting to purely instinctual responses. No one can talk to me when I'm doing this. I'm quite incapable of answering, I might lose the thread. People know that; they don't try. They watch me and enjoy the smell of cooking. I can hear their conversations, catch snatches of them. They're commenting on the menu, the weather, occasionally they complain about someone who's not there, someone I'll never actually identify but who gets a real eyeful. As winter deepens and the streets get colder I sometimes hear their voices getting louder and angrier: the door isn't properly shut. 'Were you born in a barn?' someone asks. I don't need to read the papers any more, every news item is tackled. I correct the seasoning, a bit less salt in the local news, a bit more spice in international relations, some pepper in the economy. The world comes to me. I'm at the heart of a great open concourse. I witness the inevitable simplification: the food-processor of conversation smoothes out the most tender subtleties and destroys any nuances. I consider the indispensable banality of this sort of exchange of words. While I strive to get the seasoning right on different foodstuffs, bringing out their most secret aromas without ever letting one overrun another, I wonder why people unfailingly come out with the same trite nonsense. Smoothed out, smoothed out, everything always has to be smoothed out. The steamroller of consensus moves from one continent to another as my customers talk about places they've never been to and refer to populations they will never meet. They confuse and compare things, obsessed with parallels: 'It's like the Nazis,' they often say. Everyone agrees on this point, it contains its own kind of power somewhere half-way between fascination and intellectual abdication. I notice that men adore catastrophes and what they really love is predicting the worst. 'We'll all be dead in two years' time!' one of them claims. The others nod in agreement. It's because of a mad cow or a chicken with 'flu. The melting glaciers will drown us before the terrorists wipe us out with an atomic bomb, or is it the other way round? Don't let's forget the impact of chemical weapons. The stakes are constantly being raised. Voices get louder, vying to announce the worst end for the world. I'm worried by this passion for how it will all finish. How can they keep their heads? How come they don't know the recognized fact that, unlike bad news which is always preceded by some omen, good news comes as a surprise, when we least expect it? True, we know more about our subject when we're talking about destruction, given that its opposite – construction – is often enigmatic. If Cassandra had been a man, I think to myself, she would have led a far more peaceful life. She wouldn't have worried about the horrors in her dreams, but would have made use of them to thrill her mates: 'Hey, guys, guess what, Troy's going to fall. Our heroes are going to be decimated. In a couple of weeks this place will be in ruins.' And her friends would have ordered a round of drinks to celebrate.

Vincent apologizes for not coming in for a couple of days. He had a very grand wedding to do.

'They even ordered doves,' he exclaims.

'Did it go well? Did the birds crap on the food?'

I have finished my preparations and can sit down and have a cup of coffee at last. I can feel my every joint from my toes to my hips. It feels as if they are made of iron. Rusted iron.

'I nicked this for you,' Vincent says, handing me a white orchid with a scarlet heart. 'It's indestructible,' he makes a point of adding.

So flowers aren't always perishable.

'It's so pretty. It looks like it's got a face!'

He frowns. He thinks I'm a tad too flippant. He reminds me of my husband.

'They're worth a lot of money,' he says.

'What?'

'Orchids, white ones, like that, they're worth a lot.'

He probably thinks I'm not showing enough gratitude for

this sumptuous gift. I take his hand, force myself to look him right in the eye and, with my face so close to his that anyone would think we were about to kiss, I say very quietly, 'It's really, really kind. It's beautiful.'

I notice that his breath smells of aniseed. I'd like to congratulate him but I can't see how to go about it without upsetting him. His hand stays in mine, the skin feels smooth, the flesh soft. My skin is rough, my palm scored with muscle and cuts. I feel like apologizing for it. I wonder how I could ever fall in love again. How anyone could fall in love with me. Can you make love if your hands are as calloused as your feet? Can you make love when you've got a big crease down one side of your face, like a gash, from your nostril to your chin? Why does skin have to show wear and tear like that?

'How old are you?' I ask Vincent.

'Thirty-nine.'

'I'm older than you,' I say with false pride.

'You wouldn't know.'

There is obviously a flicker of doubt on my face.

'Small women always look younger than they are,' he says.

Well, that's just given me a full set in my anthology of bar-room philosophy.

I know that from behind I really can trick people. Once when I was walking down a street with Octave a man behind us shouted out, 'Hey, you two youngsters' because one of us had dropped a glove. He couldn't see any difference between us. As far as he was concerned, I was fifteen. Like Octave. Octave picked up the glove, took my chin between his thumb and forefinger and said, 'So, my little one'. I fainted inside. I was still standing but, somewhere in the middle, all the dams had collapsed. I wasn't expecting it. How could I have foreseen that and what sort of news was it? Good or bad, a miracle or a catastrophe? Cassandra herself wouldn't have known.

Little boys' friendships. A silent country, in spite of the shouting, in spite of the fights, in spite of the voices cutting across each other and competing: 'Well, my dad…', 'Well, my dog…', 'Well, my teacher…'. From their position at the centre of the world – which is roughly the shape of the stool they are sitting on – little boys confront each other at tea-time. Then they lie down on their tummies and play, with the carpet tickling their navels right where there's a gap between their trousers and T-shirts. They hold their toy soldiers with the tips of their fingers, at arm's length, as if to erase their own bodies which shouldn't be there because, right now, their minds have taken up residence in that little plastic figure. Their new home is ten centimetres tall. It's small but you can do loads of incredible stuff in there, like flying or falling off a cliff and getting straight back up again. You can smash into each other making weird noises. When you've had enough, your fingers loosen their grip. The little figure is abandoned, sometimes it rolls under the sideboard and is lost for ever. Who cares? You want to play football now. You kick a foam ball, launch yourself flat out to stop a goal, smack your head on the bed-post, bleed. But you don't care. Afterwards your hair's wet, clinging to your head, you're dying of thirst.

The first time Hugo mentioned Octave was when he was

seven. Octave was eight. 'There's a boy in my class with a music name,' he told me.

'Ludwig,' I suggested.

'No, weirder.'

'Wolfgang?'

'No, much weirder.'

I scratched my head.

'I've got it! I remember!' he cried so suddenly it made me jump. 'Octave! He's called Octave!'

I laughed.

'And what's he like then, this Octave?' I asked my son.

'He's short. He's got a pink mouth.'

He couldn't find anything else to say.

'Is that all?'

Hugo pursed his lips, he couldn't think of anything to add.

'What's his hair like?'

'Straight.'

'What colour?'

'Beige.'

'What about his eyes?'

'Normal.'

'What colour are they?'

Hugo frowned. He didn't know. He then confided that he had never noticed people could have different-coloured eyes. 'I'll pay more attention to that from now on,' he assured me in his earnest voice.

I looked away as I always did when he tried to catch my eye. It was an almost involuntary movement, more like a reflex than a reaction. I didn't even have to think about it. Like the positive poles of magnets which can't help driving each other away, my eyes were diverted by his. I was probably afraid he would read in them what I pointlessly tried to hide from him. 'I don't love you' was the message encoded in my irises, it was the arrow that my pupils refused to shoot at him. I wanted to protect him, not because he was my flesh, not because he was my blood, simply because this was a higher-order imperative which can only be explained like this: it's so easy for an adult to hurt a child that we must forbid ourselves doing it at all costs. I defended my son from myself quite rationally with the same degree of duty that impelled me to heal an injured bird, feed a stray cat or not accelerate at a pedestrian crossing.

'Can I invite him home?' Hugo asked.

It was the first time he had talked of bringing a friend home.

'You want to invite Octave home? For tea?'

'Yes, but I'd like him to stay the night too.'

'Would his parents agree? I'll have to ring them. Have you got his phone number?'

'His parents are fine. Octave does whatever he wants.'

'How do you know?'

'He told me.'

'I'll still call his mother,' I said.

I never managed to get hold of his parents. I left messages. No one rang back. I wrote a note to which there was no reply. Octave came with a rucksack in which his carefully folded change of clothes and appropriately provisioned wash-bag proved that a grown-up had supervised his departure. He appeared with Hugo one Tuesday evening at five o'clock. His hair was straight and beige, and his eyes an indefinable colour. He said hello to me and tilted his face for me to kiss him. I leant over and kissed his cheek, instantly giving him something I had always refused Hugo. I flushed and thanked my lucky stars for wintertime which cast the hall in deep shadow from mid-afternoon. I gave the boys tea. Hugo anticipated my every move, opening cupboards, taking out the bread and jams. He was efficient and careful. Octave sat perfectly motionless on his chair waiting to be served. He didn't dare make the slightest move; I even had to pour milk into his glass and put it right next to him or he wouldn't have had a drink.

'Do you like bread and butter?' I asked him because while Hugo spread Nutella on his bread and golloped it down, Octave hadn't touched a thing.

'Yes,' he said. 'I really like it.'

'Would you like me to spread it for you?' I asked him.

'Oh, yes please. Thank you very much!'

He was all effusiveness. There again I did something for him I had never done for my son. Hugo was a champion of autonomy, he made sure he very rarely needed me.

Temptation doesn't bother with disguises. The snake offers Eve the apple in his usual reptilian attire. There was nothing in the least bit subtle about my meeting Octave, not the least ambiguous either. He systematically asked me for all the things my son had never thought to request; Hugo knew intuitively he would come up against such cruel incompetence that it was out of the question to put it to the test. Would you ask a quadriplegic to run for the bus? Or clear the table? In every area where Hugo excelled, Octave had difficulties. He had trouble reading, mumbling like a five-year-old; he didn't understand the difference between tens and units, got muddled with past participles – I had tooken, he had eated. His socks were always corkscrewed, his buttons all at sixes and sevens. He couldn't cut up his meat, had difficulty finding his sleeve when he put his coat on, and didn't know you had to look before crossing the road. He was so deficient in everything that you couldn't help helping him, especially as he was so incomprehensibly gracious. He thanked you better than anyone and displayed the most touching gratitude at every opportunity. He also had a precocious sense of the ridiculous, which meant he viewed his improbable collection of shortcomings with considerable humour.

He came for tea. He came for the night. We took him away for weekends. There was talk of taking him on holiday with us.

One night just before I went to sleep I thought to myself that I really loved Octave. It was such a sweet, comforting feeling that, for the first time in ages, I felt I was falling asleep softly and perfectly peacefully. Over a period of seven years I had got into the habit of forcibly burying myself in sleep as if having to bore a tunnel through granite. In order to succumb to sleep I had to wrest my stray mother's heart to the ground, bury it in the earth, and hush its endless lament by filling its mouth with stones. I stepped into my nights as if into my tomb except in this instance I had to do it again every evening.

The following morning Hugo told me he was no longer friends with Octave.

At first I laughed.

'What's happened? Have you had an argument?'

'No.'

'What then?'

'I don't ever want to see him again. I don't ever want to ask him here again.'

'That's not very nice,' I told my son, who suddenly seemed like my own torturer.

Why was he taking him away from me? Why did he have to remove Octave? What did he understand of my affection? I never made a show of it. I'm not like those mothers who bang on at their children about their classmates' exploits. Why aren't you more like so-and-so? Why aren't you as polite as such-and-such? Look how much what's-his-name helps his mother! I was discreet, never making any comment.

'He's the one who's not very nice,' Hugo retorted. 'He's a liar, a dirty liar.'

I'd never seen Hugo so angry.

'What are you talking about?'

As I asked the question, without realizing it, I looked him right in the eye. The arrow was shot. That look turned him to stone. I saw his lips quiver. His irises danced as if trying to find some way to take cover. He mumbled something, something incomprehensible about entities and secret planets – puerile fantasies. I didn't understand any of it and didn't want to understand. I was fascinated by the power of my own loathing. No hope of lowering my eyelids. No hope of looking away. A lava flow streamed from those scalding apertures. The windows of my soul were pulverized by the violence of that torrent.

How can I even remember that scene? How can I go back over it?

Eventually Hugo's neck drooped, overwhelmed. Very slowly, as if his whole body hurt from the impact, he went back to his room. I didn't know what border I had just crossed but as soon as my son was out of sight a wave of shame swept over me, unlike anything I had felt before but similar to the one that would ravage me several years later.

The pouting little face of Vincent's orchid is watching me crying over my onions. I forgot to chop them in advance. It's usually the first thing I do: I put on my swimming goggles and dive into those pearlescent slices. Ben's remonstrating distracted me. I dare not put on my goggles in front of customers and, however much I rinse the bulbs in cold water, my eyes are exploding. I feel like one of those dogs with undershot jaws whose eyes pop out of their heads like fat marbles. Vincent kissed my hand before leaving. I can feel the trace of his lips at the root of my fingers. I'm not sure I like it. I'm slightly repelled by his overly pale lips and the inverted commas of saliva on either side of them. And yet I can't deny that a minute lasso squeezed my navel in its slip knot. Onion skins – light, translucent, golden – swirl round the chopping board in the draft created by my knife. I think of Ali Slimane's sublime white onions, as sweet as fruit, like light bulbs because, rather than being reflected in them, the light seemed to emanate from them. I chopped without goggles in those days, but without a tear. 'You will never cry because of me,' my supplier announced as he handed me a string of luminescent spheres. 'These are mild onions. They've got just as much flavour as the others but they don't sting.' 'That's very kind,' I said. Mr Slimane lowered his eyes and curved his lips inwards modestly, lips which weren't dilute like Vincent's but brown, almost purple, like the skin of a fig. The surprise of his rare smiles like opening a fig, too. I always looked at his mouth when he was talking to me because his eyes were too sad for me. I looked at his mouth and learned it by heart as if planning to… What sort of plans would necessitate knowing a mouth so intimately? What plans with a man who would never make me cry?

Simone and Hannah push the door open and come straight over to the kitchen to kiss me hello.

'What's the matter?' they ask, horrified by my tears.

Before I can reply they too are attacked by the pungent onions which make their eyes stream. They wipe the corners of their eyes and announce that they have an impossible essay to do for the next day. Could I help them later? They've got an hour's free study after lunch. They'd like me to explain something to them.

'I'm rubbish at philosophy,' I tell them. 'I've always been rubbish at it.'

'Yes, but you've lived,' they say. 'You've got experience.'

'What's it about?'

I can't see how my experience can help me answer questions which terrified me in the sixth form and still leave me lost for words: 'Can we understand the past when we don't know the future?', 'Should we strive to demonstrate everything?', 'Can the course of history be changed?', 'Is man reasonable by nature?'. After reading the question I always felt like answering NO! An energetic and definitive no. Once free of the question I could run away. Except I had to stay sitting at the desk and not saying no, or yes, not actually answering, but constructing sentences which, like the perfect Sunday afternoon walk, took you in a loop, a sort of ellipse in which the going away simply facilitated a return to the point of departure. A succession of questions intended to reformulate the very first one. I found the process exhausting and hypocritical.

'We should always tell the truth but should the truth always be told?' Simone and Hannah chorus at me.

'Is that the question?'

They nod. A colossal NO! rears up inside me.

'I haven't a clue, girls,' I tell them with a shrug as the tears flow all the faster.

They laugh and order two bowls of soup and a knob of cheese.

Ben pins orders to the board as the customers settle and make their decisions. I notice a certain harmony in the meals and silently congratulate my regulars. They're starting to understand. They're starting to accept the good I can do them.

Just as I am carving a shoulder of lamb roasted in juniper berries, a strident voice shrieks a loud 'Hello!' behind me.

I flatten my hands on the worktop. I don't want to turn round. I want to rewind and not let this scene happen.

'Who is it?' Ben asks me quietly as he picks up a couple of *plats du jour*.

'It's Aunt Emilienne,' I say in horror.

Aunt Emilienne has got the date wrong. She missed the opening night and is here now, two months too late, to celebrate the opening of *Chez moi*.

'I'll take care of her,' says Ben, putting a hand on my shoulder.

He doesn't understand. Taking care of Aunt Emilienne is a full-time job. She's one of my many aunts, and the most calamitous. She's obese, bald, disfigured by a badly repaired hare-lip, and wears bottle-thick glasses. She's a bit deranged, always has been, and shrieks instead of talking because she refuses to acknowledge her deafness by treating it. She's extremely coquettish and capricious, a princess-and-the-pea type without the figure in the job description. I have always been kind to her – which can't be said of most members of my family. I treat her well because I admire her vitality, enthusiasm and energy. I don't know how she carries on without feeling demoralized when she has every excuse to feel sorry for herself. Having so little luck, having such a collection of defects, is worth celebrating; that's what her permanent good mood seems to proclaim.

I come out from my refuge behind the counter to greet her.

'You've lost weight!' she shrieks, victoriously, before kissing me.

Her wisps of beard scratch my cheek. I don't dare check whether the customers are staring at her.

'The opening night was two months ago,' I say right in her ear so that I don't have to raise my voice.

'The what?'

'The opening night, when the restaurant opened. You know, I sent you an invitation.'

She says nothing but drops heavily onto one of my wonky chairs. Then she opens her mouth wide, yawns without putting her hand over her mouth and cries, 'How are you?' so loudly it makes everyone jump. Some of them, probably thinking the question was addressed to them (when it was intended only for me), feel constrained to reply 'Very well, thank you, and you?'. Aunt Emilienne couldn't be less interested in them. She thinks they are mad and gives a haughty smirk, completely unaware of the impression she might have on them. I consider that a blessing.

'Would you like something to eat?'

'Is this a restaurant or not?' she asks, laughing.

Ben steps in. While my back has been turned, he has disguised himself as a waiter. The get-up is simple and convincing: he has put on his black velvet jacket, which he normally leaves on the coat stand, and has folded a clean white cloth in three and laid it over his forearm. He hands her a menu cobbled together quickly on a loose piece of paper slipped into a cardboard mount.

'Would you like me to read it for you?' he offers.

She nods. He leans towards her amiably and recites the dishes one at a time. I go back to the kitchen, relieved; he understands perfectly.

A few moments later I see him coming back with the carafe of water he put on her table.

'What's going on?' I ask him.

'Aunt Emilienne says the water tastes funny,' he says. 'She'd like me to change it.'

I hand Ben a half-bottle of Evian.

'No,' he says. 'She doesn't want mineral water. She just wants tap water.'

He empties the one he had given her and takes her a new one. During the course of the meal he reiterates this operation three times, without complaining, angelically submissive and steadfast. As soon as she has finished her first course, she calls 'Waiter!' in a strident authoritative voice. Ben comes running. She mistreats him as much as she can, insisting her cutlery is changed and complaining that there isn't an embroidered table-cloth. She takes a filthy cotton placemat from her bag and puts it under her plate. Ben congratulates her, saying it looks much better like that.

'I'm so sorry,' I say to him, not daring to come out of hiding again.

'Everything's fine,' he assures me.

We watch my aunt spitting out bits of meat she deems too tough. She lays them carefully all the way round the table. Little grey balls, duly masticated, punctuate the Formica. A few threads of salad have stuck between her teeth, and she has vinaigrette on her chin and cheeks.

'It's kind of her to have come,' Ben says to comfort me.

He's right. My aunt is responding to the invitation – it's

touching. Her two-month delay means I can spread out the pleasure. At this point I realize that not one of my first-night guests has come back to taste my cooking since the opening. Not a word from my parents. She's sorted herself out, with her little dive, they will be thinking. No need to ring her every couple of days to see if she's still alive. Nothing from my friends either. Maybe the reunion was a bit sudden. Here I am again, after six years' absence. They're relieved to know I still exist, wanted to demonstrate their indulgence. Time has done its work, they told themselves. That's that dusted under the carpet, now we can all breathe a bit more easily. Now we won't have to wait for one of those silences that breaks the flow of a conversation to ask, 'Hey, by the way, what's Myriam up to?' I wonder retrospectively how many of them knew the exact nature of the incident. I don't know how well the secret was guarded. I know I can rely on my husband to have said nothing. The emperor of silence. But my mother, my father? Corinne and Lina, my childhood friends? A scenario constructed around a bout of violent depression circulated round our acquaintances in the weeks following the revelation. 'Disappear', was my husband's advice. 'I've no desire to be dragged through the mud with you.' Those were his parting words. Such a predictable man.

My husband liked situations to be clear. He appreciated order. The house had to be impeccable, it was his favourite word, 'impeccable'. He smacked his lips as he said it. He hated confusion and paradox, abhorred sloppiness. He was astonishingly dependable. It was his solidness that attracted me straight away. I don't really know why the thought of living beside a rock was reassuring. I never suspected how opaque it would be. Or how hard.

My husband always showered after lovemaking, immediately, even in the middle of the night. He would leap out of bed and rush to the bathroom. I thought of Lady Macbeth, frantic to wipe the blood from her hands – 'Out damned spot, out I say'. Was I already so disgusting? No, surely. Cleanliness was not what this was about. I think what he hoped to find under that stream of water was something else altogether. He wanted to get back to himself. Passion worried him, he felt possessed. My husband had a very particular way of making love. Like a battering ram breaking down the door of a fort. Sometimes I felt as if he wanted to get through me, to fuck the mattress, the ground, the wall. The bones in my hips hurt. He'll break me one day, I thought. But I was more solid than I thought. And I liked what he did. I was touched by the despair, the spirit that took him over. That anger and vehemence expelled into me alone made me feel quite light-headed. It could be that I was confusing spite with desire. I left the Beatles' 'Norwegian Wood' for quite a different landscape. The new territory of my lovemaking was carved apart by seismic activity. We didn't love each other by rolling tenderly through mossy undergrowth, but trudged on a forced march towards a back-breaking summit. I was honoured by so much power. He liked sulking with me in the evening, keeping his teeth clenched all through supper, talking only to Hugo. He was preparing for the assault, furbishing his loathing. Once in bed the heat of my body, the smell of it, unleashed his furious passion. He swooped on me and I often thought he wanted to kill. That would have given him more relief than anything else.

The reason the *Letters to a Young Poet* don't feature on my shelves is that my husband's name was Rainer and I don't feel like having his name under my nose the whole time. My husband was called Rainer and that's not insignificant in our relationship. It was Lina who first mentioned him to me. We were both at the Faculty of Arts, he the Faculty of Medicine. She had met him at a party. 'Rainer?' I asked her, 'Is that really his name?' – 'Yes.' – 'Is he Austrian?' – 'I don't know.'

An Austrian, I thought to myself. That's exactly what I need. A boy who's cold as an iceberg and quite mad, torn between German rigour and Balkan licentiousness. I pictured him as terribly obsessive and, in that, I wasn't wrong. Fire beneath the ice, I liked to think. Without realizing it, I was drifting away from the truth. In Rainer there was no fire. Ice as far as the eye could see, inside, outside, a human ice field. 'It's because I'm reacting,' he explained one day. 'Reacting to what?' – 'To my origins.' We were on our third date and I felt it was already too late to back out. Whatever he could have told me, we had both made our choices and our fates were sealed. Contrary to my beliefs, he had not grown up in Vienna, his parents hadn't sung the Nazi anthem at the top of their lungs. He was born in Ventimillia to a father whose own father had been an Italian resistance fighter, and to a mother who was a Sardinian Communist. My parents-in-law – whom I hardly knew – were extremely friendly, happy people who enjoyed life and lived it to the full. He had long hair and hers was crew-cut. They smoked cannabis and earned their living by buying up ruins in Provence and selling them for a fortune once they had done them up. Emilia told me she had a good network of former Trotskyites who could afford them. 'An inexhaustible supply! And as they're buying from a former Commy they can do it with a clear conscience.' 'What about you?' I asked her. 'What, my conscience? That went up in flames more than twenty years ago. Good riddance!'

My parents-in-law died in a car crash on the dirt driveway to their Provençal farmhouse. It was a smooth, straight track. There was just one yew tree on the right-hand side. They aimed well. It was a week before our wedding.

'I think they were against it,' I told Rainer on the way to the cemetery.

'What are you talking about? They really liked you.'

'Not against me. Against the marriage. It was the institution that put them off.'

'Do you think people would die for that? As far as you're concerned, this is a political suicide then?'

I nodded.

'They were high as kites. Completely out of it,' Rainer cried. 'Two hot-air balloons of shit.'

I thought of cancelling everything. Crossing out the shared future. I didn't dare. As I put on my white dress, I thought white would always be the colour of mourning for me.

I do occasionally think things would have been different if my parents-in-law had lived. I miss them, even now. Emilia and

Francesco, my husband's parents, were good people. I sometimes saw a sparkle in Rainer that he owed entirely to them. A treasure of tenderness. Hugo was the only person who could make that nugget glow. He only had to come close to him – one word from his mouth, his hand held out, or even sitting on his knee nestled against his chest – and Rainer's face would change completely. Seeing them together, father and son, the bear and his cub, was the most intolerable sight for me. It's not true that I disappeared. It's wrong to say I was rejected. It was me who left, voluntarily. I laid a bomb in my own family. I set fire to the house. That I was wrong is in no doubt. That there was any other possibility, I don't think so. 'Should the truth always be told?' I'll think about it another day. For now, I'm dwelling on the tricky question of self-defence.

I condemned myself to six years' banishment. I can't believe the courage I displayed by sending out fifty invitations after that period of silence and isolation. I can remember the precise emotion as I wrote out those once familiar addresses on the envelopes. I told myself we were drawing a line and picking up where we had left off. My notebook. My Bible. I still knew some of the telephone numbers by heart. Every street name, as I worked my way through them, prompted memories of supper parties and celebrations. I remembered the smell and feel of friends' houses. Those that were tidy and the others, the ones that were always in pandemonium – we loved that word, 'pandemonium'. At the time Paris, the whole city, felt to me like a dot-to-dot picture: I could hop from one house to the next. Those façades which appeared anonymous to my fellow citizens' eyes harboured snug corners for me, tables to drink coffee at and armchairs to curl up in for long conversations. I remembered entry codes. That collection of numbers, a meaningless secret collection, meant I could brave the impassable frontiers of a well-guarded modern city. I adored my friends. I loved the feeling that, wherever I was, I was at home, expected, welcome. I wasn't surprised that allegiances changed so quickly. People liked one kind of Myriam, and I had altered.

Aunt Emilienne has finished her meal. She was very keen to order the shortbread with figs and her jersey dress is now a constellation of crumbs. I come and sit next to her for a minute.

'How's your husband?' she asks me.

'Very well,' I say without a moment's hesitation.

'And the little one?'

My throat tightens, but I still manage to reply.

'Wonderful. He's a big young man now.'

'And his studies?'

I nod vigorously. My voice has disappeared. I pray my predictions are right. I picture Hugo with a bag slung across his chest, striding through the cold with his chin up, his head in the air, offering his face up to the kiss of the wind. Nothing that I say to my aunt is of any consequence. She will never try to confirm my version with that of another member of the family. It wouldn't occur to her to wonder why she hasn't seen my husband for so long – she can hardly remember his name – and she will have forgotten half of what I tell her by the time she gets home. I wallow in the security of talking to someone whose brain lacks the acuity of rational thinking.

'Waiter!' Aunt Emilienne cries as Ben passes within reach. 'The bill please.'

'Don't worry,' I tell her. 'You're my guest.'

'You're very kind,' she compliments me. 'It was good. I've had a lovely meal.'

She rubs her stomach.

'I'm not hungry at all now,' she adds.

I help her put her coat on and see her to the door of *Chez moi*. For a moment I stay rooted to the spot behind the window watching her cross the street. She walks like a goose, swaying from one leg to the other with every step, proudly wielding her huge belly like a wishbone. When she reaches the pavement opposite she turns to blow me a kiss. Ben has put his hand on my shoulder.

'I've got some orders for this evening,' he tells me. 'We'll manage.'

'Do you think?'

He doesn't bother replying but goes back to the kitchen to take care of the last few desserts.

Simone and Hannah are waiting for me at their table. They have put €8 in the bakelite saucer.

'Well?' Simone asks. 'Have you thought about it?'

'Should the truth always be told?' her friend reminds me.

'What do you think?' I ask them.

They shrug.

'You must have some idea, surely?' I insist.

'I spoke to someone who's taking this year again,' explains

Hannah. 'He told me that the classic response, the one that works every time is "Yes. No. But." I can see how the first bit works: Yes, we must tell the truth because it's wrong to lie, because if we expect a bit of honesty from others we have to be sincere ourselves, and all that. Then you do the "No". So that's for when the truth is problematic; it's easy to imagine situations when the truth would do more harm than good. For example with someone who's really ill, if you tell them they're going to die, they get depressed and die… OK, they're going to die either way but this would speed it up.'

I nod, trying not to smile.

'Very good,' I say, 'then what?'

'That's where I get bogged down,' says Simone. 'We've tried but we can't find the "But". Yes, we should always tell the truth. No, we shouldn't always tell the truth. But, what? We're completely stuck, Hannah and me. We just can't see what to put after the "But".'

I wave absentmindedly to say goodbye to some regulars who are leaving, chanting my name:

'Bye, Myriam.'

'See ya, Myriam.'

'So long, Myriam.'

They know my name; but I've never actually told them what it is. Another of Ben's manoeuvres. As he puts plates down on the table he whispers, 'this is one of Myriam's own recipes. Tell me what you think.' Or, 'Myriam recommends the rice pudding. On a cold day like this it'll keep the angina at bay.' He invents all sorts of nonsense to make me seem kind.

Simone and Hannah are growing impatient.

'We'll never be able to do this!' they say, putting their heads in their hands.

'Why don't you start by asking what the truth actually is?' I say.

They look at each other, dumbfounded.

'I wouldn't have a clue,' I add quickly. 'Your friend who did it last year is bound to be right but personally I've always been very wary of that word. The truth. It's like beauty, isn't it? It depends entirely on who's looking at it.'

The girls sigh. They are disappointed.

I have a momentary flash of genius.

'We'll just have to ask Ben!'

I go over to the percolator and offer to take over from Ben for the coffees and bills.

'In exchange you can help them with their homework.'

When I tell him the question his face lights up. He's already written about the subject. He remembers his essay plan very clearly. He cites two invaluable authors whose names evoke age-old personal failures and are enough to make me shudder.

Sitting at the girls' table with his knees together and feet apart, gesticulating with his long-fingered hands to emphasize his conviction, Ben lays out his argument. The girls take notes. Several pages are covered with black scrawl. Cigarettes are lit and left to burn, un-smoked. I hear the words 'precepts', 'phenomena', 'enunciation', 'ascendancy', 'subjectivity' and 'objectivity'. Ben is juggling, as he did with my plates and glasses on the first day. His mum must be so proud of him, I think to myself. Except that she's dead, I remember, looking at him. I wipe some saucers, singing to myself. The softest feeling begins to swell gently deep in my chest. I really do have the best waiter in Paris.

The orders for the evening are unbelievable. Ben talked me through them when the girls finally left, late, unkempt and emotional.

'What do you mean unbelievable?' he asks me when I tell him how surprised I am. 'You did say we would do catering, didn't you?'

There is a note of anxiety in his voice.

'Yes, I did.'

'Is there a problem?'

I read through the list again: Exotic menu for four, tapas for eight, giant salad for sixteen. I scrutinize the names of our clients: Laferte-Girardin, N'guyen, Elkaroui.

'Who are these people?' I ask, not recognizing a single name. 'How did they know? And this one? What is it? Exotic menu. What do you think I should give them, palm hearts and bean sprouts?'

Ben looks at his feet.

'Do these people really exist, Ben?'

I suspect something, this smacks of a hoax. This boy's gentleness is suspect. Suspect too his versatility. Suspect his dedication. He wants to change the world, he told me. I agree the job needs doing but I'm afraid that this grand-scale project is only there to hide another, smaller one. Behind this Ideal with its capital 'I' so full of pride and arrogance lurks the obscure obsession for reparation. I know that vice well. If I were a psychiatrist I would call it bricklayer fever. The patient can't bear a single day between building jobs, he has to be mixing mortar, trowel in hand, filling in gaps, consolidating, reno-vating. You could also call this pattern of behaviour the fairy complex: when confronted with a difficult situation or conflict, the subject waves his wand wildly, hoping to solve problems and heal wounds. Ben has always carried the burden of the child who does everything in his power to make his parents smile, to satisfy them and surprise them; he has carried it for so long, in fact, that he has built up dangerous reserves of imagination. He wants to cheer me up, help me forget the harassment from the bank and the threatening letters; he'd like to ease my backache and, while he's at it, fill in the long crease at the corner of my mouth.

I can see exactly what he's up to. He's invented customers. What could be easier? He's the one who takes the orders and makes the deliveries: he would just have to off-load the food at the local soup kitchen (Ben's not the type to throw it away) and settle the bill with his own money. He's not rich, he told me, but I don't believe him. His clothes are beautiful, clean and new. I can still remember that elegance comes at a price. Ben is sacrificing himself for me. It's a sort of reverse-embezzlement, misusing his personal funds.

I'm waiting for his confession. He's still staring at the ground.

'Ben,' I say, 'I don't need help. I'm coping. It may not be

going as quickly as you'd like, but I'm getting there, I promise you.'

I say this very gently so as not to offend him. I take the list of orders and tear it up. Ben watches, horrified.

'What the hell am I going to tell them now, all those people?'

'Which people, Ben?'

'Them,' he says, pointing at the pieces of paper.

A flicker of doubt insinuates itself into me. 'Do you know them?'

'No,' he says.

'Well, where are they from then?'

'From the site.'

'What site?'

'*Chez moi*'s internet site.'

'Have we got an internet site?' I ask, as if that sort of thing could spring up spontaneously like warts on the backs of fingers or brambles in a garden.

Ben nods. He has set up a system for ordering food on-line. He explains that we've been very lucky because the name hadn't been registered. According to him, the site is still fairly rudimentary. The illustrations are restricted to pictures he took with his mobile. The page layout is a bit sloppy but it works. And the proof is we already have three orders when we've only been on-line twenty-four hours. I stick the torn list back together, to reconstitute our virtual customers' names.

'Are you angry?' Ben asks.

'What do you think?'

We laugh. I congratulate him for this initiative which has propelled us on our way to a fortune and to being utterly up-to-the-minute.

'How did you decide on the menus?'

'I looked at what the competition was offering. Usually it's aimed at a very specific market and too expensive. Ghettos, if you like. There are the Italians, the Asians, the Americans, the Japanese. The menus look varied but they're not really, and the desserts are depressing. Or it costs a fortune. I also took another gamble, but a more risky one.'

He hesitates. I coax him.

'I haven't got my driving licence,' he says. 'I don't have a bike or a moped; so the deliveries were going to be a bit of a problem. Specially as I'm going to have to work in the kitchen to give you a hand, well, if you want me to. So I explained on the site that we offered a local catering service and people had to come and pick their orders up themselves. I puffed this up saying it was reflected in the price and…'

Ben hesitates once more. I coax him again, I want to know the end of our story.

'… I stressed what a pleasure it would be for our dear customers to meet our chef – Myriam. I wrote stuff about you that…'

'That wasn't true?'

'No, it was true, it would just make people want to meet you.'

I don't dare ask him to recite the patter he has put together to describe my wonderful self.

'Well, then?'

'Well, it seems to be working, doesn't it?' he says waving at the Sellotaped list in my hand.

'What have we got to make?'

'An exotic menu, a giant salad and some tapas.'

I try to understand the concept, because that's what people pompously call a restaurant's style these days. Ben is putting another of his gambles between my hands. According to him, people don't like choosing any more. They have been asked their opinion too often. This is a worrying kind of weariness because it leaves them easy prey to rampant dictatorship. They don't want to make decisions any more so we make decisions for them; we are the good tyrants of dining, the enlightened dictators of culinary pleasure. Ben has drawn up a posy of deliberately vague offerings which I now have to interpret. Our menu has four formulae: Exotic, Tapas, Giant Salad and Traditional.

'Are you sure about the Traditional?'

'No one will ask for it. It's a decoy. You have to have the word 'Traditional'. But it's just a word. It's reassuring.'

I sit down at a table, pencil in hand, while Ben clears the other tables. In my head I establish the crossroads between pleasure quotients, preparation times and profitability. Here again I'm banking on my reflex responses. I have to delve deep into myself, not in the cooking I've learned, but the cooking that has been transmitted to me, the things I could do before I knew the alphabet, dishes I could put together in the dark, savours from far away, more precious than a bride's trousseau.

I make a list of my assets – caviar of aubergine, pepper salad, spiced fish, cheese pasties, potato salad with chillies, taramasalata, artichokes with oranges, broad beans with cumin, filou parcels of tuna and capers, triangular patties of meat, egg and coriander... I arrange intersections, detours, associations, improbable meetings. The exoticism will stretch from the Far East to Asia Minor. My battalions are lining up, an infantry of vegetables and a cavalry of crunchiness. I inspect my munitions between the flanks of my spice rack, curcuma and ras-el hanout standing to attention in their glass phials. Oregano, sage, poppy seeds, nigella, red berries, black peppercorns. I need mountains of garlic, pine kernels, olives, preserved lemons...

I suddenly interrupt my research as if I have stumbled across the ever absent sesame. 'I must ring Ali Slimane,' I say, lunging towards the phone.

'We haven't got time,' Ben tells me, already busy chopping herbs essential to my recipes.

I don't listen to him. I sit on the floor behind the bar, sheltered from noises and prying eyes on the street. Ben is panicking, pacing up and down, opening the fridge then closing it again. What could he do on his own? Does he know how to put together an exotic menu for four? Does he have any idea what you should put in a giant salad once you have wisely abandoned the idea of rice, tuna and sweet corn? He can't stop looking at me, a questioning look in his eye, begging me to get back to work, not to scupper his fantastic plans for expansion at this early stage.

The ring tone sounds in my ear, we are connected by a cable, Ali and I.

'Hello, it's Myriam.'

'Hello.'

'Do you remember?'

'Yes.'

'Are you well?'

'Yes.'

'Am I disturbing you?'

'No.'

I feel as if I'm talking to the sphinx. His answers are concave, opening the door on enigmas rather than closing it on doubt. I'm happy to hear his voice. I can picture him at home: top of the hill, tumbledown stone wall like a Roman ruin, frosted glass windows, clods of mud on the steel boot-scraper.

'I've opened a restaurant.'

'That's good.'

'I need you.'

He says nothing. During his pause I silently enumerate everything I know about him: his dark mouth, his assurance that he won't make me cry, his putty-coloured cotton trousers, the melancholy in his eyes, the spindly roll-ups in his elegant fingers.

'I'll come,' he promises.

I give him the address, ask when he thinks he might be able to get here, whether he needs me to fill out an order form. Does he have a fax? He answers none of my questions. He tells me he is happy to hear from me, that he feels something about me has changed.

I hang up. I take a while to get to my feet. My legs are wobbly. I have to heave myself up by gripping the edge of the bar. I totter over to the butcher's block. I feel like lying down, letting myself go, waiting.

Ben has his teeth firmly clenched, exasperated by the time I'm wasting. He's worried his initiative will be threatened by my new-found laziness. I look at the green pyramid of herbs he has chopped and mixed together, creating a mattress softer than a goose-down duvet, a little mountain of subtle pleasures – I pat the top of it gently.

'Next?' Ben asks, knife in hand.

I can't resist the pleasure of torturing him.

'Next,' I tell him, 'we have a nice little cigarette like in the good old days.'

'Like the good old days?' he repeats, dismayed.

'That's right,' I say, leaning on the back-rest of the banquette with my feet up on a stool. 'The good old days when I was twenty and you weren't even born.'

A few words too many perhaps. Now he's been punished, sitting there under my bookshelves. He's sulking. The young don't like being resented for their tender years. The old don't like being reminded of their age. No one wants to see themselves as a meaningless squashed fly on the grand scale of time. I regret my words but still manage to savour the intoxication of the forbidden cigarette. We look at each other, Ben and I, and suddenly – like an illumination – I realize that he likes men. I wouldn't be able to say the exact effect this has on me. I feel excluded. Curious too. But we don't have time to talk about this discovery. We've got work to do.

I sit up abruptly, crush the cigarette in the sink and wash my hands right up to the elbows. I feel like a surgeon in the operating theatre, with his nurse by his side. The surgeon says 'forceps' and the nurse announces 'forceps' as she hands her boss the instrument. It's very important that she repeats the word he has just uttered because he can – although it's very rare – make mistakes. He gets the wrong word. He says 'forceps' but needs the scalpel. The nurse says 'forceps' as she hands them to him and then, instead of cutting the patient's abdomen with pincers (which would be extremely hard work), he hears his mistake in his assistant's words and corrects himself in time: 'no, scalpel'. 'Scalpel' says the nurse, handing him the required instrument. With cooking, as with surgery, we have no right to slips of the tongue. I say 'salt' and Ben repeats the word as he hands it to me. I say 'butter', he says 'butter'. I say 'peppers', he says 'peppers'. I say 'six eggs', he says 'six eggs'. He understands without my needing to explain to him. He has noticed the urgency in my voice and my every move. He anticipates, constantly wipes surfaces clean, throws the peelings away as they accumulate, turns on the gas hobs and sets the oven to pre-heat. Our arms cross, our voices overlap, he tucks a stray lock of my hair back in place, knowing how much it annoys me having hair over my eyes when I'm working. I slip on a tomato skin and he catches me. I hand him knives to rinse. He supplies me with spoons and spatulas. He replaces damp tea towels and washes the lettuce. I show him how to chop tomatoes into cubes, and courgettes into thin strips. He says 'Oh, brilliant!' and copies me. His talents in the kitchen are on a par with his talents as a waiter. He is deft, patient, meticulous, focused and quick. He understands the lemon/salt balance, senses the sweet/spicy equilibrium. He has good instincts and, as I pass onto him everything I know, I can feel my heart growing lighter. The weight of knowledge is leaving me, my mind going blank. I work even faster. It makes me smile. It's almost a circus act. My hands are in the flour before I've had time to think 'pour into a bowl, chop the butter, mix, knead'. I move about carrying my head in my hand like Saint Denis, not suffering the effects of this decapitation but rejoicing in it.

Our tapas look exquisite: little squares of spiced honey-cake decorated with goat's cheese and roast pears, chicken livers in port on slices of potato with onion marmalade, rolled up radicchio with honey and haddock. Ben has been to buy some boxes from the patisserie to stow our treasures. The exotic menu is made up of taramasalata, roulade of tuna and capers, salad of peppers sautéed in garlic, and aubergine caviar. It isn't very exotic for an inhabitant of the Balkans but it probably would be for someone from Vietnam or Brittany. The giant salad really is a giant: there's a whole meal in it, from the first course to the dessert and all that with no rice and no tinned sweet corn. Slivers, slivers of all sorts of different things – vegetables, cheeses, fruit – all blended without crushing each other, side by side without working against each other.

At seven o'clock we are ready, our orders are waiting

(keeping warm or staying chilled) and our evening menu – built around wild mushrooms, smoked fish and blueberries – is arranged. We have flushed cheeks, tired hands and idiotically happy smiles on our faces. To celebrate our first night of combined activities, I open a bottle of champagne, which we cheerfully empty during the course of the evening. Our net-surfing customers are delightful and peculiarly talkative. They feel they have to chat while I pack their order. They are clearly trying to dazzle, wanting to be seen in a good light. I wonder what Ben said about me on our site. As he sees them to the door, he tells them feedback is very welcome, that we are going to set up a tasters' forum, that their comments will be published on our home page. The restaurant customers get involved, wanting to know who these invaders leaving with armfuls of cardboard boxes are. Ben works through the room handing out the leaflets he put together goodness knows when or how. They are elegant bookmarks in violet-coloured card giving the name of the restaurant and the web address. A sub-title in smaller print reads 'Chosen Caterers' and I think it's the most cryptic and the most explicit phrase I've ever read.

I cash up while Ben finishes clearing the tables. It's quarter to midnight. We're getting to bed later and later. I wonder how long we can continue at this pace. Ben pours me a cognac. I'm a bit tipsy. So is he. We clink glasses, looking into each other's eyes, hooking our arms round each other's elbows and drinking to our health, prosperity, success and future millions. I ask him how we're going to cope with his absurd idea. The internet is too big for us and we will never meet the demand. It wasn't what I was planning: I envisaged a sort of recycling, getting some value out of leftovers, struggling to avoid waste. I tell him he's a capitalist. He tells me I'm an old hippy. I tell him he reeks of business school. He tells me I reek of skipping school. Then he defends himself more seriously, patiently explaining that you can't give if you don't have the means, that you have to expand before you can spread, that Eden is synonymous with abundance, not with just getting by. I don't understand how I, who was brought up in a middle-class family, I, who grew up wanting my own middle-class family in turn, can be given a lesson in management and etiquette by some child off the streets. Who is Ben? I suddenly can't bear how little I know about him. There are a hundred things I want to ask him about his childhood and his parents, but the question that pops out is not one I had planned on submitting.

'What's it like making love with a man?' I ask.

Ben stares at me, wide-eyed.

'Sorry?' he manages.

I repeat my question – if I'm going to be blunt and indiscreet I might as well see it through. 'What's it like making love with a man?'

'You're the one who should be asked that,' he retorts.

I pour myself some more cognac. I feel as if I'm losing control, I would willingly lose control. I'm playing a part, the I-know-who-you-are part. But, it turns out, my hypothesis is wrong. I look at him: his smooth cheeks, his perfectly outlined mouth, his nostrils so intelligent (not mean, dark or repulsive), his long eyelashes closing slowly over eyes which are set quite wide apart and are slightly down-turned. To me he seems absolutely made for love: his body slim and a little stiff, cautious but quick; his hands, with their long palms and short fingers, their surprising strength. Without my asking any more questions, without making me take responsibility for the enquiry, Ben explains very simply that he has no love life.

'But you do have a sex life?' I ask, with a stupid note of hope in my voice.

'No,' he replies without sadness or joy.

'Like a priest, then? Like a nun?'

'Not really,' he says after a while. 'For me it's not a constraint, or an obligation. It's not a sacrifice.'

He hesitates for a moment. 'It's not that I don't want to either,' he adds. 'It's just the way it is.'

'Like a malformation, then?'

I've had far too much to drink. I'm talking nonsense. Being crude and aggressive. But he bursts out laughing. He's hysterical, bent double. Ben's tact is quite magical, I think to myself. He calms down and goes back to his pedagogic explanation.

'I'm normal but there's no sex in my life, like some people might have no books or music. Those people are just as alive as us but they like different things, they have other pleasures. They don't feel anything's missing because, as far as they're concerned, that thing doesn't exist.'

A violent sense of relief – as after a sustained superhuman effort – washes over me: not feeling any desire, now that would be true freedom in this combative hostile world. No more waiting, no more betrayal, or sullied hearts, or guilty bodies. An end to the torture and the hours wasted in constructing pitiful strategies. A colourless, painless internal landscape. Being transparent as glass, and never again reflecting like a mirror.

'But,' Ben goes on, interrupting my musing, 'that doesn't mean I don't know how to love, to love with a different kind of love.'

He gets up and comes over towards me. I get up too. He takes me in his arms and holds me to his tall body, which reaches beyond me in every direction, flat, spread out like a military map. He talks into the crook of my neck: 'You, for example, I really like you. Really. Really.'

His body remains mute, while mine is screaming. A poster unfurls between my legs, the words EAT ME spelled out on it in giant trembling letters.

'I've had too much to drink,' I say apologetically, pushing him away. 'Much too much.'

He strokes my head kindly. And I think of the love animals feel: the way animals love their masters, and masters their animals. How can I stall my body? I must think of Ben as my cat, Ben as an antelope. Why can I never stem the flow of this source within me? I ought to know how to stroke Ben's head as if he were a Labrador. We're not the same species. There, that's it. I would so love to be one of his kind. All that energy channelled into work and imagination. I understand why great mystics live in a state of abstinence. Except that Ben goes one further: with him it's not a case of forbidding desire, he simply doesn't experience it. That's how he finds time to carry on with his studies, work as a waiter, create an internet site and look after a madwoman like me. There's nothing holding him back. Not one gram of ballast, he's free to go. No deviations, nothing to slow him down, straight for the goal. But what is the goal? How can anyone live without the prospect of love? I would be so afraid of death if I had to launch straight towards the end like that, with no distractions and without the vast obstacle of passion! What would you cling to? I think of the suspension bridge spanning the abyss, the immeasurable work of art that only love can build and which leads us to eternity. How does Ben manage to cross the tiny dizzying chasms that open up in our everyday lives?

'You won't always be like that,' I tell him. 'It'll change.'

I would like him to listen to 'Norwegian Wood'.

'No,' he says, shaking his head. 'I don't think so. I'm not going to change. And I don't want to change. I'm not the only one, there are others like me. Lots of young people. There always have been, but it wasn't so obvious before. People used not to talk about it because they didn't talk about anything then. The proportion of virgins in the adult population is constant. Why do you think that is? Because they're shy? Well, it's true that in among them there are the disabled, the mad, the ill, and then there's us.'

How I hate that 'us'. Army of nihilists.

'And how would the world work if everyone was like you?' I ask.

'We're not asking anyone else to be like us. Not at all,' he says. 'If everyone was like you, the planet would be even more over-populated than it is. We'd all have five babies on our hands.'

'Love and babies aren't the same thing,' I tell him.

'They are the same thing,' Ben asserts. 'I don't intend to reproduce.'

Night is marching on and the shadows, exaggerated by the alcohol, start to look threatening. I can picture them, all these youngsters, bearing down on us in serried ranks, elbow to elbow. I find this union terrifying because there is no shred of jealousy or desire to break it up. They devote all their time to studying, all their energy to conquering power while we poor old things struggle on, worn down by our lustful urges.

'Naff off,' I tell Ben.

'I'll naff off tomorrow,' he says with a smile. 'I've missed the last Métro, it's cold and I haven't got enough money for a taxi.'

I take a note from the till and hand it to him. 'Here, here's some money. You'll take everything I've got anyway.'

'Yeah, right,' he says, still smiling. 'Go to bed, Myriam. I'm going to stay. It's been quite an evening and I don't want to leave you on your own.'

He takes the sleeping-bag from under the banquette – he knows all my secrets. He lies me down, tucks me in, gently strokes my hand and tells me everything is fine. Just before I go to sleep I see him lit by a tiny torch which casts a gorilla-shaped shadow on the wall: he's taking a laptop from his scruffy bag, plugging it in and setting up goodness-knows-what as he fiddles away with the wires and keys. I dream that I'm dreaming I'm going into the gardens of a palace. It's a closed circuit: as soon as I pass the rose garden I wake from the dream within the dream and it starts again.

In the middle of the night I wake up, completely lucid. There are fish swimming backwards and forwards on Ben's computer screen, wafting indifferently through black water. He has rested his head on the table and gone to sleep with his arms crossed in front of his forehead. I study the angles and broken outlines that shape him, fitting him around the wooden platform, his legs jumbled in with the chair legs. Only the repeated to-ing and fro-ing of the paler-coloured fish allows me to pick out his silhouette. The rest of the time – when it's a grey shark, an indigo barracuda or a brown moray eel drifting past – all I can see is a dark bulk not far from me. I'm worried, remembering our conversation. Unlike Ben himself, I don't think there always have been members of his tribe. In fact, these young people strike me as being the most fully realized by-product of our civilization. A whole generation of disillusionment and disgust. How can they be persuaded they are on the wrong tracks? It's a tempting emancipation: you needn't be trapped any more, no ties, no worrying about faithfulness, loyalty or territory. I don't know how to make him see the even more dangerous trap he is falling into. We are never more vulnerable than when we believe we are making a stand for revolt. Refusing the system has only ever served the system. How can I tell him that? I can barely even think it. What I do know is that desire is still the only truly subversive force. When the oppressor puts on the austere mask of economic logic it's more important than ever to nurture a reserve tank of complete nonsense, that wonderful reservoir of fickleness. While Ben sleeps I intone the merits of physical insurrection.

I feel like throwing it all out of the window, his brilliant obsessive publicity ideas, his masterful marketing techniques, his old-before-his-time business plan. If he gets his kicks out of running a business he can go and do it somewhere else. *Chez moi* isn't to do with making a fortune. *Chez moi* is for eating good food at a modest price. My customers have a wonderful time and every time they do I think to myself: there, I've made someone happy, without any pain, with no risk of it being habit-forming and no inexorable spiral of always wanting more.

I think about the seat of satiation. Some people seem not to have one. But they are rare. As far as I know there is no equivalent seat for sexual appetite. You can never have enough. It's a fire that needs constant feeding. Addiction, addiction, addiction. But in a restaurant, no thanks, I'm fine, I'm no longer hungry.

Is it possible to think one thing without immediately thinking the opposite? Simone and Hannah's philosophy questions are giving me nightmares. I don't want to be like Ben but I don't want to be like me. I'm dangerous and not very reliable. In my head I write Ben a letter of dismissal:

> *Due to divergent methods, due to ideological differences and to protect you from yourself and your illusions, I have no choice but to bring an end to our collaboration which, believe me, has been of great value to me.*

I read through it. I like the calm note of the epistolary style: anger no longer rearing its head but lying down, the blend of gentleness and betrayal that can be secreted into it. If a 'Dear John' letter three pages long, riddled with criticism and recriminations – insults even – ends with something like 'but, deep down, I know I'll never love anyone the way I loved you', then it's still a love letter. I also delight in the way a shy restrained letter can reveal the writer's feelings thanks to one word he or she couldn't hold back, flying off like a reckless butterfly, landing – it knows the exact spot – in the corner of the reader's mouth, as a quivering smile, trembling at the premonition of a secret love that has in fact been avowed.

There, I feel calm now. The last drop of cognac has blended with my blood. I resent Ben for not wanting me. It's only human – as we like to say when we dare not admit animal stupidity. It's been six years since a man held me in his arms. And even then, that last time, was he really a man? Six empty years.

Except for one evening perhaps. But that was nothing. A black sky, dotted with stars. Far too many stars, I thought. They were all over the place, up above the big top, big stars and tiny stars, clusters of stars and shooting stars. It was hot. The leaves on the trees shifted slowly like a Spanish dancer's eyelashes. The ground and the walls gave off the smell of a thwarted day, a day that has vanished but which is still there, persisting through the evening. I will not be killed, says the day. Impossible to get to sleep. You only have to inhale that air laden with regret for the sun and that's it, it will be a sleepless night. I can't get to sleep. I won't get to sleep. I'm crazy tonight.

Eloi came out because he heard the goat tugging on her tether. He had devised an act called the Wheel of Death but he also spent a lot of time looking after the animals. He was worried she might have been trying to escape. A goat in Paris. A goat climbing up to Montmartre. I was outside, breathing in the mingled smells. Together we admired Marina's rectangular pupils as she bleated imploringly. She wanted to be stroked. We laughed and stayed there, side by side, in that demented night air. A hundred times, a thousand times, our hands dreamed of touching. We stood motionless, our lungs filled with the same tempting aromas. Aromas of a summer night which bathes naked bodies in its scalding syrup. Afterwards you have to lick it off right through till morning. I could picture us rolling on top of each other in the thistles, and then crushing the chives beyond: onion-scented love. My hips wanted to leave my body, the pressure was incredible, an onslaught… phew, Eloi had already gone. Eloi, whose wife – who was much younger and prettier than me – was waiting for him in his caravan, had gone home.

I won't be able to get back to sleep now. I take a book from the shelf. A collection of letters, another one, and I read: 'So we bought the bull which my mother called Banjo, I don't know why. I always thought that if she had a dog she would have called it Azor, without a hint of irony. I would have called my dog Azor too, but ironically. You might say no one would have seen the difference.' I read through this passage from a letter Flannery O'Connor wrote to her friend 'A' on the 9th of August 1957, and I think of this incredible gift, within reach, this instant consolation for all suffering offered by the mind.

The morning wind sneaks under the metal shutter.

Good morning, I say to myself.

When Vincent comes over for his cup of coffee a few days later (he had to go to Cologne for a week to attend a convention on floral decorations), I can't help telling him: 'The boy slept here the other night.'

'Which boy?' he asks, as if he doesn't know.

'Ben. Ben slept here.'

I remember at this point that Vincent doesn't know *Chez moi* is also my home. As a result, the impact of my announcement is considerably diminished. Still, there's no question of passing up on this opportunity to show off. Our recent financial success has given me wings. The take-away orders are mounting up, we do two sittings in the evening and sometimes three at lunch time. The 'mixed bathing' is working: toddlers from nursery school eat their meatballs and mash on the same seats as bank employees, and students share a bread basket with painters from the building site nearby. Ben teases me, saying I'm elated by it. I nod and keep my ears open, listening out for the threat, the catastrophe that is bound to come and drown our little corner of paradise. I can't hear anything. I can't see where the enemy could come from. According to Ben's projections – he's got some very impressive accounting software – we'll soon be out of deep water. What goes up must come down, I tell myself; once we've achieved success we'll surely have our downfall. Perhaps it will be at the hands of a health inspector. He'll find my tights screwed up in a ball next to the dishcloths, my eau de toilette in the spice cupboard. He'll make further investigations and I'll be crippled by a fine I can't pay. But we haven't got to that stage. We've got to the stage of making revelations to our friend Vincent.

'I slept here too,' I tell him mischievously.

'What?'

Vincent's question displays more exasperation than curiosity.

'I live here, you know,' I say quietly so that the other customers don't have the benefit of this confidential information.

'What are you talking about?'

'I live in my restaurant. I didn't tell you at first because we didn't really know each other and I didn't know how you'd take it—'

'Well, I take it very badly,' he interrupts. 'I think it's grotesque, degrading, childish. No, it's not true,' he adds, smiling. 'You're taking me for a ride. How could you live in this…'

'I've got everything I need,' I tell him. 'A bed, a loo, a kitchen, a sink. And, more importantly, I can't afford to live anywhere else.'

'What about the money from selling the tea-room at Invalides?'

I'm happy to discover he's forgotten nothing of the various fabrications I've told him.

'I've never had a tea-room anywhere. I lied to you. I didn't want to disappoint you.'

'But you're disappointing me now,' he replies.

'You sound like something out of a soap opera,' I tell him.

He closes in on himself. I've hurt him.

'Don't be angry, Vincent. You were the first person to help me. Everything I've done here is thanks to you.'

'But Ben's the one you ask to stay the night,' he mutters.

He's earned his kiss. I hop over the table and, slowly, kiss him, the way you do when you haven't kissed someone for six years; with relish, curiosity and patience.

The customers haven't seen a thing, we were hidden by the coat stand.

I'm shaking.

Vincent is shaking too. He takes a pack of aniseed-flavoured pastilles from his pocket, struggles to pop one out of its aluminium bubble and sucks on it nervously. What on earth am I going to do with you? I ask myself, catching him out like that, when he's not sure what his breath smells like. I kiss him on the forehead and go back to my kitchen, carefree and courageous.

For the last few days I've been intoxicated by the giddy heights I've reached. I sit back and look at what I've achieved.

'Everything's possible,' I tell Ben.

He is sitting at his computer with his back to me, picking up the evening's take-away orders.

'You really can change the world,' I add, in the hope that he will take an interest in what I'm saying.

But no. He's concentrating. He's connected. He is quite incapable of straightening his neck and turning to face me. It doesn't bother me. I've come this far. I've reached a degree of satisfaction which makes me immune to irritations. I'm experiencing the blend of excitement and sadness that comes with realizing a dream. I now know the proud weariness of a superhero. *Chez moi* is still just as busy. We're exhausted but we're appreciated. My restaurant has become a meeting place, a haven, a lovers' refuge in the afternoon, a foodies' secret destination in the evening, a forum for the talkative in the morning, and a transient nest for single parents. We've even set up a mini self-service for the youngest children because they love helping themselves. Part of the room is set aside for them. Ben has cut a gap in the bar, one metre up from the ground, and he passes their trays through it with their raw vegetables, their warmed main dish of finger food, and their fruit purée. At first we thought it was a bad idea because babies of just four wanted to carry their food back to the table without any help. They walk so slowly. They can hardly stand on their tiny feet. But it's actually no problem at all. There's never any kind of problem here. The adults around them automatically put their hands over threatening table corners as those fragile vulnerable heads come near, arms reach out to avoid falls and, most importantly, the youngsters are getting better at it. My 'children's corner' is beginning to look like hotel school.

At first Ben worried about different generations cohabiting like this. He was afraid cigarette smoke would make the little ones cough, and the nippers' whining would annoy older customers. But no. A slight shift in timings (the children eat at about twelve and the grown-ups an hour later) makes the division of our shared space possible. 'And anyway,' I told Ben, 'at worst anyone who doesn't like it just won't come back.' We haven't registered any discontent so far. People come back. We no longer have a day off or a closing time. Customers spontaneously stop coming in at about eleven in the evening. They're sparing us – and thinking about their cup of coffee the following morning.

At one stage I thought I was distracting Ben from his studies and felt guilty, but he eventually admitted that he'd been granted a prolonged period on work placement. I signed the agreement.

'What will you say when you go back to college?' I asked him. 'What are you going to find to write in the report about your placement?'

Ben thought about this. 'I'll say I had a great time.'

'Is that what you think?'

'That's part of what I think. The rest takes up 350 pages that you won't be allowed to read.'

I don't let this mystery annoy me, accepting everything about Ben because he accepts everything about me. It's a relationship of mutual tolerance.

When I was thirteen or fourteen, I can remember fantasizing about phalansteries in history classes. There were several different sorts, those where you wore your clothes laced up at the back so that you relied on your neighbour's good will; those inspired by monasteries; and those whose primary aim was profitability. Whatever the formula, I thought they were a happy arrangement and would have liked to live in one. Our teacher handed out a sheet listing the main social utopias: it cited the creator's name, the date and place each one was founded and, at the end of the line, the word 'failed' followed by another date. How could they have failed? I was inconsolable. When I asked Mr Verdier he deemed it pointless to reply. 'We can't dwell on this for ever,' he announced. 'They're just experiments, an illustration of the innovative thinking typical of the nineteenth century.'

The innovative thinking typical of the nineteenth century, I thought on my way home after the lesson was over, whatever became of that? I looked up Fourier in the encyclopaedia and found an entry about his work and the debates it had raised. With knitted brows I read through the narrow columns of minute letters which seemed to collide with each other before my ill-accustomed eyes, but – not understanding a word of it – I was disappointed with my lack of mental agility, and devastated by my mediocre facility for concentration. Nevertheless, I have retained the vision of humanity developed in those communities: according to this merchant's son born in Besançon in 1772 and the author of *The Theory of the Four Movements and General Destinies*, published in 1808 (I happen to own – and this is both a miracle and a secret – a first edition of this work in my collection of thirty-three books; hence my ability to display such knowledge to this day when my memory, even bent double with effort, even doped with phosphorous, would never be able to reproduce it), according to Charles Fourier, then, we had reached the fifth stage in our history. Having experienced Eden, the Savage state, Patriarchy and Barbarism (for which read the beginning of capitalism), we had reached the era of Civilization, which only briefly preceded the salutary one of Harmony. This final phase, favoured by the blossoming phalansteries, was meant to last 35,000 years. People would live to the age of 144; they would grow a fifth limb, adapting them to resist the climate which would, in fact, be temperate. The overall optimism galvanized me. At last! I thought. At last someone who thinks like me. Someone who predicts that things will turn out for the best.

I now wonder what I found so attractive in this system decried by a good many people as an embryonic form of totalitarianism. I think what I had spotted in it straight away was the unprecedented opportunity it gave people to be rid of family constraints. Despite my youth, I had grasped that this was to do with opening up the stifling unit, and peacefully destroying a super-saturated intimacy in favour of a weaker solution for the common good. It meant freeing yourself from an individual body encoded with its bovine genome to dissolve into the social body, like a good-natured giant with purified free-flowing blood, light transparent blood, devoid of moods and passions. In this ideal world, as I pictured it, you were no one's child, like the heroes of certain fables who fascinated me because, even though they were very young, they never mentioned their parents; neither did the narrator feel any need to explain the protagonist's ancestry: all they needed was a first name and they were ready for adventure. I didn't like stories about kings and queens giving birth to princes and princesses, I hated biblical tales in which everyone was always the son or daughter of such-and-such or so-and-so, who in turn was son of, and so on, without end. I was all for the abolition of genealogy.

Phalansteries suited me with their seductively horizontal structure. I also suspected, although I didn't have the means to formulate this, that love and desire operated differently there. I didn't use any of these words. Didn't even think them. But I can remember sitting with the encyclopaedia on my knee, reading and re-reading the magic word 'phalanstery', and when one or other of my parents appeared snapping the huge volume shut, flushed and sweating as if I had been caught in some indecent position.

I don't know how, when I was borne by such aspirations as an adolescent, I could only a few years later have thrown myself into the narrow bottleneck of marriage and the still narrower one of motherhood. Panic probably. I relinquished my ambition to be the heart of a star, the idol of a court, the interchangeable and changing companion. Burying my dreams of a dissolute life – a dissolved life, in fact – I consented to become one of the corners of an isosceles triangle, isosceles and isolated, spinning mournfully against a gloomy azure beside other similar triangles which could never slot together without causing damage. Families and their austere geometry. Perhaps it was the world, in its incomprehensible vastness, which frightened me. Let's find a refuge, I told myself, let's shelter from statistics and put an end to dizzying calculations of probabilities which threaten to paralyse us; I would have liked to belong to everyone and be for everyone. The idea of making a choice seemed so small-minded, but I wasn't equal to my own ambitions. Having spent so much time leaping like a hare from left to right and right to left, I lost the main thread of my existence. One morning I woke to find I was tired of running. Stop! Put a steering-lock on the wheel of fortune, then it will stop turning. I drew the right number once and for all. I found Rainer and clung to him. If someone had told me to give away my lungs because I would now breathe air inhaled by my husband, I would have accepted. At the time, being oneself seemed an intolerable burden. I was in favour of sharing and, having turned away from my glorious plans for a community, I found the expected and total subservience, submission and acquiescence to a partner a good substitute for that pooling of resources, relieving me of the horrors of egocentricity. Rainer and I were one but, as there were two of us, it didn't matter. I liked thinking like him, telling myself I was wrong, fashioning my own thoughts to match his. He was rigorous while I was scatter-brained. He was patient and methodical where I had childish infatuations and absurd fads. I wanted to shake off my old skin. In fact, everything in my life is to do with skin.

When he touched me I came out of myself, left my own body. I can remember the feeling, neither pleasant nor unpleasant, something akin to anaesthesia. People – well, most people, I mean – are frightened of being put to sleep artificially. I've always loved it. I take delight in leaving myself. At least I *did*. Rainer could put one hand between my thighs and whoosh! I tumbled like a parcel in the post, light and colourless, falling into the abyss, into absence. It was a drug. I never asked myself whether or not I liked it. I just didn't imagine it could happen any other way, his hand made me forget every other hand. The whoosh! of a parcel had replaced the music of that wood in Norway. And very soon, after the baby was born, I even stopped questioning my lack of curiosity about what we did because my mind was on other things; I was alert, yes, but it was something completely different that held my attention. I was waiting, with meticulous and persistent patience, for maternal love to come back. It took absolutely all my energy. Let's behave normally, I told myself, let's make love with the husband, let's have supper parties and go out, let's play with the child, keep an eye on his homework, go on holiday, yes, all that, everything normal, and perhaps if we carry out every gesture with calm conviction, the timid little creature, the warm graceful creature of a mother's love for her son, the animal that fled, frightened by a slap on the cheek – poor little thing… perhaps it will come back, at night, treading softly, when I've even stopped waiting for it, because how many times have I mistaken the shadow of a stray cat for that too keenly awaited presence, how many times have I sat up with a start in the night and thought, there it is, it's back, but no, I had to go on waiting, to earn its return, to give up hope of it. Anne, sister Anne, can you see anything coming? Stop going up to the tower, stop using the binoculars, make believe and it will come, as faith comes to those who regularly kneel down and pray, joining their hands just as their spiritual adviser told them. Except love isn't faith. Or… is it?

Sometimes, looking back, I'm amazed by my persistence and even resent it. You should have given up, I tell myself. You were so tense, so demanding that the love could have come back without your even noticing. You missed it so much you forgot what it was like, you made such a saga of it. And what if you did actually love your son, I tell myself. But I know I didn't. I know from the tearing sound, like worn silk between brutal hands, that that sentence sends through me.

At ten past twelve Simone comes into the restaurant. She is alone. Her eyeliner has run in long trails over her cheeks. She looks like an owl: tousled hair, shining eyes, pinched nose and hunched shoulders. Ben goes over to kiss her hello but she pushes him away and sits at the table under my bookshelf, directly beneath Primo Levi's *The Periodic Table*, Ovid's *Metamorphoses* and Dylan Thomas's *Under Milk Wood*. I contemplate inverting the order of my books to create a different type of crown for her: Arnold Lobel's *Uncle Elephant*, I.B. Singer's *Shosha* and E.E. Cummings's collected poems. A benevolent headdress. A soft downy hat. I can see she's terribly upset. I note that Hannah is not there: screamingly, obscenely absent. This place is for eating, I feel like telling her. Not crying. It's bad for business. But I stop myself. I wipe my hands on a cloth, ask Ben to keep an eye on the chicken livers I have just flambéed and which are now caramelizing in the pan, and go and sit down opposite her. Using a napkin, I dab her cheeks dry. She lets me.

'What a bitch,' Simone murmurs.

And I know who she means. The bitch is her alter ego, her recently amputated right arm.

'Anyway, she's always been a hypocrite,' she adds.

I like that word 'hypocrite', which launches me far into the past all of a sudden, like a flying carpet.

'She'd got it all worked out. She told me she wasn't in love with him, but that was just her pride. That's all. Because he never even looked at her. But then afterwards, when we were together, she couldn't stand it...'

Hannah has stolen Simone's boyfriend. It's very, very serious. You have to picture a battlefield and streaming blood, a bamboo village buried by flowing lava. Her every sentence is so banal, paltry and hackneyed but you have to go with her in her suffering, accept the magnitude of it, respect the enormity of it. I remember my first disappointment in love, how it made adults laugh, how sweet they thought I was. I have no idea what I should say to console the inconsolable. What would I have wanted to hear at the time? I've forgotten. I've even forgotten what it feels like not being loved any more, being cheated on, humiliated and betrayed. Still, I find it hard convincing myself. I wonder whether Ben hasn't made the right choice – but have to remind myself that it isn't a choice, that's just the way it is, there's no love in his life. If there were no love anywhere, or desire, or sex, Hannah would be here, sitting next to her best friend. No one would cry and murderous hatred would never be hatched. I suddenly have a vision of a pacified world, a simple universe, washed clean of lust, peaceful and functional. Men and women live side by side, helping each other. Everyone has masses of time to read and go to the theatre, exhibitions and concerts. Instead of running breathlessly to clandestine meetings with our loins on fire, we head calmly through the friendly hubbub of the street towards a booth selling tickets for a ravishing dance show which moves us to tears. Our minds are free to be enlightened and our bodies – which have lost none of their energy, far from it – to enjoy every kind of sport and martial art. People massage each other in this society devoid of all ambiguity, they dance close together, and fat people are no longer ashamed to go to the swimming pool or the scrawny to the beach.

'Did you love him very much?' I ask Simone.

She utters a heart-rending yes and starts to sob helplessly. Etienne, one of the older nursery school children who particularly likes our turkey sandwiches, is watching her anxiously. He comes over and puts his tiny hand on Simone's arm but she doesn't notice.

'You'll love plenty more,' I tell her.

That's what one of my mother's friends told me when I went to her house to cry aged fifteen-and-a-half. I remember thinking she was a stupid old cow.

I take Etienne back to his table, reassuring him as best I can.

'Give Simone a bowl of soup', I tell Ben. 'Put some cream in a separate little bowl. And keep some of the chestnut mousse for her.'

I watch my livers browning, turning them with the tip of the spatula. I feel about a hundred and three.

If there was no love, or desire, or sex then Vincent wouldn't come asking for his daily kiss as well as his espresso.

Shall I pour you a coffee?

If you want.

Shall I kiss you on the mouth?

If you want.

And what else?

Whatever you want.

Except I don't know what I want.

Yesterday evening after we closed Vincent came in through the door into the hall of the building. He smelled of chrysanthemums and he had a pompom of camomile caught in his hair. He didn't see me straight away: I was behind him, busy arranging my books. I had time to breathe in the smell of him, to get used to his presence. It was after midnight and I wondered what he had done between his closing time and mine. He hadn't been home (otherwise he wouldn't have had that flower in his hair), he hadn't been to a bar (otherwise he would have smelled of cigarettes) or a restaurant (he would have smelled of burnt fat). He must have stayed at his premises when they were closed, imitating his neighbour, to see what it was like. He'd lain down on the floor, with his back on the damp surface strewn with flowerets. He had embraced armfuls of vigorous stalks, buried his face in pillowy petals, bathed his hands in the cold fragrant water in his tin-plate buckets.

He turned round when he heard my breathing. I felt like asking what he was doing there. But I knew the answer. I had started it. I had kissed him. I belonged to him now. If I wanted it to stop we would have to have a row. I would have to be unkind. Without a word he took me in his arms. His mouth was different. His mouth tastes of cinnamon, I thought; I like it.

From the application with which his tongue accomplished its circuits I could tell he was bored. It wasn't enough. I've always thought that intellectual curiosity played a part in matters of love. Before the first kiss we imagine it's going to be a monumental discovery, an opportunity to visit this other mouth and touch other teeth with the tip of our tongue. And then, after a while, we're there, we know it, we're used to it, we want to know more, to be initiated to the recesses and hidden corners, to see what no one before us has seen – how ridiculous, but we still believe it with the elation of a conquistador. Something in us wants to understand, and the light flickering at the end of the tunnel promises relief to our inquisitor's body. Personally, I've always tried to understand, but perhaps I'm alone in this. No, that's impossible, we're all looking for the same thing: we are guided by a thirst to know, and anyone who calls it a thirst for power is wrong. Vincent wants to understand me and, in order to achieve that, he slips his hand between the velvet of my trousers and that of my skin. He gets inside my clothes, with me, beside me, as if I am at last growing the fifth limb promised by Charles Fourier. His hand is cold and smells of chrysanthemums, his rather long nails scratch me where I am all tenderness. This isn't right. What he's doing is incongruous, makes me blush. I already know everything about Vincent and he knows everything about me. There's nothing to understand. Almost before becoming one, we are an old couple. We can go through all the motions but it won't be necessary, we have nothing to gain from it, or to lose. We've gone astray. We thought we were sailing towards the mysteries of the Indies and have ended up berthed in the drab bay of America.

What to do with his hand? I haven't dared take hold of his arm and tear it away from me as I would a weed in the vegetable patch. If the hand carries on, I keep thinking, it'll get lost, the boredom will send it to sleep, it will come back up to the surface, break away from me and attach itself back onto him, without shedding any light on anything, an opaque hand in an opaque body. But no, it's carrying on with its exploration and, in order not to disappoint it, so that it feels welcome (because I don't have the strength to push it away, amazed as I am by its stubborn determination) I think of something else. I think of someone else, someone I haven't allowed myself to think about for several years, but I know that his name – like a key whose weight alone can reassure the hand about to turn it in the lock – will open me. A huge smile spreads across my incorrigible face. Octave, the widest and least enigmatic interval between notes. No one's called third, no one's called fifth, and certainly not seventh, and yet… and yet… Octave, oh yes, that's a name. It's his name. It's the name of the boy I threw my life away for. And it's actually his tongue coiling round my mouth at the moment. But let's not rush things.

He had slipped out of our lives and we no longer thought about him. Hugo had driven him away because Octave had betrayed him, cheated him, humiliated him. Fine. I was sorry, but what could I do about it? He was replaced by Karims, Matthieus and Pierres. I played the game: welcoming, suggesting they came to tea and on outings. My son's friends were unanimous. They all thought I was nice. Some said I was a better cook than their mothers. Others thought I was pretty and asked Hugo how come I was so young. My big boy passed on their comments in a soft weary voice. I listened indifferently. The little brats were too much for me. They were lively and noisy, bright, well-socialized, well-adjusted; they could roller-blade and dribble and tackle, and were never tired. I thought nostalgically of Octave's laziness, his languor and ineptitude. What was the point, he had been repudiated.

One morning, succumbing to a new strategy to re-conquer my maternal feelings, I asked my son to tell me about his friends. He replied with his characteristic good grace, making lists and establishing categories. He was thirteen at the time, and his face — which should have been breaking out in spots and displaying a huge new nose, a hideous intruder between cheeks hollowed by his rapid growth — was still utterly beautiful: an elfin oval with translucent skin.

'And Octave?' I asked.

'Octave?'

'Do you remember? He was your friend in Mrs Merle's class, or was it Mrs Arnaud's, I can't remember...'

'A complete arsehole.'

I raised an eyebrow, not used to that sort of language from Hugo.

'He was crap. He couldn't do anything, but he thought he was so superior. He told me all sorts of rubbish and I went and believed him.'

'What did he tell you?'

'It was so stupid.'

'Tell me anyway.'

Hugo shook his head. He didn't want to. He was ashamed. But I would have been capable of torturing him to get him to own up, and he must have known, he was such a clever boy.

'He made me think he came from another planet,' he said eventually.

He was probably expecting me to burst out laughing, but I didn't even smile so he went on.

'One day he asked me to his house. It was weird.'

'Were his parents there?'

'I never saw his parents. There wasn't even a babysitter. It was big. There were loads of abstract paintings on the walls, huge things with colours puked over them, horrible. And sculptures too. Loads of pukey sculptures. He told me he lived alone and he'd been sent by his race... hey, I can't even remember what his stupid bloody race was called. Apparently they'd parachuted him to earth to find out about us. The worst thing is I believed him. I made notes for his research, I put together files for him. He was so useless. Do you remember? He couldn't tie his shoe-laces, he ate like a pig and, you see, I thought it was because he came from somewhere else. He convinced me he'd had lessons to be like us and he asked me to help him improve. He told me it was a secret and if anyone here on earth knew who he was, or if anyone back where he came from found out he'd confided in an earthling, he'd be destroyed.'

He stopped for a moment.

'Actually, I think he was a nutcase.'

I didn't want Hugo to stop. I didn't know what to do to set him off again. I wanted him to describe the planet to me, to give me more details. My heart quivered in my chest. Octave, my little one. I remembered the way he abandoned his light little head between my hands when I kissed him.

It was the end of our chat. Yet another failure to debit to our limping relationship.

Thinking back to that scene, I'm struck by my own stupidity, but I do know that we should never judge passion or sorrow because – whatever causes them and however they manifest themselves – we only ever see them superficially; we only see a lowly version, we remember what was visible on the surface, and have forgotten everything else when later, once we have healed, we study the painless scar of the deep-seated emotions the affair provoked in us. We have recovered. The convalescence has managed to minimize everything, to grind down the sharp shards of glass and reduce them to thousands of grains of sand so eroded by the implacable sole of reason that they have lost their cutting edge. We wipe them away with the flick of a hand, a crystal-line powder, specks of glitter. All that remains is the elusive spark picked out occasionally by a chance ray of light, just when we least expect it, but it goes out the moment we try to encourage it, or blow on it to fan those former flames. I will never know what came over me.

I've always loved it in films or books or at the theatre when a ghost from the past comes back. Everyone loved the person but they've disappeared. Everyone thought they'd died but here they are alive and well. Everyone thought they were heading for fame and fortune, but here they are back and perfectly ordinary. *Platonov* occupies a strategic position on my bookshelf, whichever way I arrange it. It's at the beginning or the end like a bookend, except that it is a book itself, and rather slimmer than the others. I don't know what it is in this pendulum motion that moves me so profoundly: the return of the hero, my favourite theme and one which – I think – conceals within it the true mystery of existence.

Vincent has undone the buttons of my blouse and unhooked my bra, and is gazing at my breasts. It's going on for ever! I feel like telling him to get a move on. I haven't got all night. I would like a few hours sleep before going to the market. Because he's taking so long to put his hand on my breast, because he can't stop wondering at how beautiful I am, so beautiful he doesn't know what to compare me with, it's quite beyond him, really, it's incredible, even the most beautiful rose, oh! my goodness! unbelievable, how can I be so soft... because he's taking so long and it's making me lose my concentration, I have no option but to imagine more going on and, instead of his motionless hands, I solder my last lover's arms to his body. Octave's vague, wandering fingers venture over my shoulders. An electric current sweeps from my head to my toes. Vincent has no idea of the passion throwing me at him. I push him to the floor. I'm going to eat him alive.

But now I'm the one at fault for being too hasty. Because we haven't got to that stage. We've got to Myriam, alone, at home, one spring afternoon. Someone rings the doorbell. But Myriam's not expecting anyone. She looks at her face in the mirror in the corridor. Her skin has a bluish tint back-lit in the gloom. She thinks about the ice fields: yes, that's it, she tells herself, I'm caught in the ice. Slowly, she makes her way to the door, puts her hand on the doorknob. The metal is ice-cold, but it's nothing compared to her hand. She opens the door and he appears. It's two years since she spoke his name for the last time. She recognizes him immediately. He has changed, though. At sixteen, Octave is much taller than her. He is well dressed, his hair tidy. 'Hello,' he says. She looks at him for some time, can't believe her eyes. He's so good-looking, his eyes so tender and mischievous. He leans forward to kiss her.

His lips have barely brushed against her cheek before Myriam's face flushes furiously. She thinks how truly ugly the dress she's wearing is, that she hasn't got any perfume on and her fingers smell of garlic. She would like to start the day again, make herself beautiful. She's not thinking of love, but dignity, yes, that's all. Being presentable. It's not like when they were little. 'How kind of you to drop by,' she tells him, unable to take her eyes off him, wondering whether he has a girlfriend, and if he has what her name is, where they meet and exactly what they get up to. She needs to know everything, urgently but ohhh! how to go about it? 'Well, don't just stand there,' she says, bursting into gales of affected laughter that she instantly loathes herself for. 'Hugo's not at home but...'; her son's name coagulates in her mouth. She didn't really succeed in pronouncing it, she said Hiuhino. 'I was just passing,' says the boy, 'so I thought...'. If he'd been truthful he would have said: I thought I'd fuck up my old friend's life, and really do it properly this time. But Octave is not truthful. He never has been, that's just the way he is. It's all part of his twisted charm. His irresistible, complete nutcase charm. He comes in and goes straight to the kitchen. Myriam pours him a glass of orange juice. She thinks of the vitamins in the drink, of the good they will do inside that tall unknown and yet familiar body. She looks at the time on the clock. More than fifty minutes before the end of lessons and Hugo coming home. 'Aren't you supposed to be at school?' Octave gives no reply. He smiles. He has a plan. Myriam doesn't know this. He knows exactly what he has to do. Talk a bit. Look at her. Wait. Come back. Look at her again. Put all sorts of intentions in his eyes. Suggest outings to her. Fill the void of her days with his total availability. Together they go to museums, the cinema, cafés. They laugh at everything and think of nothing. This all goes on during office hours. Rainer is at work; he's taken on a new medical secretary. 'It's too much work for you,' he told Myriam. 'You need to rest.' He hopes the time she spends at home will put some colour back in her cheeks. He is satisfied. After only a few weeks off work Myriam is pink-cheeked. As soon as he talks to her she flushes scarlet. Why hadn't he thought of it sooner! He congratulates himself.

Wednesdays and weekends are black days. Myriam is bored. She wants to kill her husband and kill her son: ransack the place. Friends who drop by for a cup of tea, whoosh, napalm them. Her mother, gerplonk! Remove her. Her brother, zap! In the bin. She listens to Chopin's *Nocturnes* and Prokoviev's second piano concerto, hoping to hear ever wider intervals between the notes. An octave! For pity's sake, an octave! cries her heart. But octaves are inaudible, mere echoes, the same. Myriam concentrates. She gets hold of a treatise on harmonies but doesn't understand a word of it. She's disappointed, disappointed by everything, she burns everything on her non-stick pans, can't eat, can't sleep. She thinks about the next exhibition she and Octave might go to. What an extraordinary new life! How could she have guessed? She feels much more beautiful, much more intelligent. She's growing. Filling the world. She muses about the scarf she will give... what should she call him? Her friend? My special friend, she tells herself, the only living being who understands me. A white cotton scarf, perfectly simple, to protect Octave's throat from the spring breeze. She goes shopping, buys herself T-shirts, jeans, skirts. There are piles of clothes strewn over her bedroom floor. She spends a lot of time trying them on. She has no idea what's happening to her. In front of a painting of Nicolas de Staël, Octave puts his hand on Myriam's neck. She's trying to read the name of the painting on the plaque. The letters dance. Impossible, she thinks, I'll never know the name of this picture. She narrows her eyes as something extraordinary, something un-hoped for happens between his hand and her neck. Myriam comes back. She takes a great leap back. Into the past. She has to make quite an effort to stay standing because beneath her torso she no longer has legs and beneath her legs, there are no longer feet. If she falls the hand will peel away from her skin. She absolutely must not move. Slowly, the ice field melts. Great blocks of ice break away with a thundering crunch like giant jaws. Icebergs float away, dotted across the dark blue water. My goodness it's hotting up! How it glitters!

Vincent is under me on one of the tables in my restaurant. But it isn't him, and we're not here.

It's Octave who has his arms round Myriam and is biting her in the deserted toilets of a museum at eleven o'clock in the morning. She is white as porcelain, she, the squaw, is white as a revelation. He is honeyed, he gently licks the nape of her neck. 'What am I doing?' she asks. She would like him to stop. She would like him to go on. 'What am I doing?' she cries quietly.

'You're kind,' he tells her. 'You're so kind. They don't know how lucky they are. You're the best of wives and the best of mothers. You're a gift.'

'What's going on?' Vincent asks. 'It feels like you're dead.'

That was yesterday evening and I'm now looking at the table where our bodies uncoupled. The substance of it reminds me of a coffin.

'I don't feel very well,' I told him.

He stood up while I gathered together my clothes, which seemed to have been scattered by a storm.

'I've never...' he stammered. 'I've never...'

He didn't know what to say next. I told him I liked him very much, aware of everything that this phrasing withheld.

He won't come today. I've betrayed him, cheated him, humiliated him. But tomorrow who knows?

Anyway, I seem to be up in the clouds today. A little too much so perhaps. I should be helping Simone, organizing her revenge or helping her find wisdom. I should slice up the livers before they start going black in the middle, keep their hearts pink and achingly soft. I should. I should but I'm dreaming. A hand – a new, deft one – appears from behind me and takes the pan off the hob. Ben puts the giblets onto the chopping board, cuts them up and lays them on their bed of spinach and grapefruit. He's learnt from me, without my saying anything, without my even showing him. I watch him put the sage and pancetta flans in the oven. I sit on the counter smoking a cigarette. Not doing a thing.

The only problem is I can't work out whether it's happiness or sorrow that washes over me as I exhale those scrolls of bluish smoke.

We finished just before midnight. My eyelids crackle over my irises. I dream of a bedroom. A simple square room with just a bed and two bedside tables, sheets, a blanket and a crocheted bedspread. I dream of a bathroom, or a shower room, I don't mind, tiled throughout, with a porcelain basin. I would also have a little wardrobe to hang my clothes; at the moment they are rolled up in a suitcase hidden behind the bar. My clothes never smell of washing powder. Even clean they smell of *Chez moi*. It's been six years since I've had a house. It was the same at Santo Salto, permanent insecurity. When someone new turned up I had to clear out straight away and move in with a friend in her caravan to make way. Only circus costumes were hung up, everything else was crammed into bundles. It made me think of the exodus. The sound of cartwheels on the road, the patch-work of canvas, the burlesque heaps of frying pans, books and chamber pots. I don't know which of my ancestors undertook that sort of journey. None of them, perhaps. Or it could have been my ancestors in books and films. I can no longer distinguish between true memories and those that have been grafted onto me by fiction.

At Santo Salto I felt I was alive again, not in the sense that I had rediscovered a lust for life, but rather that I was re-running a former fate. Everything was familiar, the stoves, the mattresses and cushions stuffed with old clothes, the crates which served in turn as tables, chairs, ladders, cupboards and even as swimming pools in the summer when we lined them with a thick blue tarpaulin. The lawless existence, the days spent circumventing administrative obstacles, the unenforceable rules, the agile minds matching agile bodies.

One spring morning when I was sitting down peeling carrots Rodrigo, who wanted to become a sword-swallower like his father, asked me, 'So where's your husband?'

'I don't have a husband.'

'And your children?'

I couldn't tell him I didn't have any. I didn't know what to say.

'I can tell you've got children,' he announced, indifferent to my silence.

'How can you tell?'

He shrugged.

'I can tell, I just can.'

He was walking on his hands, head down, circling round me.

'Is it difficult?'

'What?'

'Walking, like that, on your hands?'

'Yes,' he said. 'It's just as difficult as walking on your feet,' he explained after a while.

With his knees bent, he jigged his lower legs on a level with my face.

'Do you remember?' he asked.

'What?'

'When you learned to walk, do you remember it?'

'No, not at all. Do you?'

'Yes, I do. I remember everything. Do you know what my mother calls me? She calls me Memorial. Do you know what that means? It means someone who remembers everything. It's my nickname. I remember the first time I tried to walk on my feet, before that I used to walk on my knees. I remember the first time I said a word…'

'What was it, Mummy or Daddy?'

'It was clementine.'

I didn't believe him.

'Clementine? I'd be surprised, that's a very long difficult word for a baby.'

'I wasn't a baby. I was three years old. I'd done a lot of practising in my head. I chose that word specially.'

'And was your mum proud?'

'No, she'd have been happier if I'd said Mummy.'

'Could you teach me to walk on my hands?' I asked Memorial.

He dropped back down onto his feet, told me to get up, then looked me over. He touched my hips and thighs, then stood on tip-toe to feel my arms and shoulders. He shook his head.

'All your strength is down below. Your arms are all floppy and your legs all hard. You should have started earlier. You have to start everything early.'

'Can we try anyway?'

Thanks to Memorial's lessons I now know how to do a handstand for just a few seconds. I can't go backwards or forwards. He was surprisingly patient with me. As a thank-you I gave him a book, Wilhelma Shannon's *Three Adventures of a Shy Lion*.

'I can't read,' he admitted, slightly put out.

'Well, I'll teach you.'

'Is it difficult?'

'No,' I told him, very sure of myself.

Memorial must now be about thirteen or fourteen. I don't know where he is. In my purse I still have a piece of paper folded in four on which he wrote his first word: MEMORIAL in capital letters with the 'E' facing the wrong way and the 'A' upside-down. I never unfold it. I'm afraid of damaging it and it's too painful. In my head I draw a clown's costume on each of those capitals, and I can feel the weight of his pencil strokes inside my handbag like imps carved of wood. He had no difficulty learning, but I had all the trouble in the world teaching him, my throat tight and my eyes heavy with tears. That mania for reliving everything, the inability to find anything completely new. Why does it have to take me so long to understand? Why do I have to keep retracing my steps in the hopes of finding goodness knows what needle lost in a roadside haystack?

This evening I feel like sleeping in a bedroom again. I count the cracks on the ceiling, like the lines of a giant hand resting above my head.

'I swear to you,' Ben insists. 'You don't have any choice. It's pure logic.'

He picks up a pen, writes down some figures and circles them.

'Look. I don't even know why I'm asking you what you think, there's no getting away from it.'

He's drawing squares inside circles and circles inside squares. He can't think what to come up with next to make me subscribe to his cause.

'I've never had any ambition,' I tell him. 'I can't abide capitalism. I don't want to expand. I want to stay as we are. We're happy like this, aren't we?'

'No.'

Ben is serious. He's angry.

'There isn't enough room in the kitchen,' he says fierily. 'Yesterday evening we missed two take-away orders—'

'The people weren't annoyed,' I say, interrupting him.

'People are never annoyed with you, Myriam. But that's no excuse. If we carry on like this, we'll have to pay taxes. Look, it's here.' He shows me a very large figure underlined three times. 'We won't be able to.'

'They'll let us defer it.'

'Stop!' he's shouting now. 'Stop! Shit, it's not like this is complicated. Do it for me, at least. You just have to take on the lease for the haberdashery next door. We're not chucking anyone out. We're not hurting anyone. The "To Let" sign's been up there for two months. We pay, we take down the sign, we do the work and we expand!'

'With what money?'

'We borrow it.'

'He's right,' says Vincent in a quiet voice.

I can't get over the fact that he's here. Where is your pride, wounded man? I stare at him, my eyes a bit too wide. He runs his hand through my hair.

'Listen to him,' he advises as he sits down next to us.

There's a white lily stamen hanging from the collar of his pullover. His every move produces a tiny saffron shower. He isn't trying to avoid my eye. This is peace. Vincent is here as a neighbour.

We haven't cleared the place yet. The dishwasher's running but the bins still need emptying, and everything needs cleaning. I look round. I wish I could tell them I haven't the strength. I'm already so tired.

'You also need to think about taking on staff,' Ben tells me gently.

'What a thought!'

I jump up, grab the broom, wring out the floor cloth, descend on the bins and wipe all the surfaces down.

'I don't want to take anyone on, Ben, do you understand. No one! It's you and me, and that's all. If you stop, I stop. If it's too much for me, I'll close. I couldn't give a damn about closing. None of it means anything to me, this restaurant, this shitty life, I'll give it all up, with no regrets, give it all up. Don't need anyone. Look.'

I tip buckets of scalding water over the floor, squirt washing-up liquid into the dirty casseroles, run a cloth over the chairs and buff up the banquette.

My banquette, my little banquette for the ladies that I bought from a charity shop. I lie down on it, and the cool moleskin welcomes my cheeks flushed from my exertions. I'm crying. I don't know how to explain to them that this wasn't at all what I intended. I just wanted… I just wanted… I'm trying to find the word. It won't come. I clutch at another one. I wanted to do something good. No. That's not it. It's the sentence next to it that I'm trying to say, but I can't seem to. I can't find it any more.

'I'm sorry,' I say, sobbing. 'I'm sorry.'

That's the word I was looking for.

Ben and Vincent wait for me to calm down. They don't come over. I would rather have spared them this performance. They don't know anything about my life and don't understand why I'm crying. I'm worried they both think they are responsible; when neither of them is. After a while, when my sobs are spaced further apart, Vincent decides to speak.

'Anyway, it would be good for the area,' he says. 'As a shopkeeper myself…'

He's so neutral, so professional. Vincent isn't afraid of being down to earth, he's my pragmatic genius.

'As a shopkeeper myself, it's in my best interests for your… your…'

'Her restaurant,' Ben prompts.

'Yes, that's right, for your restaurant to get bigger. It'll give everything else a boost.'

There then follows a discussion between him and Ben about the inevitability of growth. They very soon forget I'm sad, and even forget I'm there. They exchange opinions – which, to their great delight, are the same – about my venture, well thought-out orders, and the longevity of neighbouring businesses. Bit by bit, they build me an empire, taking on waiters, waitresses and an accountant. The word 'chef' wakes me from my torpor.

'Oh no!' I say hoarsely. 'You're not putting anyone else in the kitchen instead of me.'

They laugh, glad to see me defending myself. They talk all night and I think to myself that our lives are like glasses. Glasses that need filling. We pour in love and desire and longing. I came very close to being the liquid in Vincent's glass. I got away, and he's pouring something else in there now. I wonder what I'd like to find in my own at the moment.

'DRINK ME', read the inscription on Alice's little bottle. She drank and felt herself getting smaller like a telescope. 'EAT ME', read another inscription, on the cake. Alice ate it and stretched up like a sapling. Too small, too big, my life keeps changing proportions and I'm never the right size for what I'm trying to do. I would so like to get back to my original size, the one which meant I could slip into the glove of each day without feeling either too exposed or too cramped.

My pair of tempters, who have had a little too much to drink, beg me to join them in their ambitious dreams. I'm resisting. I don't want anything to change, but they talk over each other and in unison, telling me what I want is inadmissible. It's market pressure, they say, expand or perish, those are the only options.

'How can people always want more? Doesn't it make your head spin just thinking about it?'

'She's read too many books,' Vincent decrees.

'Or not enough,' Ben suggests. 'Not the right ones.'

I've read books in which greed is punished and modesty rewarded. I've read some in which it was the other way round, success stories where people climbed up the ladder. I've read tales where love happens without ever being declared, and where it is declared without ever happening. I've followed the adventures of a billionaire who started his career with a nail in his pocket, nothing else, just a nail. I've read fables populated with talking animals and people turned into creatures: a toad/prince, a young man/cockroach. I've read stories of murder, stories of rape, those about war, those about boredom. I've lost the titles and forgotten the authors and now all I have left is Alice, Alice who's trying to solve the hopeless equation of time and space: she needs to get smaller to go through the tiny door but once she has shrunk she realizes she's left the key on the table that's now four times her height, so she has to stretch again, to grow bigger by biting into the magic cake, to make amends for her previous negligence. I'm never the right size either.

Last night we did away with sleep. In the morning my face looks grey in the mirror: a shelled walnut. Knife handles burn me, damp cloths chill me, the fridge light dazzles me. I have to sit on a stool to check over my filets mignons. Every movement comes at a price. A potato weighs as much as a wild boar, a sprig of parsley as much as an ancient oak. The peppercorns bursting under the pressure of my blade and the coriander seeds breaking up in the mill squeal and scream. A customer puts his coffee cup down on his saucer a little too violently and the clatter of china startles me. I say 'ah!' but no one hears me. My voice is buried somewhere in the depths of my stomach. I get up to fetch some prunes from a jar on the shelf and collapse half-way there. As my head smacks the floor I check that the knife I had in my hand hasn't planted itself in my body. No, there it is, a few centimetres from my face. Phew! I'm not dead.

When I wake up I'm in a bedroom. The sun is filtering between drawn curtains. Beneath my head, a pillow of goose-down. Over my body, white sheets. I'm fully clothed, in an unfamiliar bed. The room is small, with bare walls. I sit up. My jaw feels stiff. I slowly heave myself to my feet, pushing off from the single mattress. I check that I can stand and, walking along the walls in case I lose my balance, make my way out of my cell. The rest of the apartment is plunged in deep shadow striped with sunlight: rays of light stream through gaps in the closed shutters. It smells of mothballs and washing powder. Most of the furniture is covered with see-through nylon sheets. Lengths of white cloth cover the ornaments. I lift the skirt on a clock and find two naked golden cherubs smiling beneath a glass cover. There are display cabinets harbouring tea sets, sets of glasses and dessert services. The bookcase, a meagre one, contains only the complete works of the Marquis de Sade, three apparently identical editions of a treatise on sexology and five leather-bound volumes dedicated to skin diseases. I'm just heading towards what I imagine to be the kitchen when I hear a key turn in the lock a few metres from me.

'Ah, you're awake,' says Charles, seeing me standing there in the corridor.

I don't understand what my brother's doing here. Maybe I'm at his house. Maybe he's moved. I'm ashamed of his pitiful bookcase. I'm also ashamed of the nylon covers. I think what the carpets and gilt-framed mirrors must have cost, now punished under their shrouds of sheeting.

'I was as quick as I could be,' he apologizes. 'How are you?'

I don't say anything. He comes over and sweeps a lock of hair off my face. He laughs.

'You did that properly,' he congratulates me. 'You look like elephant woman.'

I feel my head. There's a huge bump, like the beginnings of a horn, distorting my forehead.

'Am I ugly?'

'Hideous,' Charles tells me.

He looks at me and laughs.

'But I'm obviously funny.'

'I've just come from your harem,' he explains. 'They got in touch with me.'

'What are you talking about?'

'What are they called again? I've forgotten their names. Your staff at the restaurant. They called me at work.'

'I don't have any staff,' I tell Charles.

'Right, go back to bed.'

'Who are you talking to like that?'

'To a little girl I'm going to take for an X-ray as soon as she comes round properly. How many fingers?' he asks, hiding his hands behind his back.

'You've got the same number of fingers as me and I don't need an X-ray. I feel absolutely fine. I've been wanting a little snooze for a few days. Well I've had one now so I'm going back to work.'

I go to get my coat from the bedroom.

'Your place is so big!' I call from the end of the corridor. 'And so ugly!'

'It's not my place,' Charles calls back. 'But you're right, it *is* ugly.'

We're at Ben's house. Or, to be precise, at Ben's late parents' house. Charles opens the living-room shutters and shows me, bang opposite, on the other side of the street, my restaurant with its lack of sign and its bare windows. Ben the local boy, I think to myself. Then I remember the evening when he claimed to have missed the last Métro so he could sleep at the restaurant. I'm touched by his lie, more than I would have been by an admission. I screw up my eyes to try to see through the panes whether the restaurant is empty or full. I can't make out any movement. It's the quietest time of day, mid-afternoon. From up on the second floor I look at our short wide street in the late winter sunlight. The buildings are dirty, leaning slightly, growing beards of straggly weeds, metal shutters half-lowered like weary eyelids, vast porches opening onto wizened little courtyards along a vice-like formation of façades bouncing the sun's reflection back at each other, quickly, quickly, in a billiard game of light. A little further down on the right-hand side, parked by the pavement in front of Vincent's shop, I notice a blue van, a unique blue, a blue from our childhood, clear and hard.

'Shit!' I say. 'Shit! Shit! Shit! Shit! Shit!'

Charles looks at me inquiringly. He can't help smiling. It's because of my bump. That bump has made his day.

'You see that van?' I ask him.

He nods.

'Well... that vehicle is extremely important to me.'

I'm conscious of the fact that this sentence has no hope of reassuring him about my mental faculties, but I don't know how else to explain things. I stand facing him, in the light, and pull my hair back: I want him to tell me honestly how I look. He bursts out laughing.

'That bad?'

'Look at yourself in the mirror,' he tells me. 'It's brilliant. No, really. And it's beginning to go quite a colour now, tending towards greens, and purples... a bit of yellow too.'

I don't want a mirror. I drag as much hair as I can over my face. 'And like that,' I ask him, 'how's that?'

'Like a dog,' he says without a moment's hesitation.

A dog, I think to myself, perfect. It is as a dog, then, that I will see my old friend, Ali Slimane.

'Are you sure you're OK?' Charles asks me.

He looks so sad, I think to myself. Why do we never see each other? I don't look after him. I don't deserve to be a big sister. That makes it a full house for me then. What's that all about, growing up together, bound together like the fingers of a hand and then losing touch like boats set adrift? No one warned me. As children we were a fortress. I came home from school and there he was with his Lego and cars. I thumped him. He bit me. We watched TV, huddled together. He rifled through my things. I passed my ear infections onto him. He wore my trousers and jumpers. We were each other's alibi, against our parents. Occasionally we betrayed each other. We hated each other. I made fun of his spelling. Then we would club together to buy a purse on mother's day or a tie on father's day. We were in the same boat. How could I have believed it would go on forever? How could I have let the moorings break away?

'I've been useless,' says Charles.

'What?'

'All these years. I've been useless.'

'What are you talking about?'

'About your fuck-ups, and my own.'

I laugh.

'Oh,' I say philosophically, 'my fuck-ups!'

I want to ask him for news of Hugo. It's almost there, on the tip of my tongue. I know he's seen him. There have been Christmases, birthdays, funerals. Where is my son? Just that. I want to know where he lives. I want to see him. I miss my son.

'Which one of them's your lover?' asks Charles.

I don't understand.

'The young one or the up-tight one?'

'It's none of your business.'

'Go on, tell me.'

He has opened the apartment door. Once we are out on the landing he locks it up.

'Did he give you his keys?' I ask.

'He's very polite. What's-his-name.'

'Ben.'

'Ben's very polite', Charles tells me. 'He told me he found my number in your notebook.'

Ben really hesitated but he thought it would be good to let a member of the family know. He felt guilty because he thought I should possibly have gone to hospital but he couldn't miss a shift, he thought I would be furious with him if he shut up shop.

'The other one, the up-tight one,' Charles says, 'came and gave him a hand.'

'He's not up-tight,' I say. 'He's a florist.'

'I don't see the connection.'

'Well, I do.'

We go our separate ways outside the building.

'Go back to work,' I tell my brother.

'You too.'

He straightens my dog-like hairstyle and I give a little bark in reply.

'By the way,' I say when he's already a little way away, 'what did you think of *Chez moi*?'

I wave my hand in the direction of the restaurant.

'Very you,' he tells me. 'But it's a bit small, isn't it?'

This male conspiracy is beginning to get on my nerves.

'Come and eat there some time.'

He doesn't answer but smiles, then disappears on his huge and impeccably clean motorbike.

I cross the street, shakily. The blue van is staring at me with its wide-set headlights on either side of its metal grill snout. I've got a metallic taste in my mouth, the taste of blood. When I get to the door I take an elastic band from my pocket and put my hair in a ponytail. Goodbye dog. Goodbye beauty. I go home as a novice unicorn. There are three knights waiting for me.

My return is a success. Their expressions, their laughter. They invite me to sit at their table. I shake Ali's hand, without meeting his eye. Never in my life have I felt so intimidated.

'Mr Slimane agrees with us,' announces Vincent.

'Yes, fine, that's enough,' I say. 'Do you really think I'm in a fit state to conquer the world?'

I run the tips of my fingers over my bruise. The pain brings tears to my eyes.

'You know some people think the bumps on our heads mean something?' Ben says playfully, 'well yours means you're a born businesswoman.'

'Did you shut your shop?' I ask Vincent.

'No, we sorted it out. Simone didn't have any lessons so we gave her the choice between washing-up and selling bouquets. She chose the bouquets.'

Why are you helping me? I want to ask them. What is this new world where people come to the aid of their neighbour? Are we actually creating the first viable phalanstery? I'm terrified by the mystery of goodness. Everything suddenly seems unbearably solemn. I don't deserve this. I don't feel I belong here as queen of the kindly kingdom of gentleness and fine feelings. I'm a dangerous woman. I'm a wicked woman. The biggest fucker-upper the world has ever brought forth. Prison is what I deserve. No one has actually complained but that's no excuse. I should have given myself up, gone to the first police station I could find and asked them to put me in handcuffs for sleeping with an adolescent, corrupting him, giving in to my abject urges, failing to protect him from his own folly. Did I harm him? What was he avenging? Because it was to do with revenge, and premeditated, with recordings and photos to back it up. Documents he made a point of passing on to my son and my husband.

I don't remember seeing Hugo again after that. Only the settings are still imprinted on my memory, empty of actors. I can picture the ransacked apartment, my clothes strewn all over the place, even down the loos, the broken doors, upturned chairs, shattered mirrors, crockery in the corridor, books torn and trampled. I can hear Rainer's voice bellowing 'You had no right! You had no right!' He should have killed me. He certainly could have done and wanted to. I know what stopped him: he didn't want both Hugo's parents to be criminals. He kept a modicum of restraint for his sake, for our child. 'Your mother's mad,' he told him. 'Your poor mother doesn't know what she's doing.' Where was my son at this point? Holed up in his bedroom with his head on his knees, struggling to blot out the memory of his mother's moaning and gasping, her thighs, her breasts. Try as I might, I can't find him anywhere. My memory is very good and very bad. I can remember the exact angle of one of my skirts which had waltzed over onto a lampshade, the folds in the silk, the light from the bulb filtering through the pattern; I can remember the rose in the middle of a plate broken in four under the bathroom cabinet, my eyes locked onto it when I crawled in there with my head on the tiles, looking for shelter; I can remember the perfume bottle spilt on the bedroom carpet, the sickening smell, the orangey stain; I can remember the sense of relief now that, at last, my life was just as chaotic on the outside as it was on the inside as if, for all those years, maintaining order had been the most unbearable lie. In any event, we were there. We no longer had to fear the worst, it had happened. Those images are as clear in my mind as if I had spent hours constructing them and organizing them. Terror brought an end to terror, swallowing itself up, and slowly – even though everything was happening very quickly – I started to think thank you, thank you.

Rainer dragged me from one room to another, pulling me by my hair. 'Look,' he said. 'Look what you've done.' I registered every last detail. Every garment turned inside out, every piece of furniture hurled upside-down was a reward. I had thoroughly demolished the pretty life of buttered bread and hemlines, the pleasant existence of Sunday roasts and freshly-ironed clothes. At the beginning I probably took a bit too much of a run-up for the simple somersault that turns a young girl into a wife and mother: I had landed, head over heels, infinitely grotesque.

Hugo! Hugo! I call him, in vain, in my memories. No one answers.

A period scene springs to mind. Lit by candlelight, smell of hay and cattle, blood trickling lazily into an enamel bowl. 'The mother or the child?' the doctor asks the weeping father. 'Which of them should I keep alive? Which of them, sir, will make you happier?' 'The mother and the child,' replies the father, emphasizing the co-ordinating conjunction which gives his life meaning. But the doctor completely misunderstands, instead of saving them both he assassinates them. There, you can be happy now. No mother, no child. No jealousy.

The sun is sinking. Ali Slimane takes me on a tour of my kitchen. When he walks, not a sound. When he talks, a gentle murmur.

'Preserved food there.'

The butcher's block is adorned with two rows of multicoloured jars.

'Fresh vegetables there.'

He leans forward and I lean with him; my knees crack, his don't. He has created an opening under the window and built a larder cupboard of wicker and bamboo. Luxurious cabbages, self-satisfied leeks, arching chard, earthy carrots, ravishing little turnips and all sorts of different squashes, some with markings like an ocelot, some shaped like gourds and others sheltering under impish bonnets of stalk.

'Dried vegetables.'

In wooden pails, raised off the ground by hollow bricks, there are black-eyed beans watching me, lentils sleeping, haricot beans slithering and chickpeas tumbling.

'Dairy products.'

There is now a portable chiller cabinet above my fridge. It is opened by means of a large aluminium handle which you lift then turn. It's a precious old-fashioned kitchen unit harbouring the cool half-light so beneficial to goat's and ewe's cheese, fresh cream and yoghurt in strainers.

'As for the meat,' he says, 'I've given you lamb, poultry, and a few partridges too. I supply every two days. I can sort something out for fish but it's more complicated.'

'Forget about the fish,' I tell him. 'All this is wonderful as it is. Have you got a bill for me?'

He hands me a piece of paper and quickly turns away. He whistles a slow tune between his teeth. His prices are lower than in the market. It's a very good deal for me, but for him too. I'm sure of that.

'You've given me a special price as a friend,' I point out.

'As an acquaintance,' he rectifies. 'It'll be more expensive in the summer. With all that delicate fruit which is difficult to pick, raspberries, gooseberries, blackcurrants.'

'Will it always be you who delivers it?'

'Always me.'

I dare not ask how he will find time to run his business if he spends so much of the week on the road.

'You need looking after,' he says, his eyes on my bump.

My eyes scoot about, zigzagging in every direction to avoid meeting his. He waves at me to sit down under the light. Outside on the pavement I can see Vincent and Ben having a cigarette and making goodness knows what sort of deductions.

Mr Slimane examines me. He takes my face between the palms of his hands and tilts it from right to left and back to front.

'I should have put some ice on it,' I say.

He shakes his head.

'Lie down.'

I obey him. Lying on the banquette, I look at the cracks on the ceiling and wonder which is the line of luck, of life and of money. All three of them are very long and that doesn't surprise me because recently I've had a lot of luck, I've earned too much money and I've had enough energy to take me galloping beyond 120. I wait for my treatment, letting myself be lulled by the occasional sounds Mr Slimane makes in the kitchen. He asks no questions, understands where all the utensils live, knows how to light the gas cooker, and doesn't confuse salad servers with wooden spatulas. After a few minutes an unfamiliar smell reaches my nostrils: a mixture of sage, irises, caramel and tar. The lemon only comes through as an after-thought. How strange, I think, lemon usually comes first. Ali comes over to me with a saucepan in his hand, stirring its contents so gently it borders on laziness.

'What is it?'

'You mustn't move. I'm going to spread the cataplasm on your forehead, but it mustn't get in your eyes; or here,' he adds, pointing to the open summit of my wound, where the skin has opened out like a star, sketching a little spider of blood.

'Will it sting?' I ask anxiously.

'It stings eyes and open wounds. On the skin it warms and

cools at the same time.' He spreads his strong-smelling pitch from my eyebrows to my hairline, taking care not to press too hard. It has a grainy texture like eggs beaten with sugar, it is liquorice black and its effect is instant. It heats and chills at the same time.

He leans over me and looks at me attentively. 'How old are you?' he asks me.

'Why do you want to know how old I am?'

He laughs. He says bumps like this only happen to children. That it's the first time he's treated an adult with his preparation.

'I'm forty-three,' I tell him.

'That's good,' he says. 'That's very good. And your restaurant, is it doing well?'

'I don't know. I think so. I'm not very good with figures. Ben takes care of all that. He says we need to expand.'

'He says you need to *reinvest*,' he corrects.

I don't see the difference.

'He's right,' adds Mr Slimane.

As he peels the layer of sticky paste from my face, I have a surreptitious look at him. I see his mouth, his flat inward-sloping lips. His teeth – which are revealed by a grimace because the gloop is resisting his efforts – are not very straight, they overlap and I have no idea why but they bowl me over like an unexpected piece of architecture. As the paste comes away, he throws it into the pan. When it's done he smiles, satisfied.

'It's much better,' he says.

I pat my forehead tentatively with the tips of my fingers. The bump is noticeably smaller. He hands me a pocket mirror, having wiped it carefully. It's spectacular: the colours have melted into each other and the bump has flattened out, only the scarlet spider is still there in the top right-hand corner.

'It was my neighbour who gave me that recipe,' he explains. 'When the children were little we spent the whole time going to the doctor for the slightest thing. Their mother was a real worrier. Then one day Mme Dubrême who lived over the road invited me round and taught me how to make various unguents. She didn't want me to tell my wife about them. She said "city people don't understand anything about witchcraft". My wife was from the city. "But what with you being an Arab, it doesn't frighten you, am I right?" She was right. But I don't know if it's because I'm Arab or because I was fed up with spending a fortune on doctors.'

'What else did she teach you?'

'Plaster made with mustard and nettles, thyme honey for sprains, the fifty-three virtues of rhubarb. And love potions, of course.'

'Do they exist?'

'No, that was a joke, they don't exist. If they did my wife wouldn't have left with the mayor from the next village.'

His wife has gone. What a good idea that was of hers. I'm so happy she found love with her rural politician. It fills me rather disturbingly with joy.

'Was it a long time ago?'

'What?'

'Your wife.'

'Four years.'

'I remember your sadness,' I tell him. 'There was something in your eyes.'

'I loved her.'

'Do you still love her?'

'She still loves me too,' he answers evasively.

I've had enough of talking about his wife. This conversation doesn't suit me at all.

'Love,' he goes on, 'never ends. It changes but it never ends.'

'What does it change into?'

'Into everything, into anything. Into hate, very often. Into coldness. Into friendship…'

'I'm not following this, not following at all.'

I have sat up. My bump is no longer hurting. I just need to sort out this little problem with love and I can pick my day back up exactly where it stopped.

'It's too easy to say it changes,' I tell Ali who is busy cleaning out the saucepan. 'If it turns into hate, then it no longer exists. It's been replaced by hate. There's nothing of it left.'

'There is day even in the night,' he replies.

'Your neighbour was right, you're very much an Arab.'

That makes him laugh.

'There's nothing particularly Arab about saying there's day in the night,' he informs me. 'It's one of your great French poets who wrote that. I learnt it at school.'

'And what does it mean?'

'It means that a relationship between a man and a woman is like a firmament. The hate you feel for someone you've loved is nothing like other kinds of hate. It's fuelled by the old love.'

'Supposing it is,' I say, 'what difference does that make?'

'You like discussions,' Ali tells me.

I nod, lowering my eyes, as if caught out. I so love ideas, the way they collide, drown inside each other, turn their backs on each other and confuse each other's issues. But I'm ashamed of this fascination, because I so quickly run out of words, because I've never learned to think, because I have about as much rhetoric as a farmyard goose.

'I like them too,' he says, slapping his thighs as if giving his legs the signal to leave.

He checks that everything is as it should be and tells me when he will next be here.

'You were sad too,' he says in the doorway. 'I could see it in your eyes.'

We finally make eye contact. There will be night in our day, I tell myself, looking at his eyes, which are dark as juniper berries.

Job interviews terrify me. Ben has insisted: I absolutely have to conduct them in person. People need to know who's the boss here, he explained.

We've run an advertisement and it's raining applications. The CVs and covering letters flood into the letter-box, drowning out the bills in their gleeful torrent. I receive candidates in a small office that we have managed, I'm not sure how, to fit in behind the bar. They come during the rare slack periods, and our conversations are punctuated by the strident whirr of hand-held drills, the shudder of pneumatic drills and the thud of sledgehammers on walls. The former haberdashery has begun its moult. Men in orange, yellow or white hard hats come and go. They seem to feed off nothing but cheese sandwiches and apples. They're a funny bunch, not very talkative but quick to laugh. They chat among themselves in a language I don't know, and address me in a French full of rolled 'R's and devoid of definite articles. But they prefer speaking to Ben; I don't inspire their confidence.

In the course of the interviews I meet mostly young girls. Some are limp as cucumber peelings, others smell of tobacco from three metres away; there are the very stupid ones who can only come up with one answer – 'Dunno'; then there are the clever ones who have terrible trouble expressing themselves, flushing, rolling their eyes and stammering with nerves. One Thursday afternoon I see Mlle Malory Rouleau. I'm in love with her name, and pray she will be the perfect candidate. Malory Rouleau, Roleau Malory, I say, making a nursery rhyme of it. I picture her as vivacious and sensual, exotic and reassuring. I don't read any CVs, don't ask for any certificates or diplomas, not the least bit of experience, because I know how easy it is to fake all that. So I know nothing about Malory Rouleau.

When she walks in I think she looks like a banana and, even though it's a fruit I like – so nourishing, so unfairly belittled – I'm immediately disappointed. She sits opposite me, both stiff and limp, rather like her emblematic fruit. Her cheeks are long and beige, boring as a winter's day.

I amuse myself delving through my list of interviewees.

'So you must be...' I say, as if I didn't know who I had in front of me.

'Malory Rouleau?'

She pronounces her own name with a note of interrogation. Is she expecting me to confirm her identity?

'And how old are you?'

'Twenty-five?'

Here again she wants reassurance.

'Diplomas?' I ask simply, hoping my laconic tone will encourage her to say a bit more.

'I've been to catering school?'

And is that where they taught you to speak like that? I feel like asking her. I don't. I carry on with the interrogation, thinking of the diverse tortures that parents inflict on their children, and teachers on their pupils for them to turn out like this, unnerved and amorphous. Malory Rouleau reminds me not so much of a banana as fruit purée.

These meetings are discouraging. I'm too demanding. You would have thought I was looking for the love of my life, and a woman at that! After three days of interviews, I've become allergic to dandruff, the least pimple of acne disgusts me, and bare midriffs send shivers down my spine. Ben teases me.

'You weren't so picky when you took me on,' he points out.

'It's not the same at all,' I tell him. 'You were the only one and you were perfect.'

He smiles. His whole face is carved in two with suffering.

'You're not going to cry?' I say belligerently.

'I am,' he replies.

One tear falls. Solitary and perfect.

'You know, Ben, soon I'm going—'

He clamps his hand over my mouth. How does he know I want to talk about leaving? How does he understand I wanted to tell him about my succession? I will make him my heir. I can feel the end is near. I'm probably not the only one. He keeps his hand over my mouth, and it is at that exact moment that Barbara comes into my life.

Barbara is tall, very tall even. She is about thirty years old, has a wide luminous forehead and thick red hair held in a bun at the back of her head. She walks with purposeful strides, she is not shy.

'Am I disturbing you? Would you like me to come back later? It's for the job.'

Ben takes his hand away.

'Please sit down,' I say.

She puts her bag on a chair, sits facing me and looks around. She nods her head, smiling radiantly. I'm dying to know what she thinks. She's only been here a minute and I'm already so used to her I can anticipate how much it will hurt when she leaves. She smells of soap. She looks cunning.

Barbara is a top-flight maths teacher and extraordinarily badly qualified.

'I might as well be honest with you,' she says, 'I'm not a cook. I can't even boil an egg.'

'I was the same,' I say in a slightly motherly voice. 'But anyone can learn!'

'I won't learn', she replies.

I'm delighted by her authoritative tone. I take her on then and there, and I'm proud of my choice. Within three days she's the boss and I'm the employee, and that's absolutely fine.

It's difficult to explain what Barbara's job consists of. Since she's been with us, Vincent has grasped that *Chez moi* is a restaurant. He says things like 'I'll pop by and see you at the restaurant', or 'By the way, I picked up some cut-price white carnations for the restaurant'. Nothing has changed but everything happens even more quickly. Even the building work is accelerating. She is the oil in the cogs, the wind in the sails. Ben adopted her immediately. I'm not jealous, I'm relieved. When I ask her why, with her diplomas, she isn't looking for better paid work, more worthy of her abilities, why she isn't teaching, for example, she explains that she has spent her life in classrooms and can't picture going back to one straight away. She wants to see people. 'You won't be disappointed,' I tell her, 'there's a lot of coming and going here.' She wants to know how a small business works, and she needs to put some money aside to go round the world in a few years' time. For a moment I toyed with the idea that her teaching qualification could be as fictitious as my work experience at the Ritz, but I didn't give that possibility the time of day. I don't need to know more about her. Barbara knows how to do all the things I don't. She delegates, organizes, sorts. Barbara sings as she works and has an admirable way of making the most of Vincent's flowers. She is an ace at housework and the rational use of space. I let her choose the new furniture for the haberdashery, and she negotiates even better rates than me with the supplier on the Avenue de la République.

A month after her arrival we inaugurate the big new dining-room. Ben wants to have a party and I say 'Yes, why not, that's a good idea,' and something inside my chest – something heavy and solemn like the pendulum of a clock – shifts with menacing slowness. Time is doubling back on itself now, and here comes this second launch to remind me of the first, except that this time everything is perfect. My parents, my friends, and even my brother – who finally has the good grace to come and see me – drink to my success. We have invited our most loyal customers, and the whole neighbourhood pops in. Simone and Hannah start the dancing, magically reconciled. Everyone eats, drinks and dances. This is great, people tell me, the most wonderful party, the best evening of their lives. I look at the smiling faces, the shimmying hips, the handshaking. I hear it all, the music, the words, the popping champagne corks, the laughter, but it's as if I'm inside a glass cage. Nothing I eat satisfies me, nothing I drink has any effect on me. I feel as if I'm attending my own funeral. I focus on tiny details, concentrating all my attention on the join between two floor tiles which is a little wider than the others, a crust of bread stuck between the zinc circumference and the Formica top of a round table. People kiss me and hug me and talk to me. My eye keeps escaping towards the big blue lacquered door that I've had painted in a trompe-l'oeil on the back wall. I would like to call Mrs Cohen back and tell her there's no problem for her son's bar mitzvah, everything's ready. I would like to go through that door and disappear into the garden my mind's eye has painted behind it. The grass there is soft and sweet, there are bulrushes bowing along the banks of a river. I put lime trees in it, hornbeams, weeping elms, blossoming cherries and liquidambars. I plant it with ancient roses, daffodils, dahlias with their melancholy heavy heads, and flowerbeds of forget-me-nots. Pimpernels, armed with all the courage peculiar to such tiny entities, follow the twists and turns between the stones of a rockery. Triumphant artichokes raise their astonished arrows towards the sky. Apple trees and lilacs blossom at the same time as hellebores and winter magnolias. My garden knows no seasons. It is both hot and cool. Frost goes hand in hand with a shimmering heat haze. The leaves fall and grow again. Grow and fall again. Wisteria climbs voraciously over tumbledown walls and ancient porches leading to a boxwood alley with a poignant fragrance. The heady smell of fruit hangs in the air. Huge peaches, chubby-cheeked apricots, jewel-like cherries, redcurrants, raspberries, spanking red tomatoes and bristly cardoons feast on sunlight and water, because between the sunbeams it rains in rainbow-coloured droplets. At the very end, beyond a painted wooden fence, is a woodland path strewn with brown leaves, protected from the heat of the skies by a wide parasol of foliage fluttering in the breeze. You can't see the end of it, just keep walking, and breathe.

Ali has brought me a present. He is late. I thought he wasn't going to come. Too shy, I told myself. In his arms he's cradling a parcel wrapped in newspaper. Enigmatic smile.

'Can I open it?'

'It's fragile,' he tells me.

He hands the thing to me, awkward but light. What is about the shape of a balloon, weighs nothing and mustn't be knocked? It's a riddle. He advises me to sit down in a quiet corner to unwrap it. We hide behind the bar. Crouching beneath the counter, we give each other a conspiratorial wink. People are calling me: 'Myriam, where do the empty bottles go?', 'Myriam, is there any more bread?', 'Myriam, what did you do with the corkscrew?' I can't be found. I peel the layers from my present, in no hurry, and at the heart of that printed envelope I find a big ball, disturbingly white and soft as the skin on a baby's tummy. I press my index finger hesitantly against the surface. It is both pliable and resistant. It smells of woods and trees. I examine this large spongy sphere carefully, trying to find a crease, a flaw. But no, it is perfectly smooth.

'Is it for telling the future?' I ask.

Ali bursts out laughing.

'It's a mushroom, you city girl,' he tells me.

I don't believe him. I've never seen such a perfectly huge, white, round mushroom.

'But it hasn't got a stem!' retorts the latent mycologist in me.

Ali turns it over gently and shows me a slightly crumpled, brownish area.

'That's how it's attached,' he says.

'Are you joking?'

'No. It's called a giant puffball. It's edible.'

'Where did you find it?'

'In my garden.'

'Is it good?'

'It's delicious. You slice it like… like rump steak, and fry it, in olive oil.'

'You picked this in your garden?'

He nods. It reminded him of me, he explains. Like a face with no eyes or mouth, no nose or ears, a face that is a soul. He thought of me and felt I would like it, and it would make me want to see the country. Because I'm inquisitive. Because I always ask masses of questions. He says that yes, actually, it's true, you can read the future in it.

'What do you mean?'

'The future is what we don't know, what we too readily refuse to believe.'

I ask him whether there are smaller ones.

'They come in all sizes.'

'How come?'

He shrugs: 'Nature's like that. It makes things in every shape and size.'

'But why?'

'So that it can carry on. As contingencies.'

He tells me about different varieties of blackcurrant, freckles on pear skin, humour in cows and the sheer nerve of hares. Paths, shadows, holes, underground streams, grass which can cut, grass which can whistle, periwinkles and snapdragons. He describes everything in minute detail but not poetically, as if we urgently need to compile a topographical statement.

I stroke the extraordinarily soft white ball and let its encrypted message travel up through my fingers. Ali puts his hand on mine. I look at the perfect graduation from his brown skin to my pale skin on the white surface. I dare not look up. I would like the soft opaque crystal of this magic fungus to take us far away from here, to a place where the meaning of life comes down to the bland urge to live it.

'Shall we go?' he asks.

'Let's go.'

I let Barbara know I'm leaving.

'I'll be back in a couple of days.'

She will have to say goodbye to the guests for me, apologize for me, explain to Ben. I gabble away and she listens kindly, reassures me.

'It's not a problem, they're all completely pissed anyway.'

I leave *Chez moi* by the side door with a full moon under my arm. Once out on the street I succumb to a mental inventory:

seventy chairs, two banquettes, twenty tables, six hobs, two fridges… I want to know what I'm leaving behind. I lean on this reassuring itemization because my body can barely take a step forward. It's beating far too fast in there. The blood's boiling. It's trembling. It's scattering. I'm so frightened. Frightened like never before. I want to lose everything. Shake it all off. Have nothing left so that I'll stop worrying about being ransacked and robbed because suddenly everything seems precious. Every memory is moaning softly inside me. Don't leave me, begs the past. Don't abandon us, weep the images. Time itself is talking to me, admonishing me. I draw up my legacy against its inexorable tide. After the lists of things come the lists of people. Faces tumble and clink like coins in a slot-machine, the tinkle of cheeks against noses and ears. Don't leave us, scream the mouths before falling into oblivion. I haven't forgotten you, I tell them. I haven't forgotten anything. I'm counting you and gathering you together, sorting you out the better to see you. Nothing sinister, a statement of account with no conclusion. An escalation. To see whether, if I pile you up, if I lay you one on top of the other like bricks, I'll be able to climb up, to build the enormous staircase I need to go and hang this moon up in my sky. I tell the people they will be the framework, and the things the substance. I need to build it straight away. I have to be up to the task. But how? Tipping over all the rubbish bins of my existence, mixing up the rubbish with my most recent and most expensive acquisitions, and carrying on climbing when in my veins there isn't a single drop of blood left, beneath my skin not a single drop of sweat.

I've gone and evaporated. Only the menacing pendulum is left, its expressionless copper face travelling from right to left, and left to right, the tiny distance of every second, which tells me it is time.

The blue van speeds through the night. A vertiginous fall away from the city, far from the lights, into the silent darkness of the countryside. But my eyes and ears soon get used to it. Once I have my feet in the grass, when the engine has been switched off and the headlights have stopped projecting their halo, I can see and hear. The curtain is raised on a nocturnal scene, revealing little winter stars and scarves of cloud stretching, grey or perhaps blue, from one constellation to another. Evergreen foliage emerges against the sky. I can make out thickets shaped like giant bears; the outline of a forest, slightly to our left, sketches the silhouette of a dinosaur sleeping on the hillside. Between the fallen branches there is a rustling, a teeming, then nothing. A smell of moss, strangled by the cold, reaches me, almost spent. A bird calls. Nothing. A bird answers. Nothing. Two arms wrap round my shoulders, then my waist, then my hips, then my knees. His hands around my ankles. They come back up and rest on my thighs, my stomach, my breasts, my eyes, my ears. The mouth that I know by heart, the one that belongs to the man who will never make me cry, the man standing behind me holding me fast, encircling me, bites the skin on my neck. And that's it. The man who was never meant to make me cry, who had promised he wouldn't, makes the tears stream down my cheeks, over my armpits and down my legs. I won't hold the lie against him. The strong grip of this betrayal is better than anything. I want him to lie to me, go back on his word and contradict himself. He thinks he knows but he knows nothing. And I don't know anything about him and long to know everything. The clothes thrown to the ground around us depict continents, ridged with mountain ranges, harbouring rivers of dew. We make love in the woods. Burn all the beds, sheets and pillows. No more blankets, no more bedsprings. A huge fire – its flames licking at furniture and consuming it, consuming the comfort of roofs over heads and the cushioned softness of eiderdowns – explodes into the night. I can hear it crackling as my body spreads from one valley to another. An elbow on the hill, a toe at the foot of the cliff, the nape of my neck on the rocks by the waterfall, my shoulder blade rolling on the beaten earth of a track, my index finger straight up against the trunk of an oak, the small of my back rubbing on a bed of lichen, my kneecap pressing against the sheer side of a plateau, my head moulding into the silt beside the sea, my hair saltier than kelp as it wafts through the waves. I cry out. I call to the atoms of my skin one by one, collecting them together at last, and shrink back to size. When the cold starts to needle us, we crawl to the house which is only a few metres away, leaving our clothes to rest beneath the stars.

When I open my eyes I am saddened by the drab whiteness of the morning. I would have liked sunshine, but no. The sky is indistinct, muted. I'm alone in an unknown bed. I screw up the thick cotton sheet and stuff it into my mouth. I feel the bottomless loneliness of a child waking in a strange house. He was brought there in his sleep. He doesn't know whose arms laid him down during the night, or whose smile will greet him on waking, he is unfamiliar with the customs of the household and dare not get up for fear of disturbing the others. He is afraid that no one in this new place will know how to make the hot chocolate which is the only thing that could reassure him.

I raise my head shyly and look at the square of garden visible through the window. The van with its scowling snout is parked a few metres away. I sit up further so that I can see the ground, looking for the clothes I took off the night before. They have disappeared. Ali must have got up at dawn to pick them up, harvesting the evidence. What would Mme Dubrême, the witch opposite, have said seeing jumpers, socks, underwear and trousers immortalized by a light glazing of white frost?

I wonder what would be the right thing to do now. I don't want to be here. I'm frightened of morning-after conversations and perhaps, even more, of the eye contact. I want to get back to my world, where every object is familiar, where ordinariness reigns, where I don't have to think. I try to envisage what will happen next. I imagine a smell of coffee wafting under the door, breakfast in bed – I've always refused to eat lying down, it's bad for digestion and afterwards you go back to sleep in all the crumbs. In another version I get up, wrapping myself in a toga of sheets as they do in films, and I go and sit in the kitchen where a blue and white china bowl is waiting for me. I dare not say I prefer drinking from a cup. We share embarrassed laughter and unfortunate words. We are drowned out by shame and awkwardness, and confront them with a pitiful dam of buttered bread – when I actually like mine with just cheese. Next I picture a little note left on the table: 'The station is three kilometres away, you can take the bike from behind the house. It was really great. See you soon.'

These various hypotheses paralyse me. I can't see how to cope with what will happen next. I would like to simplify the encounter, to hand over a video of my past and say: there you are. That's what I've been up to till now. Watch it and then we'll talk. I feel too old to talk about my childhood, my parents, my marriage and the rest, but I don't believe in new beginnings. What's he going to do with me? I'm angry with Ali. I hate him for not knowing me sooner. I resent him for needing to have everything explained. I succumb to the lethargy of a demoralized teacher confronted with a stupid pupil. No question of him getting any ideas. I've got to disappear as quickly as possible. I'll walk to the main road and then hitch a lift. I'll make it clear that I don't want to see him again. No more deliveries. He reeled me in with his organic vegetables. It's high time I got to know the wholesalers at Rungis. I've made a mistake but I'm used to that, it was small fry for a delinquent like me. I leap out of bed, determined to escape as quickly as possible.

On a chair, properly folded, I find my clothes. So the cinematographic toga won't be necessary. I throw them all on in a frenzy. My jumper is inside out. The sleeves of my T-shirt are twisted over my elbows and stopping my circulation. I pinch the skin on my stomach with the zip of my jeans. It makes me choke with rage. I throw the door open like a hurricane ready to ravage the house. Where's the fucking kitchen? This house is huge. There are bedrooms all over the place. Is this a hotel or something? I walk heavily, kicking out at door frames, alerting the population. But no one answers. This place is empty. The bathroom is tiled with silver mosaic. It isn't a hotel it's a Turkish brothel! 'Fucking Turkish brothel!' I cry. As I run along the corridor a mirror throws back the image of a madwoman whose make-up has run. Her hair has formed a halo round her forehead. I stop abruptly, take a few steps back and study my reflection. I don't know this face. Beneath the trails of mascara my cheeks are pink. No sign of bags under my eyes. I'm pretty. I go back to my searching rather more calmly and eventually come to a small room on the ground floor, lit by three windows and dominated by a reassuring range cooker. Someone has lit a fire in the stove. It's warm. No steaming coffee, no bowl on the waxed blue cloth. A grey and white cat sitting on the window ledge casts a friendly eye over me. I get the feeling he's smiling at me.

Through the window I can see Ali, with his back to me, strolling through the garden. I wait for him to turn round. When he sees me he gives a whistle. I automatically wipe the traces of make-up from my face and smooth my hair. He nods. He utters a few inaudible words. I answer, although no sound comes from my mouth. He waves me over. I wave him in.

I stroke the grey and white cat who almost closes his eyes.

Ali is walking away with his hands in his pockets. He is disappearing to the right, round the corner of the house. I wait for him to come back, my heart burning in my chest.

The next few hours I spend in his arms, on his back: he carries me. He loves it, throwing me from one shoulder to the other like a bundle. At nightfall we are very hungry and I decide to make a dish which takes three hours to cook. Ali agrees. While we wait patiently we try to remember everything we learned in our school gym classes; demonstrations are compulsory and follow swiftly on from an announcement of each exploit. 'Forward roll?' – 'Yup.' We do it. Backward roll landing with legs apart. Harder. Long jump. High jump. Shot put. Triple jump. Balancing. 'Walking on your hands!' I cry, caught up in the competitive spirit. Now I have to do it. Night fell long ago in the garden which is acting as the arena for our private Olympics. I take a long slow breath and with almost no run up, thinking this is really only walking – what difference does it make if it's upside down? – I tip myself up and move forward, agile as an insect. The strength in my own arms amazes me. It's not tiring at all. It's like walking on your feet.

Back at the restaurant I keep making mistakes. I put my hand up to take coffee from the shelf above when it's in the cupboard below. I confuse the drawer of utensils with the one for cutlery, reach for the fridge handle on the right when it's on the left. My body has secretly made the absurd decision to integrate the geography of Ali's kitchen perfectly. In two days, during which I haven't prepared more than three meals, my hands have recorded a useless new set of information and ousted the old one which is so essential. My efficiency is under threat. I'm slow, I'm clumsy, I laugh idiotically. Barbara wonders whether my neck is sore because I keep bringing my hand up to it gently.

Ben is sulking.

'A girl came,' he tells me icily.

'And?'

'She wanted to talk to you.'

'About what?'

'She didn't say.'

'Didn't you ask her?'

'She showed me a picture in the paper. She wanted to check it was you.'

'A picture?'

Ben hands me a free paper they give out at the Métro station. He has opened it on the restaurants page. In the section for the Eleventh Arrondissement the only establishment mentioned is *Chez moi*: there's an article which I don't manage to read and a rather hazy photograph. I study the picture, my hands shaking.

'It's not very clear because it was taken through the window,' Ben points out.

'I'm going to sue.'

He bursts out laughing.

'Who do you think you are, Britney Spears?'

'*Myriam welcomes you…*' I re-read the beginning of the sentence a dozen times and feel ashamed. '*… into the cheerful shambles…*'. What do they mean cheerful? What do they mean shambles?

'Do you think this place is shambolic?' I ask indignantly.

'This is very good news for us. For you,' Ben corrects himself, pointing at the three stars the journalist has honoured us with.

'Did you do this?' I ask him.

'No. I don't have any contacts in the Press,' he replies in a perfectly neutral voice. 'But if I did, I wouldn't have hesitated for a minute. It's a very good paper. They even mention the take-away service and the children's canteen. All our inventions…'

He's enthused. He wants me to read the article.

'That's it,' I say. 'It's over.'

I'm not looking at Ben, I'm talking to my picture, my picture in the paper.

'What are you talking about?' asks Ben.

'We're closing,' I say. 'I've had it. We're closing.'

'Stop being ridiculous,' he interrupts. 'You can't have a nervous breakdown because of a picture in the paper.'

I can't find anything to say in reply. I'm genuinely convinced that we need to stop everything, although I can't explain why. I recognize the sign of decadence all too clearly. I don't want to go through another downfall. I couldn't cope with the comedown. I can only go up.

'She was very pretty, this girl,' says Ben.

'Which girl?'

'The one who wanted to talk to you.'

'How old?'

'Eighteen, twenty.'

'Everyone's pretty at eighteen-twenty,' I snap. 'I was pretty at eighteen-twenty too.'

Ben is exasperated.

'Is it because you're in love that you're such a pain in the arse?' he asks.

And I know that everything in that sentence is difficult for him: the cloying noun 'love', the vulgar extravagance of 'pain in the arse'.

'I'm sorry,' I say, biting my lip. 'It's just it all seems so real, so definitive.'

'She said she'd come back,' he mumbles, taking the newspaper from me.

He bundles it into his bag, afraid I might use it to wrap the potato peelings.

'When?'

'She didn't give a time. I said you were coming back today.'

A horrible feeling of foreboding takes hold of me. Danger never comes from where we expect it. I suspect this could be a health and safety inspection. Nothing here is up to standard. I dread being questioned, judged and punished by a woman younger than me. She won't have any qualms. The merciless blade of immaturity is terrifying: expert eye and suspicious nostrils, she won't miss a thing.

And then what? She'll file her report, we won't be able to pay the astronomical fine and I'll go bankrupt. Actually, this is a good thing. We're closing. We're stopping everything. Blessings never come from where we expect them. I accept condemnation in advance. I can't wait to be accused and dispossessed. Then I'll run away.

When he took me to the station, Ali said, 'You're the wildest person I've ever met.' I thought back to the bed which I had made so carefully, the sauté of veal with lemon and sage which was so tender and so prettily arranged on the dish, the neat swish of a broom over the floor after the meal. I had settled into his house as if I were going to live there for ever. I had been his perfect wife. My brows furrowed.

'I don't understand.'

'Good,' he said. 'A wild farmer is just what's needed. I was worried you would be a townie but you're not in fact.'

He started to laugh and hugged me to him. He didn't tell me to come back. He didn't ask me to stay. He stroked my head the way he would a rabbit's, a tom-cat's, a heifer's or a chicken's before killing them, but not necessarily, also because he loved them. Then he heaved a deep sigh and, still laughing, said something I didn't hear because the train came into the station with a screech of rails.

I learned this at school. We humans are on the fringes of the food chain. We don't really play the game. A fly is eaten by a frog and he is gobbled up by a heron who, in turn, is gobbled up by... or there's the worm who's eaten by the bird who gets ripped apart by the cat... you can also start with a fish.

There are of course big predators, animals which aren't sandwiched between those they eat and those that eat them. No one eats the big predators. But they are killed. Humans kill them sometimes.

I should also mention minor prey, the sort of creatures who – rather like the big predators – miss out on the sandwich and only ever get to see a single slice of bread: something eats them but they, the minor prey, don't eat anything, or at least nothing animate, nothing that suffers, nothing that bleeds.

We humans stand alone. One notch above the big predators. Pariahs to this wonderful system. Occasionally an animal can eat one of us, but we still know it's a non-chain incident.

I do wonder whether this isolation is our greatest misfortune. It is thanks to this, this tiny breach, that life loses its meaning, like a tyre losing air. As nothing does us any harm, it falls to us to invent our own adversity.

I contemplate organizing a sort of council of big predators (how many of us would have a legitimate claim to attend?).

Lions, crocodiles, killer whales, tigers, bears… I'm not well up on animal behaviour, so I could be getting things wrong. What I'm interested in is the principle. We would meet every year to debate a variety of subjects such as 'Danger as a necessity', 'The mechanism of fear' and 'Passions and their management in non-threatened species'. Humans would be honorary members of this glorious commission. Coming together with the elite assassins would help us feel less isolated. Of course his majesty the herbivorous pachyderm, Professor Elephant, would also be there to mediate the symposium.

There would be a lot of talk about the melancholy of dominant species, their vague sense of threat which never actually manifests itself, insomnia linked to guilt. We would inevitably end up envying the fate of our victims. The prey. Our gentle prey which makes the best of life until the day when, without any warning, it is decapitated with the snap of a jaw.

I try to imagine the satisfactions of a bullfinch: Yum! I've found a maggot, phew! I got away from the cat. What a good day!

Would it be possible, in the context of extreme destitution, for a man to end up identifying with a bullfinch? Imagine famine hand in hand with guerrilla war: Yum! says bullfinch-man, I've found a worm; phew! he then cries as the machete or the bullet narrowly misses him. What a great day! But it doesn't work. Man's happiness has nothing to do with his survival. It lies somewhere else. Because of our awareness, because of hope, because of the infinite possibilities.

At certain points in my life I have been a bullfinch-woman.

Surviving. It was a miracle waking up alive each day, so insistent was the temptation to end it all. Sometimes, seeing dazzling March sunlight throwing a golden glow over the white stone façades along the banks of the Seine, I tried to remember: How do you do that again? How do you find this beautiful? How do you enjoy it? I remembered the pleasure of looking at something, the luxury that came for free, and I could see that I needed to construct some sort of framework for it, that the joyous sense of beauty could only reign if it were enthroned like a pasha on top of other feelings, that it would never be the first. Why ask for more? I thought indignantly. Isn't it an insult to life to insist on happiness? Be a good bullfinch and make do with being alive.

I've got my strength back, I'm on my feet again with my feathers puffed up. Staying alive isn't enough any more. My eagerness and appetite are awakened now and, as a result, my agitated heart is flooded with fear. I got something wrong earlier, one important detail escaped my vigilance: true, we don't participate in the great cycle of killing, but within our own caste we have a very satisfying system for devouring each other. I'm thinking of the young girl Ben told me about, the pretty one, who wants my picture and who, some day soon, will come to kill me. I can't imagine she means me any good. She is my exterminating angel, I recognized the beat of her wings. In her hand, a sword. In her eyes, daggers. I feel old. Old and grotesque with my bucolic escapades.

With an apron round my hips I slice and chop half-heartedly. I struggle to put menus together. I'm bored with food. I fall back on my classics and no one notices the difference. But I myself know that the intoxicating pleasure of invention has deserted me. Now that the first battle is won, it doesn't bother me whether I win the war. I've opened a restaurant. My business makes a profit. I raise my employees' salaries, hand out bonuses, invest in a new food-processor. As soon as a pan starts sticking, I give it to a charity shop and buy a new one. Ali has stopped delivering. He sends a solemn, sullen and excruciatingly punctual boy.

I think of the tiny firmament that we carved, my lover and I, in space, of the canopy beneath which we exchanged our silent vows. I know it exists somewhere but I can't shelter beneath it.

I haven't answered the telephone. I haven't opened the letters. I've behaved like an idiot. I don't know if he's crying, if he misses me, if he regrets me. I don't know what love is any more, what it consists of. All that I have left is desire. Once the physical amazement is over, there's nothing more. At night I bang my head against the wall, clench my jaws and wring my hands. In the morning I wake with an empty mind, and go over the things I will have to do through the day, the words I will have to say. I stock up in advance on the smiles I will have to give out. I'm rather like one of those mechanical pianos you feed perforated scores into. I churn out the notes soullessly a minute at a time. Reciting them. The days are getting longer and they seem to go by unbearably slowly. As soon as dawn breaks I set my eye on nightfall and the solitary rest it brings, the truth of those hours of insomnia during which, released from my role as a fulfilled restaurant owner, I can wander aimlessly with drooping eyelids and down-turned mouth.

One morning Ben arrives an hour early. I haven't had time to put on my armour or practise my lines for the day.

'Something's wrong,' he says.

I say nothing, my eyes on the floor.

'Something's wrong,' he says again.

My teeth start chattering.

'Are you ill?' he asks. 'Would you like me to call the doctor?'

I put my hands over my cheeks and squeeze. I'd like my teeth to stop their performance. Ben comes over, touches my shoulder shyly. I let him. He comes closer and takes me in his arms.

'It's nothing,' he says. 'It's nothing.'

He rocks me gently, swaying from one foot to the other, like inexperienced teenagers risking their first slow dance.

'You're tired,' he explains. 'That's why. It's hardly surprising. You haven't stopped. You work the whole time. It's too much. There. That's what it is. You've done too much. But everything's fine. Barbara and I can manage on our own. You should get some rest. You should go away to the country.'

I burst into sobs.

'Have I said the wrong thing?' Ben asks.

I don't answer. He stands still and hugs me very tightly.

'Tell me what I can do. I can do anything. I've written down the recipes, I've watched you do them. I've practised at home.'

It's so unfair, I tell myself. This boy's goodness is so unfair.

He'll do anything for me and I deserve nothing. Can't he see the mark on my forehead, the stigmata of a cold-hearted woman?

'You're the first person who's made me want to do something. The first person who's taught me anything.'

'So you agree then?' I ask hoarsely.

'Agree to what?' he asks, pulling back slightly.

'To taking over the restaurant. I want to give it to you. It's your work as much as mine. I can't deal with it any more. I'll find out about health and safety standards and we'll do whatever alterations need doing. You won't have to worry about anything. We're going to sort the whole place out.'

I grind to a halt, hesitating to go on.

'I want it to be a present, Ben. I don't want it to be a burden.'

I can see the glint of protest in his eye and start talking again before he can put his case together.

'You've worked for months without pay. You don't owe me anything. I'm the one who owes you everything. So I'm giving you what I've got. We're going to go to the solicitor and put the lease in your name.'

He shakes his head.

'Not that,' he says. 'Not that.'

'Take it, please.'

He thinks for a long time.

'I'm very happy to take care of the business,' he says, 'but you mustn't give it to me.'

There is so much authority in his voice. How does he know? How can he have guessed that I have no right to make him my heir? By what stroke of luck has he saved me from this ultimate betrayal?

'You're right,' I say. 'I'll appoint you as manager of *Chez moi*.'

'What are you going to do?' he asks. 'Where are you going to go?'

I haven't thought about that.

'You don't have a home,' he reminds me.

'That's true.'

'Do you have any savings?'

I shake my head.

'But I don't need anything to live,' I tell him. 'Hardly anything.'

Monday passes like a day of mourning, like coming back from a funeral. We're sad, Ben and I, each knowing our sadness is the same as we comfort each other. The air is mild and the sun, which has finally succeeded in warming up our short wide street, is modestly announcing that we can assume spring is here at last. Barbara is wearing a dress dotted with little flowers. Her large, dancing body is a meadow. I tell her about our plans, afraid she will refuse to be Ben's employee because he is a few years younger than her.

'That's perfect,' she reassures me. 'My favourite role is being the governess, the underling who runs everything from behind the scenes. I've got a weakness for clandestine arrangements.'

She's so clever, I think to myself, and enjoy watching her waltzing from one table to another, noting down orders in her big legible handwriting. She laughs with customers, crouches down to talk to the under-fours, doesn't let the whingers, fussers and downright pains walk all over her. She has a fearsome understanding of time and space. With her here, it's as if the dining-room is carved up into a grid, every scrap of information, every request has its own X and Y co-ordinates. No hold-ups in the kitchen, no customers kept waiting, no mistakes serving out plates. It's a privilege watching her work.

At five o'clock, when Vincent drops in for a cup of tea to talk to Barbara about the shrubs she would like round the edge of the terrace, a silhouette appears in the doorway. I don't notice it straight away because I'm leaning over a file trying to find the measurements allocated to us by the local authorities and therefore the area of pavement we are allowed. Our terrace must not exceed two metres by six, all told. I hand the document to Vincent who has brought a pile of plant catalogues. I notice that he's turned his head towards the door, and follow his gaze.

A tall young woman with high cheek-bones is standing on the doorstep. She has plaits coiled on top of her head, which immediately reminds me of the portrait of Vassilissa Primoudra, the very wise Vassilissa, heroine of the Russian fables of my childhood. I can't make out her eyes, and her expression is difficult to read because of the blinding sunlight behind her. She is standing absolutely still. It's disquieting. We all fall silent, petrified, waiting for her to move.

Ben murmurs, 'It's her'.

I gather up the scattered documents on the table and hand them over to Vincent. 'Could you three go to your place?' I ask.

Without a word, Barbara, Vincent and Ben get up and head for the door. The young woman steps aside to let them past. As she makes way, a ray of sunlight that she was blocking streams into my eyes, faster than any arrow, blinding me. When I open my eyes she has disappeared. I think I am alone, then hear someone gently clearing their throat behind me. She has sat down at the table we were using a few moments earlier.

'Are you Myriam?' she asks.

I sit down facing her and put out my hand. She shakes it, my fingers against her soft warm palm. Her eyes are black and her hair the colour of ripe wheat. Her lips are pale, pale pink and her neck long and white. She is wearing a black velvet jacket over a white lace blouse. You could be forgiven for thinking she has stepped out of a nineteenth-century painting. I think she looks odd. Not at all what I expected of a health inspector.

'My name is Tania,' she says.

We look at each other and I have no idea what sort of protocol we are supposed to observe. She lowers her eyes and smiles.

'I'm Hugo's girlfriend.'

I beg the ground to break open and suck me deep inside it. My hands shake on the table. I hide them and ram them under my thighs.

'We saw your picture in the paper,' she explains.

I'm struck by the clarity of her voice, no affectation or shyness.

'We were in the Métro, heading for lectures…'

What lectures? I want to ask her. Which university? Where's

my son? Where had you set off from? Where had he spent the night?

'... and I took the free paper because I like reading the restaurant reviews. I like my food. I said to Hugo, "Look, that's a nice idea, a restaurant called *Chez moi*," and I showed him the article. He didn't say anything. He brought the paper right up to his face. He said, "That's my mother, the woman, there, she's my mother." He recognized you. I thought he was joking at first. Because he talks about you all the time and it winds me up.'

What does he say about me? I want to ask. Does he hate me? But I'm muzzled by my shame. By my relief, too.

'I gathered very early on that you were... separated. He told me everything. As soon as we started going out. Because he couldn't sleep at night, so I asked him what he thought about for all those hours he spent walking up and down the room.'

What room? Do you live together? How long have you known him? Is he sleeping better?

But the muzzle won't slacken.

'He was angry. He cried when he told me that. I'd never seen a boy my age cry. I thought it was very weird. I thought it was very moving too. He told me he sometimes saw the bloke – what was his name again? Auguste? No, Octave. He said when he saw him he wanted to kill him. That frightened me. I thought it was stupid. "But this is all so childish", I told him and he went berserk.'

She roars with laughter.

'He was furious. He told me I was the stupid one, I wouldn't understand. That he'd been traumatized. And, well, I just can't put up with that sort of thing, do you see what I mean? People who've been traumatized. Everyone's traumatized these days, don't you think? Am I being too blunt?'

I can't answer. I think she is right. I would love to talk to her about the excesses of trauma. I would also like to thank her, to tell her how beautiful I think she is. To ask her how come she is so mature for her age. To find out about her origins.

'Everyone says so, that I'm too blunt. It's because of my origins.'

This echo surprises me. Reading the curiosity I cannot disguise in my eyes, she explains what she means: 'I'm not from here. I was born in Smolensk. I came to Paris when I was twelve. I couldn't speak French.'

She laughs again.

'There's just one word I still can't pronounce without an accent. It's not really a word, it's the name of a shop. Monoprix. Can you hear it? I don't say the "O"s properly.'

I smile.

'Well, I told Hugo. A woman is like a man. Women have bodies too. Do you find that shocking? Am I being crude? But it's true, isn't it? Boys are hopelessly uptight in reality. They're the ones who invented the concept of the Madonna. The Virgin and Child turns them on. But it makes me sick. Still, I understand him too. It's true. He was little and when it's your mother it's not the same. No one wants to know about their parents' love lives. You want that packed away in a box. Nothing odd about that. But I told him it had gone on long enough now. I don't want to live with some bloke who keeps on about his mother the whole time. It's very simple. No need for a shrink. I told him that if he missed you he just had to find you, it wasn't complicated. You've got parents, relations, you won't have evaporated, you're not dead. But he told me he didn't know how to go about it, that he didn't want to mention you to the others, Gizèle and André, your parents. He found it embarrassing. And I understand. It's true, it is embarrassing. So I said "What then? What are you waiting for? What are you going to do? Because traumatized orphans aren't really my thing." He said he was waiting for a sign. When he saw the photo I gave him a dig in the ribs. "There's your sign." We haven't talked about it but I know he's counting on me. You know what it's like. All men want is for you to relieve them of decision making. You just have to take responsibility for it. Well, I accept the responsibility. I can't see what's wrong with that. If you go wrong, you go wrong. It's not the end of the world.'

'Myriam?'

Someone's calling me. It's coming from the big dining-room. I can't seem to move.

'Myriam?'

'Go on,' says Tania. 'You see to your customers. I'll wait.'

I turn very slowly and get up, unsteady on my feet. Denis and Nico, two trainees from the dental prosthetics lab opposite, are waiting for their coffee.

'Have you got any dessert?' asks Nico.

'There's some chocolate fondant left,' I say like an automaton.

I serve them in slow motion. I haven't got the will to cut up the leftover pudding and arrange it on little plates: I take the whole mould to their table.

'You clean that up, my boys,' I tell them. 'It's on the house.'

I tear up the till receipt. I don't intend to be interrupted a second time, afraid I won't have the strength to take their money and give them their change.

I sit back down opposite Tania. She has stopped talking. She takes a deep breath and opens her eyes wide. She looks just like a clown and I wonder what's happening to her. Why's she not saying anything? Has the chatterbox ground to a halt? But what else could she add? It's my turn. I must not cry. I'm afraid that she will judge me. That she will laugh at me, furiously young and healthy as she is, that she won't tolerate my sorrow, my terror, my anxiety. I try to formulate something, in my mind. I assemble some words, but no sentences emerge. I have a huge problem with syntax. Syntax and pronunciation. I feel as if the words will come out of my mouth deformed by the appalling wail I'm trying to repress.

An idea saves me. Tania likes her food. I'm going to feed her. That will keep her waiting. She'll wait until I can manage speech again. Without getting up, I reach over to the work surface and put a slice of carrot and walnut cake in front of her.

Her face lights up.

'Can I have a cup of tea with it?' she asks.

My Hirschmüller percolator gleams in the light of the setting sun. I boil the water and put a spoonful of Russian tea in the teapot. A cloud of steam goes up and the deafening hiss of the spout spitting scalding water reminds me of the funnel on an old steam engine, the mournful whistle as it leaves, the moaning goodbyes and reunions.

Her spoon digs deep into the unctuous lemon-flavoured icing, breaks into the grainy sponge.

Eat me, my girl. Eat me and understand.

With her eyes closed she savours the delicate alloy of cinnamon and brown sugar.

'This is so good!' she exclaims.

She sighs and looks at her plate.

'It would be a hell of a waste if our children didn't taste this', she says. 'We haven't got any yet, but I want several. Maybe two, maybe four. It would be a real shame, wouldn't it?'

I shrug my shoulders, holding my tears back so hard that my forehead hurts.

She finishes her plateful conscientiously, stopping occasionally to shake her head in incredulity. She can't get over the texture, the flavour, the softness.

She goes to find another cup, pours some tea into it and puts it in front of me.

'Cheers?' she says, raising her cup.

'Cheers.'

Now all I have to do is wait: a meticulous activity which requires my full attention. It's inhuman not knowing how long this will last, jumping every time the door creaks, with every footstep. I interrupt what I'm doing the whole time, my life has lost all continuity. I keep having to look up, turn round, just to check, be ready.

Ben has been in the kitchen for two days now. He sees it as the last part of his training before he qualifies. He has a divine hand for pastry. It's a gift. It can't be learned. His tarts are infinitely better than mine. His Swiss roll with poppy seeds and cherry jam is celestial. He hasn't got the knack of cooking meat quite right yet, but that's a science which holds no mystery. You just have to obey the rules.

As for orders, Barbara takes care of them. Forward planning and lists are her speciality.

We're hurtling headlong towards my disappearance but still the time stagnates round the edge of every hour.

I summon an expert from the department of hygiene standards. He is a hateful man who pulls ridiculous faces as he takes notes, moves tables and chairs, and turns the dining-room upside-down. He waves his arms about and goes bright red when he tries to look in the fridge. I think there's a terrible smell of sweat about him. You're getting sweat all over the place, I want to tell him. He tells me about anti-bacterial gel, the cold chain and synthetic sponges. He refuses everything I offer him, a slice of asparagus flan, a bowl of pumpkin soup, a blueberry mousse with almond cream, a coffee for the road. He says he will send his report, and leaves without shaking my hand. Two days later we receive a printed document announcing conditionally favourable findings, followed by a few suggested but not compulsory minor changes.

Everything is ready. Ben is officially appointed manager. His training comes to an end triumphantly when he announces he has created a fabulous dessert which is like a cross between a millefeuille and Black Forest gâteau, practically impossible to achieve according to me, child's play according to him.

I can go.

But I can't go.

Because I'm waiting, and struggling not to look at the wretched calendar or my watch with its impotent hands.

An eyelash falls on my cheek.

'Make a wish,' says Ben. 'Pat one of your cheeks and make a wish.'

I wish my son would get here very soon.

I pat my left cheek.

'It was the other one,' says Ben. 'Bad luck.'

I couldn't say how many days have passed since Tania, the harbinger, came to see me, but here he is now, coming in after tapping on the window. Hugo is here, right in front of me, and so tall. It's knocked the breath out of me. I flatten myself instinctively against the wall, as if under fire. But he has no weapon, apart from his smile, a wide open smile like a segment of orange, apart from his eyebrows which are raised high on his smooth forehead, apart from his eyes, the only pair of eyes I have ever been afraid of.

He looks amused, pleased with himself for giving me this surprise. I recognize that look of his, like a shrewd baby. I'm so afraid of disappointing him. I try to smile but none of my muscles respond. I feel as if my whole body fits in the palm of a hand and that the hand is crushing me. I look at my son's face with curiosity, as you would a new-born baby, trying to find likenesses. Is he more like his mummy or his daddy? No, no, neither. He's a grown man. A very good-looking young man, rather distinguished, dressed with a studied elegance all his own.

I'm in pain. I don't realize straight away because of the tide unfurling within me. Or is it me unfurling? I feel something hurting. Ow. It's terrible, it makes my eyes water like a punch on the nose. Ow. In my stomach and my back too. It's stretching and tunnelling. What's wrong with me?

Hugo comes over and holds out his hand inquisitively. His every move is made with a note of humour. I don't understand how that's possible. How does my son manage to be funny?

I take his hand in mine and pull him to me. I sit on the banquette and pat my knees. He shakes his head but isn't against the idea. He laughs as he sits down on my lap. He crushes me completely. He's too big, too thin, too old.

'My darling,' I say. 'My beloved boy.'
'Still just as mad!' he says, pinching my cheek.
I press my head to his chest. I can hear his heart.

A little while later the blue van comes round the end of the street.

My suitcase weighs nothing. The same one I came with. Standing on the pavement opposite, I look at *Chez moi* with its spruce façade newly painted in lilac and the Mexican orange trees round the edge of the terrace. Ben and Barbara are standing on the doorstep waving to me. Vincent is busy in his shop. We've had a farewell cup of coffee. He's promised to keep an eye on the youngsters.

'What shall we do with your books?' asks Ben.

I think about my survival kit books, my treasure. I shrug.

'Read them.'

A PENGUIN READERS GUIDE TO

CHEZ MOI

Agnès Desarthe

An Introduction to
Chez Moi

Forty-three years old, trailing secrets and extravagant lies, Myriam has just convinced a bank to give her a loan to open a small restaurant in the Eleventh Arrondissement of Paris. Chez Moi is a modest place, but the name alone signifies its importance. Too poor to rent an apartment, Myriam must live in the restaurant, sleeping on a banquette and bathing in the (thankfully) deep kitchen sink. The restaurant could be her last chance to create a new, stable life for herself.

Six years earlier, Myriam did the unthinkable; she initiated an affair with her son Hugo's friend. Humiliated and embarrassed, and unable to make amends, Myriam decided to leave her family. With her only possessions a small suitcase and a thirty-three book library, she managed to secure a position cooking for the Santo Salto circus. The misfits and talented strays of the circus gave her a home, but they could not shelter her from her past indiscretion. Myriam had to find her own way back into the world.

With the establishment of Chez Moi, she cautiously opens her life back up for business. Still tender from the loss of her family, she has little faith in herself or in the future of her restaurant, and is skeptical of the people around her. Despite her misgivings, she puts all the love that she cannot give her family into the food she prepares. Gradually, whether she wants to admit it or not, the restaurant begins to change her.

Myriam has always felt that her life has been predetermined, but with the opening of Chez Moi, things begin to take a positive turn. Ben, an outwardly awkward yet astoundingly graceful waiter, appears at the very moment she needs him, and Vincent, the uptight florist next door, becomes her dear friend after a fraught beginning. Though she is a self-taught cook, her dishes are skillfully executed, and her vivid dreams and intoxicating visions for the restaurant create a haven for the local community. But as her success grows, so does her fear that her life could crumble again, leaving her with nothing.

By reaching out to Ali, a farmer she knew during her years cooking for the circus, Myriam hopes to bring his magic to her new venture. But Ali does much more than transform her kitchen; he transforms Myriam's entire perspective, allowing her to love again. And when, after six years of silence, her son seeks her out with the help of the new love in his own life, Myriam finally begins to make peace with herself.

ABOUT AGNÈS DESARTHE

Agnès Desarthe was born in Paris in 1966 and has written books for children, teenagers, and adults. She has had two previous novels translated into English: *Five Photos of My Wife* (2001), which was shortlisted for both the Independent Foreign Fiction Prize and the Jewish Quarterly Fiction Prize, and *Good Intentions* (2002). *Chez Moi* is her first book to be published in the United States.

A CONVERSATION WITH AGNÈS DESARTHE

In Chez Moi, *you deal with serious themes of maternal and romantic love, betrayal and redemption, yet despite the difficult subject matter, you generally keep a light or even fablelike tone. Why did you choose to write the book in this way? Did you purposefully set out to make* Chez Moi *a positive, redemptive story, or did that notion evolve during the course of your writing?*

Keeping a light tone has always been my way, whether I'm writing for children or for adults. It's a question of both aesthetics and culture. To me, humor is one of the most exciting literary devices.

"Redemptive" is not a word I would use. A book just has to end. Isaac Bashevis Singer used to say that in literature as well as in dreams death did not exist. I always have this in mind. There is something utterly not serious in fiction.

You write so evocatively about food it must be a love in your own life, in some form. Are you a cook yourself? Why is food such an integral part of this story? What did you hope to convey by making Myriam a chef?

At one point in my life I noticed that I spent more time cooking than writing. I love cooking, but still I found it alarming. I started wondering what the problem was with me and realized that when you cook, you do it for people who are hungry. The average human being is hungry three times a day. That's an awful lot. When you write, nobody seems to be especially hungry (for fiction, I mean). There's something absurdly romantic in keeping up this activity. I often say to myself that my life would be happier if I were a cook.

The reason why food is so important in the novel is because it allows the perfect give-and-take relationship that will always be missing in art. Myriam is a chef because she has a problem with desire. Cooking is the only way she has found to give herself to others without being too threatening. In France the book is called *Eat Me*. The sexual tension is made much more obvious than in the English title.

Myriam is a voracious reader and many of her favorite books are mentioned in Chez Moi. *Which books have the most personal resonance for you? Are your tastes similar to Myriam's?*

All of the books that are mentioned in the novel are part of my ideal list—but that list includes many more than thirty-three volumes.

You started as a translator, and you've now written many children's books, two plays, and this is your sixth novel for adults. Is there one form you enjoy most? Do you still work in all of these forms?

What I enjoy most is going from one form to the other. I don't think I'll ever stop translating or writing for children. Recently I've translated Cynthia Ozick's *The Puttermesser Papers* and Virginia Woolf's *Jacob's Room,* and both were such nourishing experiences that I don't see how I could do without them. It gives me the impression that I'm a better writer than I really am, and it's ego-free work, which is a wonderful holiday for an artist.

What other writers have most influenced your work? Or if not directly influenced by any, who do you admire?

That is a particularly difficult question. Very often in magazines, I read interviews in which the author cites Flaubert, Dostoevsky, Faulkner (very few women in general), and I think, "Wow, he must be really good having received such wonderful influences," but once I get down to read the actual work, I'm disappointed. I'll answer all the same, because, as we say in French: *Le ridicule ne tue pas* (ridicule never killed anyone). I admire and would gladly be influenced by: Virginia Woolf, I. B. Singer, Sylvia Townsend Warner, Primo Levi, Cynthia Ozick, Henry Roth, Marguerite Duras, and many, many more.

What are you working on now?

I'm translating Gail Carson Levine's *Fairest* and writing a novel for teenagers about three issues that torment me: beauty, adulthood, and novel writing.

Questions for Discussion

1. Myriam says she cooks "with and out of love" (p. 3), yet is unable to feel love for her son. Is it possible to stop loving your child? What circumstances do you believe would cause something like that to happen?

2. The way Myriam describes flowers and food is deeply affectionate and almost anthropomorphic. Why do you think she is able to so lushly convey her love for these things, yet has such trouble with people?

3. Were you surprised by Rainer's slap and the aftermath? Do you believe that love can die so suddenly? What are some other reasons that could cause a relationship to end swiftly and without argument?

4. When Myriam's betrayal and the reason for her abandonment are revealed, does it change your view of her? How were you able to understand or empathize with her unfaithfulness? If you were in her position, would you have made the same decision to leave?

5. Myriam has elaborate, realistic dreams that reflect her state of mind and desires. Why do you think she remembers them so clearly? What effect do they have on her? How do your own dreams effect your waking life?

6. At the end of *Chez Moi*, Hugo and Myriam reunite after six years apart. It can be argued that often it is much easier to remain estranged from a person than to make strides to patch things up. Have you had an experience in your own life when you had to choose whether or not to repair a relationship that

had grown distant? Who made the first move toward contact, and how did it work out in the end? Was it worth the effort?

7. Ali tells Myriam, "You're the wildest person I've ever met" (p. 237). Myriam has taken such risks in her life but in her mind, she is merely a cook. Why do you think she's still so unaware of others' perceptions of her? Do you think your own self-perception is accurate? Are you surprised at what others see in you?

8. Myriam feels that she needs to leave behind the restaurant and everything that she's created if she's going to give herself wholly to Ali. What did the restaurant say about her that has now changed? Do you agree with her decision?

9. Desire, physical and emotional, plays a large role in the book. So does destiny. How are the ideas of desire and destiny intertwined? Do you think it is possible to will something to happen?

For more information about or to order other Penguin Readers Guides, please e-mail the Penguin Marketing Department at reading@us.penguingroup.com or write to us at:

Penguin Books Marketing Dept.
Readers Guides
375 Hudson Street
New York, NY 10014-3657

Please allow 4–6 weeks for delivery.
To access Penguin Readers Guides online, visit the Penguin Group (USA) Inc. Web site at www.penguin.com and www.vpbookclub.com.